PENGUIN BOOKS

SALVATION OF A FORSYTE
AND OTHER STORIES

John Galsworthy, the son of a solicitor, was born in 1867 and educated at Harrow and New College, Oxford. He was called to the Bar in 1890; while travelling in the Far East he met Conrad, who became a lifelong friend. In 1897 he published *Four Winds* (short stories) under another name, and later two novels. *The Man of Property* (1906), the first book in *The Forsyte Saga*, together with his first play, *The Silver Box*, established him in the public mind. Other novels and plays followed, but it was not until after the First World War that he completed the first Forsyte trilogy with *In Chancery* (1920) and *To Let* (1921). The complete edition of *The Forsyte Saga*, first published in 1922 has since been through fifty-six impressions. The second Forsyte trilogy, *A Modern Comedy*, appeared in 1929, and the third, *End of the Chapter*, posthumously in 1934. Galsworthy was the first president of the P.E.N. Club, was awarded a Nobel Prize, and received the Order of Merit in 1929. He lived on Dartmoor for many years and afterwards at Bury on the Sussex Downs. He died in 1933. All nine volumes of *The Forsyte Chronicles* are now available in Penguins.

SALVATION OF A FORSYTE
AND OTHER STORIES

John Galsworthy

PENGUIN BOOKS

Penguin Books Ltd, Harmondsworth, Middlesex, England
Penguin Books Australia Ltd, Ringwood, Victoria, Australia

—

First published by William Heinemann Ltd 1907
Published in Penguin Books 1971

—

Made and printed in Great Britain
by C. Nicholls & Company Ltd
Set in Linotype Granjon

TO
My Wife

This volume of 'tales falling short of the novel in length' has been taken from a larger volume of such tales selected by Galsworthy in 1925 and first published as *Caravan* in that year.

The basis of Galsworthy's selection in that volume was to 'rope them two by two, an early tale behind and a late tale in front' and, he wrote, 'I have tried to find tales which have some likeness in theme or mood so that any reader who has the curiosity can mark such difference as time brings to technique or treatment.'

Contents

SALVATION OF A FORSYTE

SWITHIN FORSYTE lay in bed. The corners of his mouth under his white moustache drooped towards his double chin. He panted: 'My doctor says I'm in a bad way, James.'

His twin-brother placed his hand behind his ear. 'I can't hear you. They tell me I ought to take a cure. There's always a cure wanted for something. Emily had a cure.'

Swithin replied: 'You mumble so. I hear my man, Adolf. I trained him... You ought to have an ear-trumpet. You're getting very shaky, James.'

There was silence; then James Forsyte, as if galvanized, remarked: 'I s'pose you've made your will. I s'pose you've left your money to the family; you've nobody else to leave it to. There was Danson died the other day, and left his money to a hospital.'

The hairs of Swithin's white moustache bristled. 'My fool of a doctor told me to make my will,' he said, 'I hate a fellow who tells you to make your will. My appetite's good; I ate a partridge last night. I'm all the better for eating. He told me to leave off champagne! I eat a good breakfast. I'm not eighty. You're the same age, James. You look very shaky.'

James Forsyte said: 'You ought to have another opinion. Have Blank; he's the first man now. I had him for Emily; cost me two hundred guineas. He sent her to Homburg; that's the first place now. The Prince was there – everybody goes there.'

Swithin Forsyte answered: 'I don't get any sleep at night, now I can't get out; and I've bought a new carriage – gave a pot of money for it. D'you ever have bronchitis? They tell me champagne's dangerous; it's my belief I couldn't take a better thing.'

James Forsyte rose.

'You ought to have another opinion. Emily sent her love; she would have come in, but she had to go to Niagara. Everybody goes there; it's *the* place now. Rachel goes every morning: she overdoes it – she'll be laid up one of these days. There's a fancy ball there tonight; the Duke gives the prizes.'

Swithin Forsyte said angrily: 'I can't get things properly cooked here; at the club I get spinach decently done.' The bedclothes jerked at the tremor of his legs.

James Forsyte replied: 'You must have done well with Tintos; you must have made a lot of money by them. Your groundrents must be falling in, too. You must have any amount you don't know what to do with.' He mouthed at the words, as if his lips were watering.

Swithin Forsyte glared. 'Money!' he said; 'my doctor's bill's enormous.'

James Forsyte stretched out a cold, damp hand. 'Good-bye! You ought to have another opinion. I can't keep the horses waiting: they're a new pair – stood me in three hundred. You ought to take care of yourself. I shall speak to Blank about you. You ought to have him – everybody says he's the first man. Good-bye!'

Swithin Forsyte continued to stare at the ceiling. He thought: 'A poor thing, James! a selfish beggar! Must be worth a couple of hundred thousand!' He wheezed, meditating on life . . .

He was ill and lonely. For many years he had been lonely, and for two years ill; but as he had smoked his first cigar, so he would live his life – stoutly, to its predestined end. Every day he was driven to the club; sitting forward on the spring cushions of a single brougham, his hands on his knees, swaying a little, strangely solemn. He ascended the steps into that marble hall – the folds of his chin wedged into the aperture of his collar – walking squarely with a stick. Later he would dine, eating majestically, and savouring his food, behind a bottle of champagne set in an ice-pail – his waistcoat defended by a napkin, his eyes rolling a little or glued in a stare on the waiter. Never did he suffer his head or back to droop, for it was not distinguished so to do.

Because he was old and deaf, he spoke to no one; and no

one spoke to him. The club gossip, an Irishman, said to each newcomer: 'Old Forsyte! Look at 'um! Must ha' had something in his life to sour 'um!' But Swithin had had nothing in his life to sour him.

For many days now he had lain in bed in a room exuding silver, crimson, and electric light, and smelling of opopanax and of cigars. The curtains were drawn, the firelight gleamed: on a table by his bed were a jug of barley-water and *The Times*. He made an attempt to read, failed, and fell again to thinking. His face with its square chin looked like a block of pale leather bedded in the pillow. It was lonely! A woman in the room would have made all the difference! Why had he never married? He breathed hard, staring frog-like at the ceiling; a memory had come into his mind. It was a long time ago – forty odd years – but it seemed like yesterday . . .

It happened when he was thirty-eight, for the first and only time in his life travelling on the Continent, with his twin-brother James and a man named Traquair. On the way from Germany to Venice, he had found himself at the Hôtel Goldene Alp at Salzburg. It was late August, and weather for the gods: sunshine on the walls and the shadows of the vine-leaves, and at night, the moonlight, and again on the walls the shadows of the vine-leaves. Averse to the suggestions of other people, Swithin had refused to visit the Citadel; he had spent the day alone in the window of his bedroom, smoking a succession of cigars, and disparaging the appearance of the passers-by. After dinner he was driven by boredom into the streets. His chest puffed out like a pigeon's, and with something of a pigeon's cold and inquiring eye, he strutted, annoyed at the frequency of uniforms, which seemed to him both needless and offensive. His spleen rose at this crowd of foreigners, who spoke an unintelligible language, wore hair on their faces, and smoked bad tobacco. 'A queer lot!' he thought. The sound of music from a *café* attracted him; he walked in, vaguely moved by a wish for the distinction of adventure, without the trouble which adventure usually brought with it; spurred too, perhaps, by an after-dinner demon. The *café* was the *bier-halle* of the 'Fifties, with a door at either end, and lighted by a large wooden lantern. On a small dais three musicians were fiddling. Solitary men, or groups, sat at some dozen tables, and the waiters hurried about replenishing glasses; the air was thick with smoke. Swithin sat down. 'Wine!' he said sternly. The astonished waiter brought him wine. Swithin pointed to a beer-glass on the table. 'Here!' he said, with the same ferocity. The waiter poured out the wine. 'Ah!' thought Swithin, 'they can understand if they like.' A group of officers close by were laughing; Swithin stared at them uneasily. A hollow cough sounded almost in his ear. To his left a man sat reading, with his elbows on the corner of a journal, and his gaunt shoulders raised almost to his eyes. He had a thin, long nose, broadening suddenly at the nostrils; a black-brown beard, spread in a savage fan over his chest; what was visible of the face was the colour of old parchment. A strange, wild, haughty-looking creature! Swithin observed his clothes with some displeasure – they were the clothes of a journalist or strolling actor. And yet he was impressed. This was singular. How could he be impressed by a fellow in such clothes! The man reached out a hand, covered with black hairs, and took up a tumbler that contained a dark-coloured fluid. 'Brandy!' thought Swithin. The crash of a falling chair startled him – his neighbour had risen. He was of immense height, and very thin; his great beard seemed to splash away from his mouth; he was glaring at the group of officers, and speaking. Swithin made out two words: *'Hunde! Deutsche Hunde!'* 'Hounds! Dutch hounds!' he thought: 'Rather strong!' One of the officers had jumped up, and now drew his sword. The tall man swung his chair up, and brought it down with a thud. Everybody round started up and closed on him. The tall man cried out, 'To me, Magyars!'

Swithin grinned. The tall man fighting such odds excited his unwilling admiration; he had a momentary impulse to go to his assistance. 'Only get a broken nose!' he thought, and looked for a safe corner. But at that moment a thrown lemon struck him on the jaw. He jumped out of his chair and rushed at the officers. The Hungarian, swinging his chair, threw him a look of gratitude – Swithin glowed with momentary admiration of himself. A sword blade grazed his arm: he felt a sudden dislike of the Hungarian. 'This is too much,' he thought, and, catching up a chair, flung it at the wooden lantern. There was a crash – faces and swords vanished. He struck a match, and by the light of it bolted for the door. A second later he was in the street.

2

A voice said in English, 'God bless you, brother!'

Swithin looked round, and saw the tall Hungarian holding out his hand. He took it, thinking, 'What a fool I've been!' There was something in the Hungarian's gesture which said, 'You are worthy of me!' It was annoying, but rather impressive. The man seemed even taller than before; there was a cut on his cheek, the blood from which was trickling down his beard. 'You English!' he said. 'I saw you stone Haynau – I saw you cheer Kossuth. The free blood of your people cries out to us.' He looked at Swithin. 'You are a big man, you have a big soul – and strong, how you flung them down! Ha!' Swithin had an impulse to take to his heels. 'My name,' said the Hungarian, 'is Bölcsey. You are my friend.' His English was good.

'Bults-shai-ee, Burlts–shai-ee,' thought Swithin; 'what a devil of a name!' 'Mine,' he said sulkily, 'is Forsyte.'

The Hungarian repeated it.

'You've had a nasty jab on the cheek,' said Swithin; the sight of the matted beard was making him feel sick. The Hungarian put his fingers to his cheek, brought them away wet, stared at them, then with an indifferent air gathered a wisp of his beard and crammed it against the cut.

'Ugh!' said Swithin. 'Here! Take my handkerchief!'

The Hungarian bowed. 'Thank you!' he said; 'I couldn't think of it! Thank you a thousand times!'

'Take it!' growled Swithin; it seemed to him suddenly of the first importance. He thrust the handkerchief into the Hungarian's hand, and felt a pain in his arm. 'There!' he thought, 'I've strained a muscle.'

The Hungarian kept muttering, regardless of passers-by,

'Swine! How you threw them over! Two or three cracked heads, anyway – the cowardly swine!'

'Look here!' said Swithin suddenly; 'which is my way to the Goldene Alp?'

The Hungarian replied, 'But you are coming with me, for a glass of wine?'

Swithin looked at the ground. 'Not if I know it!' he thought.

'Ah!' said the Hungarian with dignity, 'you do not wish for my friendship!'

'Touchy beggar!' thought Swithin. 'Of course,' he stammered, 'if you put it in that way –'

The Hungarian bowed, murmuring, 'Forgive me!'

They had not gone a dozen steps before a youth, with a beardless face and hollow cheeks, accosted them. 'For the love of Christ, gentlemen,' he said, 'help me!'

'Are you a German?' asked Bölcsey.

'Yes,' said the youth.

'Then you may rot!'

'Master, look here!' Tearing open his coat, the youth displayed his skin, and a leather belt drawn tight round it. Again Swithin felt that desire to take to his heels. He was filled with horrid forebodings – a sense of perpending intimacy with things such as no gentleman had dealings with.

The Hungarian crossed himself. 'Brother,' he said to the youth, 'come you in!'

Swithin looked at them askance, and followed. By a dim light they groped their way up some stairs into a large room, into which the moon was shining through a window bulging over the street. A lamp burned low; there was a smell of spirits and tobacco, with a faint, peculiar scent, as of rose leaves. In one corner stood a czymbal, in another a great pile of newspapers. On the wall hung some old-fashioned pistols, and a rosary of yellow beads. Everything was tidily arranged, but dusty. Near an open fireplace was a table with the remains of a meal. The ceiling, floor, and walls were all of dark wood. In spite of the strange disharmony, the room had a sort of refinement. The Hungarian took a bottle out of a cupboard and, filling some glasses, handed one to Swithin. Swithin put it gingerly to his nose. 'You never know your luck! Come!' he thought, tilting it slowly into his mouth. It was thick, too sweet, but of a fine flavour.

'Brothers!' said the Hungarian, refilling, 'your healths!'

The youth tossed off his wine. And Swithin this time did the same; he pitied this poor devil of a youth now. 'Come round tomorrow!' he said, 'I'll give you a shirt or two.' When the youth was gone, however, he remembered with relief that he had not given his address.

'Better so,' he reflected. 'A humbug, no doubt.'

'What was that you said to him?' he asked of the Hungarian.

'I said,' answered Bölcsey, ' "You have eaten and drunk; and now you are my enemy!" '

'Quite right!' said Swithin, 'quite right! A beggar is every man's enemy.'

'You do not understand,' the Hungarian replied politely. 'While he was a beggar – I, too, have had to beg' (Swithin thought, 'Good God! this is awful!'), 'but now that he is no longer hungry, what is he but a German? No Austrian dog soils my floors!'

His nostrils, as it seemed to Swithin, had distended in an unpleasant fashion; and a wholly unnecessary raucousness invaded his voice. 'I am an exile – all of my blood are exiles. Those Godless dogs!' Swithin hurriedly assented.

As he spoke, a face peeped in at the door.

'Rozsi!' said the Hungarian. A young girl came in. She was rather short, with a deliciously round figure and a thick plait of hair. She smiled, and showed her even teeth; her little, bright, wide-set grey eyes glanced from one man to the other. Her face was round, too, high in the cheekbones, the colour of wild roses, with brows that had a twist-up at the corners. With a gesture of alarm, she put her hand to her cheek, and called, 'Margit!' An older girl appeared, taller, with fine shoulders, large eyes, a pretty mouth, and what Swithin described to himself afterwards as a 'pudding' nose. Both girls, with little cooing sounds, began attending to their father's face. Swithin turned his back to them. His arm pained him.

'This is what comes of interfering,' he thought sulkily; 'I might have had my neck broken!' Suddenly a soft palm was placed in his, two eyes, half-fascinated, half-shy, looked at him; then a voice called, 'Rozsi!' the door was slammed, he was alone again with the Hungarian, harassed by a sense of soft disturbance.

'Your daughter's name is Rosy?' he said; 'we have it in England – from rose, a flower.'

'Rozsi (Rozgi),' the Hungarian replied; 'your English is a hard tongue, harder than French, German, or Czech, harder than Russian, or Roumanian – I know no more.'

'What?' said Swithin, 'six languages?' Privately he thought, 'He knows how to lie, anyway.'

'If you lived in a country like mine,' muttered the Hungarian, 'with all men's hands against you! A free people – dying – but not dead!'

Swithin could not imagine what he was talking of. This man's face, with its linen bandage, gloomy eyes, and great black wisps of beard, his fierce mutterings, and hollow cough, were all most unpleasant. He seemed to be suffering from some kind of mental dog-bite. His emotion indeed appeared so indecent, so uncontrolled and open, that its obvious sincerity produced a sort of awe in Swithin. It was like being forced to look into a furnace. Bölcsey stopped roaming up and down. 'You think it's over?' he said; 'I tell you, in the breast of each one of us Magyars there is a hell. What is sweeter than life? What is more sacred than each breath we draw? Ah! my country!' These words were uttered so slowly, with such intense mournfulness, that Swithin's jaw relaxed; he converted the movement to a yawn.

'Tell me,' said Bölcsey, 'what would you do if the French conquered you?'

Swithin smiled. Then suddenly, as though something had hurt him, he grunted, 'The "Froggies"? Let 'em try!'

'Drink!' said Bölcsey – 'there is nothing like it'; he filled Swithin's glass. 'I will tell you my story.'

Swithin rose hurriedly. 'It's late,' he said. 'This is good stuff, though; have you much of it?'

'It is the last bottle.'

'What?' said Swithin; 'and you gave it to a beggar?'

'My name is Bölcsey-Stefan,' the Hungarian said, raising his head; 'of the Komorn Bölcseys.' The simplicity of this phrase – as who shall say: What need of further description? – made an impression on Swithin; he stopped to listen. Bölcsey's story went on and on. 'There were many abuses,' boomed his deep voice, 'much wrong done – much cowardice. I could see clouds gathering – rolling over our plains. The Austrian wished to strangle the breath of our mouths – to take from us the shadow of our liberty – the shadow – all we had. Two years ago – the year of '48, when every man and boy answered the great voice – brother, a dog's life! – to use a pen when all of your blood are fighting, but it was decreed for me! My son was killed; my brothers taken – and myself was thrown out like a dog – I had written out my heart, I had written out all the blood that was in my body!' He seemed to tower, a gaunt shadow of a man, with gloomy, flickering eyes staring at the wall.

Swithin rose, and stammered, 'Much obliged – very interesting.' Bölcsey made no effort to detain him, but continued staring at the wall. 'Good night!' said Swithin, and stamped heavily downstairs.

3

When at last Swithin reached the Goldene Alp, he found his brother and friend standing uneasily at the door. Traquair, a prematurely dried-up man, with whiskers and a Scotch accent, remarked, 'Ye're airly, man!' Swithin growled something unintelligible, and swung up to bed. He discovered a slight cut on his arm. He was in a savage temper – the elements had conspired to show him things he did not want to see; yet now and then a memory of Rozsi, of her soft palm in his, a sense of having been stroked and flattered, came over him. During breakfast next morning his brother and Traquair announced their intention of moving on. James Forsyte, indeed, remarked that it was no place for a 'collector', since all the 'old' shops were in the hands of Jews or very grasping persons – he had discovered this at once. Swithin pushed his cup aside. '*You* may do what you like,' he said, '*I'm* staying here.'

James Forsyte replied, tumbling over his own words: 'Why! what do you want to stay here for? There's nothing for you to do here – there's nothing to see here, unless you go up the Citadel, an' you won't do that.'

Swithin growled, 'Who says so?' Having gratified his perversity, he felt in a better temper. He had slung his arm in a silk sash, and accounted for it by saying he had slipped. Later he went out and walked on to the bridge. In the brilliant sunshine spires were glistening against the pearly background of the hills; the town had a clean, joyous air. Swithin glanced at the Citadel and thought, 'Looks a strong place! Shouldn't wonder if it were impregnable!' And this for some occult reason gave him pleasure. It occurred to him suddenly to go and look for the Hungarian's house.

About noon, after a hunt of two hours, he was gazing about him blankly, pale with heat, but more obstinate than ever, when a voice above him called 'Mister!' He looked up and saw Rozsi. She was leaning her round chin on her round hand, gazing down at him with her deep-set, clever eyes. When Swithin removed his hat, she clapped her hands. Again he had the sense of being admired, caressed. With a careless air, that sat grotesquely on his tall square person, he walked up to the door; both girls stood in the passage. Swithin felt a confused desire to speak in some foreign tongue. 'Maam'selles,' he began, 'er – *bong jour* – er, your father – *père, comment?*'

'We also speak English,' said the elder girl; 'will you come in, please?'

Swithin swallowed a misgiving and entered. The room had a worn appearance by daylight, as if it had always been the nest of tragic or vivid lives. He sat down, and his eyes said: 'I am a stranger, but don't try to get the better of me, please – that is impossible.' The girls looked at him in silence. Rozsi wore a rather short skirt of black stuff, a white shirt, and across her shoulders an embroidered yoke; her sister was dressed in dark green, with a coral necklace: both girls had their hair in plaits. After a minute Rozsi touched the sleeve of his hurt arm.

'It's nothing!' muttered Swithin.

'Father fought with a chair, but you had no chair,' she said in a wondering voice.

He doubled the fist of his sound arm and struck a blow at space. To his amazement she began to laugh. Nettled at this, he put his hand beneath the heavy table and lifted it. Rozsi clapped her hands. 'Ah! now I see – how strong you are!' She made him a curtsey and whisked round to the window. He found the quick intelligence of her eyes confusing; sometimes they seemed to look beyond him at something invisible – this, too, confused him. From Margit he learned that they had been two years in England, where their father had made his living by teaching languages; they had now been a year in Salzburg.

'We wait,' suddenly said Rozsi; and Margit, with a solemn face, repeated, 'We wait.'

Swithin's eyes swelled a little with his desire to see what they were waiting for. How queer they were, with their eyes that gazed beyond him! He looked at their figures. 'She would pay for dressing,' he thought, and he tried to imagine Rozsi in a skirt with proper flounces, a thin waist, and hair drawn back over her ears. She would pay for dressing, with that supple figure, fluffy hair, and little hands! And instantly his own hands, face, and clothes disturbed him. He got up, examined the pistols on the wall, and felt resentment at the faded, dusty room. 'Smells like a pot-house!' he thought. He sat down again close to Rozsi.

'Do you love to dance?' she asked; 'to dance is to live. First you hear the music – how your feet itch! It is wonderful! You begin slow, quick – quicker; you fly – you know nothing – your feet are in the air. It is wonderful!'

A slow flush had mounted into Swithin's face.

'Ah!' continued Rozsi, her eyes fixed on him, 'when I am dancing – out there I see the plains – your feet go one – two – three – quick, quick, quick, quicker – you fly.'

She stretched herself, a shiver seemed to pass all down her. 'Margit! dance!' and, to Swithin's consternation, the two girls – their hands on each other's shoulders – began shuffling their feet and swaying to and fro. Their heads were thrown back, their eyes half-closed; suddenly the step quickened, they swung to one side, then to the other, and began whirling round in front of him. The sudden fragrance of rose leaves enveloped him. Round they flew again. While they were still dancing, Bölcsey came into the room. He caught Swithin by both hands.

'Brother, welcome! Ah! your arm is hurt! I do not forget.' His yellow face and deep-set eyes expressed a dignified gratitude. 'Let me introduce to you my friend Baron Kasteliz.'

Swithin bowed to a man with a small forehead, who had appeared softly, and stood with his gloved hands touching his waist. Swithin conceived a sudden aversion for this cat-like man. About Bölcsey there was that which made contempt impossible – the sense of comradeship begotten in the fight; the man's height; something lofty and savage in his face; and an obscure instinct that it would not pay to show distaste; but this Kaseliz, with his neat jaw, low brow, and velvety, volcanic look, excited his proper English animosity. 'Your friends are mine,' murmured Kasteliz. He spoke with suavity, and hissed his s's. A long, vibrating twang quavered through the room. Swithin turned and saw Rozsi sitting at the czymbal; the notes rang under the little hammers in her hands, incessant, metallic, rising and falling with that strange melody. Kasteliz had fixed his glowing eyes on her; Bölcsey, nodding his head, was staring at the floor; Margit, with a pale face, stood like a statue.

'What can they see in it?' thought Swithin; 'it's not a tune.' He took up his hat. Rozsi saw him and stopped; her lips had parted with a faintly dismayed expression. His sense of personal injury diminished; he even felt a little sorry for her. She jumped up from her seat and twirled round with a pout. An inspiration seized on Swithin. 'Come and dine with me,' he said to Bölcsey, 'tomorrow – the Goldene Alp – bring your friend.' He felt the eyes of the whole room on him – the Hungarian's fine eyes; Margit's wide glance; the narrow, hot gaze of Kasteliz; and lastly – Rozsi's. A glow of satisfaction ran down his spine. When he emerged into the street he thought gloomily, 'Now I've done it!' And not for some paces did he look round; then, with a forced smile, turned and removed his hat to the faces at the window.

Notwithstanding this moment of gloom, however, he was in an exalted state all day, and at dinner kept looking at his brother and Traquair enigmatically. 'What do they know of life?' he thought; 'they might be here a year and get no farther.' He made jokes, and pinned the menu to the waiter's coat-tails. 'I like this place,' he said, 'I shall spend three weeks here.' James, whose lips were on the point of taking in a plum, looked at him uneasily.

4

On the day of the dinner Swithin suffered a good deal. He reflected gloomily on Bölcsey's clothes. He had fixed an early hour – there would be fewer people to see them. When the time approached he attired himself with a certain neat splendour, and though his arm was still sore, left off the sling . . .

Nearly three hours afterwards he left the Goldene Alp between his guests. It was sunset, and along the river-bank the houses stood out, unsoftened by the dusk; the streets were full of people hurrying home. Swithin had a hazy vision of empty bottles, of the ground before his feet, and the accessibility of all the world. Dim recollections of the good things he had said, of his brother and Traquair seated in the background eating ordinary meals with inquiring, acid visages, caused perpetual smiles to break out on his face, and he steered himself stubbornly, to prove that he was a better man than either of his guests. He knew, vaguely, that he was going somewhere with an object; Rozsi's face kept dancing before him, like a promise. Once or twice he gave Kasteliz a glassy stare. Towards Bölcsey, on the other hand, he felt quite warm, and recalled with admiration the way he had set his glass down empty, time after time. 'I like to see him take his liquor,' he thought; 'the fellow's a gentleman, after all.'

Bölcsey strode on, savagely inattentive to everything; and Kasteliz had become more like a cat than ever. It was nearly dark when they reached a narrow street close to the cathedral. They stopped at a door held open by an old woman. The change from the fresh air to a heated corridor, the noise of the door closed behind him, the old woman's anxious glances, sobered Swithin.

'I tell her,' said Bölcsey, 'that I reply for you as for my son.'

Swithin was angry. What business had this man to reply for him!

They passed into a large room, crowded with men and women; Swithin noticed that they all looked at him. He stared at them in turn – they seemed of all classes, some in black coats or silk dresses, others in the clothes of workpeople; one man, a cobbler, still wore his leather apron, as if he had rushed there straight from his work. Laying his hand on Swithin's arm, Bölcsey evidently began explaining who he was; hands were extended, people beyond reach bowed to him. Swithin acknowledged the greetings with a stiff motion of his head; then seeing other people dropping into seats, he, too, sat down. Someone whispered his name – Margit and Rozsi were just behind him.

'Welcome!' said Margit; but Swithin was looking at Rozsi. Her face was so alive and quivering! 'What's the excitement all about?' he thought. 'How pretty she looks!' She blushed, drew in her hands with a quick tense movement, and gazed again beyond him in the room. 'What is it?' thought Swithin; he had a longing to lean back and kiss her lips. He tried angrily to see what she was seeing in those faces turned all one way.

Bölcsey rose to speak. No one moved; not a sound could be heard but the tone of his deep voice. On and on he went, fierce and solemn, and with the rise of his voice, all those faces – fair or swarthy – seemed to be glowing with one and the same feeling. Swithin felt the white heat in those faces – it was not decent! In that whole speech he only understood the one word – 'Magyar' – which came again and again. He almost dozed off at last. The twang of a czymbal woke him. 'What?' he thought, 'more of that infernal music!' Margit, leaning over him, whispered: 'Listen! Rácóczy! It is forbidden!' Swithin saw that Rozsi was no longer in her seat; it was she who was striking those forbidden notes. He looked round – everywhere the same unmoving faces, the same entrancement, and fierce stillness. The music sounded muffled, as if it, too, were bursting its heart in silence. Swithin felt within him a touch of panic. Was this a den of tigers? The way these people listened, the ferocity of their stillness, was frightful! . . . He gripped his chair and broke into a perspiration; was there no chance to get away? 'When it stops,' he thought, 'there'll be a rush!' But there was only a greater silence. It flashed across him that any hostile person coming in then would be torn to pieces. A woman sobbed. The whole thing was beyond words unpleasant. He rose, and edged his way furtively towards the doorway. There was a cry of 'Police!' The whole crowd came pressing after him. Swithin would soon have been out, but a little behind he caught sight of Rozsi swept off her feet. Her frightened eyes angered him. 'She doesn't deserve it,' he thought sulkily; 'letting all this loose!' and forced his way back to her. She clung to him, and a fever went stealing through his veins; he butted forward at the crowd, holding her tight. When they were outside he let her go.

'I was afraid,' she said.

'Afraid!' muttered Swithin; 'I should think so.' No longer touching her, he felt his grievance revive.

'But you are so strong,' she murmured.

'This is no place for you,' growled Swithin. 'I'm going to see you home.'

'Oh!' cried Rozsi; 'but papa and – Margit!'

'That's their look-out!' and he hurried her away.

She slid her hand under his arm; the soft curves of her form brushed him gently, each touch only augmented his ill-humour. He burned with a perverse rage, as if all the passions in him were simmering and ready to boil over; it was as if a poison were trying to work its way out of him through the layers of his stolid flesh. He maintained a dogged silence; Rozsi, too, said nothing, but when they reached the door, she drew her hand away.

'You are angry!' she said.

'Angry,' muttered Swithin; 'no! How d'you make that out?' He had a torturing desire to kiss her.

'Yes, you are angry,' she repeated; 'I wait here for papa and Margit.'

Swithin also waited, wedged against the wall. Once or twice, for his sight was sharp, he saw her steal a look at him, a beseeching look, and hardened his heart with a kind of pleasure. After five minutes Bölcsey, Margit, and Kasteliz appeared. Seeing Rozsi they broke into exclamations of relief, and Kasteliz, with a glance at Swithin, put his lips to her hand. Rozsi's look said, 'Wouldn't you like to do that?' Swithin turned short on his heel, and walked away.

5

All night he hardly slept, suffering from fever, for the first time in his life. Once he jumped out of bed, lighted a candle, and going to the glass, scrutinized himself long and anxiously. After this he fell asleep, but had frightful dreams. His first thought when he woke was, 'My liver's out of order!' and, thrusting his head into cold water, he dressed hastily and went out. He soon left the house behind. Dew covered everything; blackbirds whistled in the bushes; the air was fresh and sweet. He had not been up so early since he was a boy. Why was he walking through a damp wood at this hour of the morning? Something intolerable and unfamiliar must have sent him out. No fellow in his senses would do such a thing! He came to a dead stop, and began unsteadily to walk back. Regaining the hotel, he went to bed again, and dreamed that in some wild country he was living in a room full of insects, where a housemaid – Rozsi – holding a broom, looked at him with mournful eyes. There seemed an unexplained need for immediate departure; he begged her to forward his things, and shake them out carefully before she put them into the trunk. He understood that the charge for sending would be twenty-two shillings, thought it a great deal, and had the horrors of indecision. 'No,' he muttered, 'pack, and take them myself.' The housemaid turned suddenly into a lean creature; and he awoke with a sore feeling in his heart.

His eye fell on his wet boots. The whole thing was scaring, and jumping up, he began to throw his clothes into his trunks. It was twelve o'clock before he went down, and found his

26

brother and Traquair still at the table arranging an itinerary; he surprised them by saying that he too was coming; and without further explanation set to work to eat. James had heard that there were salt-mines in the neighbourhood – his proposal was to start, and halt an hour or so on the road for their inspection: he said: 'Everybody'll ask you if you've seen the salt-mines: I shouldn't like to say I hadn't seen the salt-mines. What's the good, they'd say, of your going there if you haven't seen the salt-mines?' He wondered, too, if they need fee the second waiter – an idle chap!

A discussion followed; but Swithin ate on glumly, conscious that his mind was set on larger affairs. Suddenly on the far side of the street Rozsi and her sister passed, with little baskets on their arms. He started up, and at that moment Rozsi looked round – her face was the incarnation of enticement, the chin tilted, the lower lip thrust a little forward, her round neck curving back over her shoulder. Swithin muttered, 'Make your own arrangements – leave me out!' and hurried from the room, leaving James beside himself with interest and alarm.

When he reached the street, however, the girls had disappeared. He hailed a carriage. 'Drive!' he called to the man, with a flourish of his stick, and as soon as the wheels had begun to clatter on the stones he leaned back, looking sharply to right and left. He soon had to give up thought of finding them, but made the coachman turn round and round again. All day he drove about, far into the country, and kept urging the driver to use greater speed. He was in a strange state of hurry and elation. Finally, he dined at a little country inn; and this gave the measure of his disturbance – the dinner was atrocious.

Returning late in the evening he found a note written by Traquair. 'Are you in your senses, man?' it asked; 'we have no more time to waste idling about here. If you want to rejoin us, come on to Danielli's Hotel, Venice.' Swithin chuckled when he read it, and feeling frightfully tired, went to bed and slept like a log.

6

Three weeks later he was still in Salzburg, no longer at the Goldene Alp, but in rooms over a shop near the Bölcseys'. He had spent a small fortune in the purchase of flowers. Margit would croon over them, but Rozsi, with a sober 'Many tanks!' as if they were her right, would look long at herself in the glass, and pin one into her hair. Swithin ceased to wonder; he ceased to wonder at anything they did. One evening he found Bölcsey deep in conversation with a pale, dishevelled-looking person.

'Our friend Mr Forsyte – Count D—,' said Bölcsey.

Swithin experienced a faint, unavoidable emotion; but looking at the Count's trousers, he thought: 'Doesn't look much like one!' And with an ironic bow to the silent girls, he turned, and took his hat. But when he had reached the bottom of the dark stairs he heard footsteps. Rozsi came running down, looked out at the door, and put her hands up to her breast as if disappointed: suddenly with a quick glance round she saw him. Swithin caught her arm. She slipped away, and her face seemed to bubble with defiance or laughter; she ran up three steps, stopped, looked at him across her shoulder, and fled on up the stairs. Swithin went out bewildered and annoyed.

'What was she going to say to me?' he kept thinking. During these three weeks he had asked himself all sorts of questions: whether he were being made a fool of; whether she were in love with him; what he was doing there, and sometimes at night, with all his candles burning as if he wanted light, the breeze blowing on him through the window, his cigar, half-smoked, in his hand, he sat, an hour or more, staring at the wall. 'Enough of this!' he thought every morning. Twice he packed fully – once he ordered his travelling carriage, but countermanded it the following day. What definitely he hoped, intended, resolved, he could not have said. He was always thinking of Rozsi, he could not read the riddle in her face – she held him in a vice, notwithstanding that everything about her threatened the very fetishes of his existence. And Bölcsey! Whenever he looked at him he thought, 'If he were only clean!'

and mechanically fingered his own well-tied cravat. To talk with the fellow, too, was like being forced to look at things which had no place in the light of day. Freedom, equality, self-sacrifice!

'Why can't he settle down at some business,' he thought, 'instead of all this talk?' Bölcsey's sudden diffidences, self-depreciation, fits of despair, irritated him. 'Morbid beggar!' he would mutter; 'thank God *I* haven't a thin skin.' And proud too! Extraordinary! An impecunious fellow like that! One evening, moreover, Bölcsey had returned home drunk. Swithin had hustled him away into his bedroom, helped him to undress, and stayed until he was asleep. 'Too much of a good thing!' he thought, 'before his own daughters, too!' It was after this that he ordered his travelling carriage. The other occasion on which he packed was one evening, when not only Bölcsey, but Rozsi herself had picked chicken bones with her fingers.

Often in the mornings he would go to the Mirabell Garden to smoke his cigar; there, in stolid contemplation of the statues – rows of half-heroic men carrying off half-distressful females – he would spend an hour pleasantly, his hat tilted to keep the sun off his nose. The day after Rozsi had fled from him on the stairs, he came there as usual. It was a morning of blue sky and sunlight glowing on the old prim garden, on its yew-trees, and serio-comic statues, and walls covered with apricots and plums. When Swithin approached his usual seat, who should be sitting there but Rozsi!

'Good morning,' he stammered; 'you knew this was my seat then?'

Rozsi looked at the ground. 'Yes,' she answered.

Swithin felt bewildered. 'Do you know,' he said, 'you treat me very funnily?'

To his surprise Rozsi put her little soft hand down and touched his; then, without a word, sprang up and rushed away. It took him a minute to recover. There were people present; he did not like to run, but overtook her on the bridge, and slipped her hand beneath his arm.

'You shouldn't have done that,' he said; 'you shouldn't have run away from me, you know.'

Rozsi laughed. Swithin withdrew his arm; a desire to shake her seized him. He walked some way before he said, 'Will you have the goodness to tell me what you came to that seat for?'

Rozsi flashed a look at him. 'Tomorrow is the *fête*,' she answered.

Swithin muttered, 'Is that all?'

'If you do not take us, we cannot go.'

'Suppose I refuse,' he said sullenly, 'there are plenty of others.'

Rozsi bent her head, scurrying along. 'No,' she murmured, 'if *you* do not go – I do not wish.'

Swithin drew her hand back within his arm. How round and soft it was! He tried to see her face. When she was nearly home he said good-bye, not wishing, for some dark reason, to be seen with her. He watched till she had disappeared; then slowly retraced his steps to the Mirabell Garden. When he came to where she had been sitting, he slowly lighted his cigar, and for a long time after it was smoked out remained there in the silent presence of the statues.

7

A crowd of people wandered round the booths, and Swithin found himself obliged to give the girls his arms. 'Like a little Cockney clerk!' he thought. His indignation passed unnoticed; they talked, they laughed, each sight and sound in all the hurly-burly seemed to go straight into their hearts. He eyed them ironically – their eager voices, and little coos of sympathy seemed to him vulgar. In the thick of the crowd he slipped his arm out of Margit's, but, just as he thought that he was free, the unwelcome hand slid up again. He tried again, but again Margit reappeared, serene, and full of pleasant humour; and his failure this time appeared to him in a comic light. But when Rozsi leaned across him, the glow of her round cheek, her curving lip, the inscrutable grey gleam of her eyes, sent a thrill of longing through him. He was obliged to stand by while they parleyed with a gipsy, whose matted locks and skinny hands inspired him with a not unwarranted disgust. 'Folly!' he muttered, as Rozsi held out her palm. The old woman mumbled, and shot a malignant look at him. Rozsi drew back her hand, and crossed herself. 'Folly!' Swithin thought again; and seizing the girls' arms, he hurried them away.

'What did the old hag say?' he asked.

Rozsi shook her head.

'You don't mean that you believe?'

Her eyes were full of tears. 'The gipsies are wise,' she murmured.

'Come, what did she tell you?'

This time Rozsi looked hurriedly round, and slipped away into the crowd. After a hunt they found her, and Swithin, who was scared, growled: 'You shouldn't do such things – it's not respectable.'

On higher ground, in the centre of a clear space, a military band was playing. For the privilege of entering this charmed circle Swithin paid three *gulden*, choosing naturally the best seats. He ordered wine, too, watching Rozsi out of the corner of his eye as he poured it out. The protecting tenderness of yesterday was all lost in this medley. It was every man for himself, after all! The colour had deepened again in her cheeks, she laughed, pouting her lips. Suddenly she put her glass aside. 'Thank you, very much,' she said, 'it is enough!'

Margit, whose pretty mouth was all smiles, cried, '*Lieber Gott!* is it not good – life?' It was not a question Swithin could undertake to answer. The band began to play a waltz. 'Now they will dance. *Lieber Gott!* and are the lights not wonderful?' Lamps were flickering beneath the trees like a swarm of fireflies. There was a hum as from a gigantic beehive. Passers-by lifted their faces, then vanished into the crowd; Rozsi stood gazing at them spellbound, as if their very going and coming were a delight.

The space was soon full of whirling couples. Rozsi's head began to beat time. 'O Margit!' she whispered.

Swithin's face had assumed a solemn, uneasy expression. A man, raising his hat, offered his arm to Margit. She glanced back across her shoulder to reassure Swithin. 'It is a friend,' she said.

Swithin looked at Rozsi – her eyes were bright, her lips tremulous. He slipped his hand along the table and touched her fingers. Then she flashed a look at him – appeal, reproach, tenderness, all were expressed in it. Was she expecting him to dance? Did she want to mix with the riff-raff there; wish *him* to make an exhibition of himself in this hurly-burly? A voice said, 'Good evening!' Before them stood Kasteliz, in a dark coat tightly buttoned at the waist.

'You are not dancing, *Rozsi Kisaszony*?' (Miss Rozsi). 'Let me, then, have the pleasure.' He held out his arm. Swithin stared in front of his him. In the very act of going she gave him a look that said as plain as words: 'Will you not?' But for answer he turned his eyes away, and when he looked again she was gone. He paid the score and made his way into the crowd. But as he went she danced by close to him, all flushed and panting. She hung back as if to stop him, and he caught the glistening of tears. Then he lost sight of her again. To be deserted the first minute he was alone with her, and for that jackanapes with the small head and the volcanic glances! It was too much! And suddenly it occurred to him that she was alone with Kasteliz – alone at night, and far from home. 'Well,' he thought, 'what do I care?' and shouldered his way on through the crowd. It served him right for mixing with such people here. He left the fair, but the further he went, the more he nursed his rage, the more heinous seemed her offence, the sharper grew his jealousy. 'A beggarly baron!' was his thought.

A figure came alongside – it was Bölcsey. One look showed Swithin his condition. Drunk again! This was the last straw!

Unfortunately Bölcsey had recognized him. He seemed violently excited. 'Where – where are my daughters?' he began.

Swithin brushed past, but Bölcsey caught his arm. 'Listen – brother!' he said; 'news of my country! After tomorrow –'

'Keep it to yourself!' growled Swithin, wrenching his arm free. He went straight to his lodgings, and, lying on the hard sofa of his unlighted sitting-room, gave himself up to bitter thoughts. But in spite of all his anger, Rozsi's supply-moving figure, with its pouting lips, and roguish appealing eyes, still haunted him.

8

Next morning there was not a carriage to be had, and Swithin was compelled to put off his departure till the morrow. The day was grey and misty; he wandered about with the strained, inquiring look of a lost dog in his eyes.

Late in the afternoon he went back to his lodgings. In a corner of the sitting-room stood Rozsi. The thrill of triumph, the sense of appeasement, the emotion, that seized on him, crept through to his lips in a faint smile. Rozsi made no sound, her face was hidden by her hands. And this silence of hers weighed on Swithin. She was forcing him to break it. What was behind her hands? His own face was visible! Why didn't she speak? Why was she here? Alone? That was not right surely.

Suddenly Rozsi dropped her hands; her flushed face was quivering – it seemed as though a word, a sign, even, might bring a burst of tears.

He walked over to the window. 'I must give her time!' he thought; then seized by unreasoning terror at this silence, spun round and caught her by the arms. Rozsi held back from him, swayed forward and buried her face on his breast . . .

Half an hour later Swithin was pacing up and down his room. The scent of rose leaves had not yet died away. A glove lay on the floor; he picked it up, and for a long time stood weighing it in his hand. All sorts of confused thoughts and feelings haunted him. It was the purest and least selfish moment of his life, this moment after she had yielded. But that pure gratitude at her fiery, simple abnegation did not last; it was followed by a petty sense of triumph, and by uneasiness. He was still weighing the little glove in his hand, when he had another visitor. It was Kasteliz.

'What can I do for you?' Swithin asked ironically.

The Hungarian seemed suffering from excitement. Why had Swithin left his charges the night before? What excuse had he to make? What sort of conduct did he call this?

Swithin, very like a bull-dog at that moment, answered: What business was it of his?

The business of a gentleman! What right had the Englishman to pursue a young girl?

'Pursue?' said Swithin; 'you've been spying, then?'

'Spying – I – Kasteliz – Maurus Johann – an insult!'

'Insult!' sneered Swithin; 'd'you mean to tell me you weren't in the street just now?'

Kasteliz answered with a hiss, 'If you do not leave the city I will make you, with my sword – do you understand?'

'And if you do not leave my room I will throw you out of the window!'

For some minutes Kasteliz spoke in pure Hungarian while Swithin waited, with a forced smile and a fixed look in his eye. He did not understand Hungarian.

'If you are still in the city tomorrow evening,' said Kasteliz at last in English, 'I will spit you in the street.'

Swithin turned to the window and watched his visitor's retiring back with a queer mixture of amusement, stubbornness, and anxiety. 'Well,' he thought, 'I suppose he'll run me through!' The thought was unpleasant; and it kept recurring, but it only served to harden his determination. His head was busy with plans for seeing Rozsi; his blood on fire with the kisses she had given him.

9

Swithin was long in deciding to go forth next day. He had made up his mind not to go to Rozsi till five o'clock. 'Mustn't make myself too cheap,' he thought. It was a little past that hour when he at last sallied out, and with a beating heart walked towards Bölcsey's. He looked up at the window, more than half expecting to see Rozsi there; but she was not, and he noticed with faint surprise that the window was not open; the plants, too, outside, looked singularly arid. He knocked. No one came. He beat a fierce tattoo. At last the door was opened by a man with a reddish beard, and one of those sardonic faces only to be seen on shoemakers of Teutonic origin.

'What do you want, making all this noise?' he asked in German.

Swithin pointed up the stairs. The man grinned, and shook his head.

'I want to go up,' said Swithin.

The cobbler shrugged his shoulders, and Swithin rushed up-stairs. The rooms were empty. The furniture remained, but all signs of life were gone. One of his own bouquets, faded, stood in a glass; the ashes of a fire were barely cold; little scraps of paper strewed the hearth; already the room smelt musty. He went into the bedrooms, and with a feeling of stupefaction stood staring at the girls' beds, side by side against the wall. A bit of ribbon caught his eye; he picked it up and put it in his pocket – it was a piece of evidence that she had once existed. By the mirror some pins were dropped about; a little powder had been spilled. He looked at his own disquiet face and thought, 'I've been cheated!'

The shoemaker's voice aroused him. *'Tausend Teufel! Eilen Sie, nur! Zeit is Geld! Kann nit länger warten!'* Slowly he descended.

'Where have they gone?' asked Swithin painfully. 'A pound for every English word you speak. A pound!' and he made an O with his fingers.

The corners of the shoemaker's lips curled. *'Geld! Mff! Eilen Sie, nur!'*

But in Swithin a sullen anger had begun to burn. 'If you don't tell me,' he said, 'it'll be the worse for you.'

'Sind ein komischer Kerl!' remarked the shoemaker. *'Hier ist meine Frau!'*

A battered-looking woman came hurrying down the passage, calling out in German, 'Don't let him go!'

With a snarling sound the shoemaker turned his back, and shambled off.

The woman furtively thrust a letter into Swithin's hand, and furtively waited.

The letter was from Rozsi.

"Forgive me" – it ran –

that I leave you and do not say good-bye. Today our father had the call from our dear Father-town so long awaited. In two hours we are ready. I pray to the Virgin to keep you ever safe, and that you do not quite forget me. – Your unforgetting good friend,

Rozsi.

When Swithin read it his first sensation was that of a man sinking in a bog; then his obstinacy stiffened. 'I won't be done,' he thought. Taking out a sovereign he tried to make the woman comprehend that she could earn it, by telling him where they had gone. He got her finally to write the words out in his pocket-book, gave her the sovereign, and hurried to the Goldene Alp, where there was a waiter who spoke English. The translation given him was this:

'At three o'clock they start in a carriage on the road to Linz – they have bad horses – the Herr also rides a white horse.'

Swithin at once hailed a carriage and started at full gallop on the road to Linz. Outside the Mirabell Garden he caught sight of Kasteliz and grinned at him. 'I've sold *him* anyway,' he thought; 'for all their talk, they're no good, these foreigners!'

His spirits rose, but soon fell again. What chance had he of catching them? They had three hours' start! Still, the roads were heavy from the rain of the last two nights – they had luggage and bad horses; his own were good, his driver bribed – he might overtake them by ten o'clock! But did he want to? What a fool he had been not to bring his luggage; he would then have had a respectable position. What a brute he would look without a change of shirt, or anything to shave with! He saw himself with horror, all bristly, and in soiled linen. People would think him mad. 'I've given myself away,' flashed across him, 'what the devil can I say to them?' and he stared sullenly at the driver's back. He read Rozsi's letter again; it had a scent of her. And in the growing darkness, jolted by the swinging of the carriage, he suffered tortures from his prudence, tortures from his passion.

It grew colder and dark. He turned the collar of his coat up to his ears. He had visions of Piccadilly. This wild-goose chase appeared suddenly a dangerous, unfathomable business. Lights, fellowship, security! 'Never again!' he brooded; 'why won't they let me alone?' But it was not clear whether by 'they' he meant the conventions, the Bölcseys, his passions, or those haunting memories of Rozsi. If he had only had a bag with him! What was he going to say? What was he going to get by this? He received no answer to these questions. The darkness itself was less obscure than his sensations. From time to time he took out his watch. At each village the driver made inquiries. It was past ten when he stopped the carriage with a jerk. The stars were bright as steel, and by the side of the road a reedy lake showed in the moonlight. Swithin shivered. A man on a horse had halted in the centre of the road. 'Drive on!' called Swithin, with a stolid face. It turned out to be Bölcsey, who, on a gaunt white horse, looked like some winged creature. He stood where he could bar the progress of the carriage, holding out a pistol.

'Theatrical beggar!' thought Swithin, with a nervous smile. He made no sign of recognition. Slowly Bölcsey brought his lean horse up to the carriage. When he saw who was within he showed astonishment and joy.

'You?' he cried, slapping his hand on his attenuated thigh, and leaning over till his beard touched Swithin. 'You have come? You followed us?'

'It seems so,' Swithin grunted out.

'You throw in your lot with us. Is it possible? You – you are a knight-errant then!'

'Good God!' said Swithin. Bölcsey, flogging his dejected steed, cantered forward in the moonlight. He came back, bringing an old cloak, which he insisted on wrapping round Swithin's shoulders. He handed him, too, a capacious flask.

'How cold you look!' he said. 'Wonderful! Wonderful! you English!' His grateful eyes never left Swithin for a moment. They had come up to the heels of the other carriage now, but Swithin, hunched in the cloak, did not try to see what was in front of him. To the bottom of his soul he resented the Hungarian's gratitude. He remarked at last, with wasted irony:

'You're in a hurry, it seems!'

'If we had wings,' Bölcsey answered, 'we would use them.'

'Wings!' muttered Swithin thickly: 'legs are good enough for me.'

Arrived at the inn where they were to pass the night, Swithin waited, hoping to get into the house without a 'scene', but when at last he alighted the girls were in the doorway, and Margit greeted him with an admiring murmur, in which, however, he seemed to detect irony. Rozsi, pale and tremulous, with a half-scared look, gave him her hand, and, quickly withdrawing it, shrank behind her sister. When they had gone up to their room Swithin sought Bölcsey. His spirits had risen remarkably. 'Tell the landlord to get us supper,' he said; 'we'll crack a bottle to our luck.' He hurried on the landlord's preparations. The window of the room faced a wood, so near that he could almost touch the trees. The scent from the pines blew in on him. He turned away from that scented darkness, and began to draw the corks of wine-bottles. The sound seemed to conjure up Bölcsey. He came in, splashed all over, smelling slightly of stables; soon after, Margit appeared, fresh and serene, but Rozsi did not come.

'Where is your sister?' Swithin said. Rozsi, it seemed, was tired. 'It will do her good to eat,' said Swithin. And Bölcsey, murmuring, 'She must drink to our country,' went out to summon her, Margit followed him, while Swithin cut up a chicken. They came back without her. She had 'a megrim of the spirit.'

Swithin's face fell. 'Look here!' he said, '*I'll* go and try. Don't wait for me.'

'Yes,' answered Bölcsey, sinking mournfully into a chair; 'try, brother, try – by all means, try.'

Swithin walked down the corridor with an odd, sweet, sinking sensation in his chest; and tapped on Rozsi's door. In a minute, she peeped forth, with her hair loose, and wondering eyes.

'Rozsi,' he stammered, 'what makes you afraid of me?, *now*?'

She stared at him, but did not answer.

'Why won't you come?'

Still she did not speak, but suddenly stretched out to him her bare arm. Swithin pressed his face to it. With a shiver, she whispered above him, 'I will come,' and gently shut the door.

Swithin stealthily retraced his steps, and paused a minute outside the sitting-room to regain his self-control.

The sight of Bölcsey with a bottle in his hand steadied him.

'She is coming,' he said. And very soon she did come, her thick hair roughly twisted in a plait.

Swithin sat between the girls; but did not talk, for he was really hungry. Bölcsey too was silent, plunged in gloom; Rozsi, was dumb: Margit alone chattered.

'You will come to our Father-town? We shall have things to show you. Rozsi, what things we will show him!' Rozsi, with a little appealing movement of her hands, repeated, 'What things we will show you!' She seemed suddenly to find her voice, and with glowing cheeks, mouth full, and eyes bright as squirrels, they chattered reminiscences of the 'dear Father-town,' of 'dear friends,' of the 'dear home.'

'A poor place!' Swithin could not help thinking. This enthusiasm seemed to him common; but he was careful to assume a look of interest, feeding on the glances flashed at him from Rozsi's restless eyes.

As the wine waned Bölcsey grew more and more gloomy, but now and then a sort of gleaming flicker passed over his face. He rose to his feet at last.

'Let us not forget,' he said, 'that we go perhaps to ruin, to death; in the face of all this we go, because our country needs — in this there is no credit, neither to me nor to you, my daughters; but for this noble Englishman, what shall we say? Give thanks to God for a great heart. He comes — not for country, not for fame, not for money, but to help the weak and the oppressed. Let us drink, then, to him; let us drink again and again to heroic Forsyte!' In the midst of the dead silence, Swithin caught the look of suppliant mockery in Rozsi's eyes. He glanced at the Hungarian. Was he laughing at him? But Bölcsey, after drinking up his wine, had sunk again into his seat; and there suddenly, to the surprise of all, he began to snore. Margit rose and, bending over him like a mother, murmured: 'He is tired — it is the ride!' She raised him in her strong arms, and leaning on her shoulder Bölcsey staggered from the room. Swithin and Rozsi were left alone. He slid his hand towards her hand that lay so close, on the rough table-cloth. It seemed to await his touch. Something gave way in him, and words came welling up; for the moment he forgot himself, forgot everything but that he was near her. Her head dropped on his shoulder, he breathed the perfume of her hair. 'Good night!' she whispered, and the whisper was like a kiss; yet before he could stop her she was gone. Her footsteps died away in the passage, but Swithin sat gazing intently at a single bright drop of spilt wine quivering on the table's edge. In that moment she, in her helplessness and emotion, was all in all to him – his life nothing; all the real things – his conventions, convictions, training, and himself – all seemed remote, behind a mist of passion and strange chivalry. Carefully with a bit of bread he soaked up the bright drop; and suddenly he thought: 'This is tremendous!' For a long time he stood there in the window, close to the dark pine-trees.

II

In the early morning he awoke, full of the discomfort of this strange place and the medley of his dreams. Lying with his nose peeping over the quilt, he was visited by a horrible suspicion. When he could bear it no longer, he started up in bed. What if it were all a plot to get him to marry her? The thought was treacherous, and inspired in him a faint disgust. Still, *she* might be ignorant of it! But was she so innocent? What innocent girl would have come to his room like that? What innocent girl? Her father, who pretended to be caring only for his country? It was not probable that any man was such a fool; it was all part of the game – a scheming rascal! Kasteliz, too – his threats! They intended him to marry her? And the horrid idea was strengthened by his reverence for marriage. It was the proper, the respectable condition; he was genuinely afraid of this other sort of *liaison* – it was somehow too primitive! And yet the thought of that marriage made his blood run cold. Considering that she had already yielded, it would be all the more monstrous! With the cold, fatal clearness of the morning light he now for the first time saw his position in its full bearings. And, like a fish pulled out of water, he gasped at what was disclosed. Sullen resentment against this attempt to force him settled deep into his soul.

He seated himself on the bed, holding his head in his hands, solemnly thinking out what such marriage meant. In the first place it meant ridicule, in the next place ridicule, in the last place ridicule. She would eat chicken bones with her fingers – those fingers his lips still burned to kiss. She would dance wildly with other men. She would talk of her 'dear Fathertown,' and all the time her eyes would look beyond him, somewhere or other into some d—d place he knew nothing of. He sprang up and paced the room, and for a moment thought he would go mad.

They meant him to marry her! Even she – she meant him to marry her! Her tantalising inscrutability; her sudden little tendernesses; her quick laughter; her swift, burning kisses; even the movements of her hands; her tears – all were evidence against her. Not one of these things that Nature made her do counted on her side, but how they fanned his longing, his desire, and distress. He went to the glass and tried to part his hair with his fingers, but being rather fine, it fell into lank streaks. There was no comfort to be got from it. He drew his muddy boots on. Suddenly he thought: 'If I could see her alone, I could arrive at some arrangement!' Then, with a sense of stupefaction, he made the discovery that no arrangement could possibly be made that would not be dangerous, even desperate. He seized his hat, and, like a rabbit that has been fired at, bolted from the room. He plodded along amongst the damp woods with his head down, and resentment and dismay in his heart. But, as the sun rose, and the air grew sweet with pine scent, he slowly regained a sort of equability. After all, she had already yielded; it was not as if – ! And the tramp of his own footsteps lulled him into feeling that it would all come right. 'Look at the thing practically,' he thought. The faster he walked the firmer became his conviction that he could still see it through. He took out his watch – it was past seven – he began to hasten back. In the yard of the inn his driver was harnessing the horses; Swithin went up to him.

'Who told you put them in?' he asked.

The driver answered, '*Der Herr*.'

Swithin turned away. 'In ten minutes,' he thought, 'I shall be in that carriage again, with this going on in my head! Driving away from England, from all I'm used to – driving to – what?' Could he face it? Could he face all that he had been through that morning; face it day after day, night after night? Looking up, he saw Rozsi at her open window gazing down at him; never had she looked sweeter, more roguish. An inexplicable terror seized on him; he ran across the yard and jumped into his carriage. 'To Salzburg!' he cried; 'drive on!' And rattling out of the yard without a look behind, he flung a sovereign at the hostler. Flying back along the road faster even than he had come, with pale face, and eyes blank and staring like a pug-dog's, Swithin spoke no single word; nor, till he had reached the door of his lodgings, did he suffer the driver to draw rein.

12

Towards evening, five days later, Swithin, yellow and travel-worn, was ferried in a gondola to Danielli's Hotel. His brother, who was on the steps, looked at him with an apprehensive curiosity.

'Why, it's you!' he mumbled. 'So you've got here safe?'

'Safe?' growled Swithin.

James replied, 'I thought you wouldn't leave your friends!' Then, with a jerk of suspicion, 'You haven't brought your friends?'

'What friends?' growled Swithin.

James changed the subject. 'You don't look the thing,' he said.

'Really!' muttered Swithin; 'what's that to you?'

He appeared at dinner that night, but fell asleep over his coffee. Neither Traquair nor James asked him any further question, nor did they allude to Salzburg; and during the four days which concluded the stay in Venice Swithin went about with his head up, but his eyes half-closed like a dazed man. Only after they had taken ship at Genoa did he show signs of any healthy interest in life, when, finding that a man on board was perpetually strumming, he locked the piano up and pitched the key into the sea.

That winter in London he behaved much as usual, but fits of moroseness would seize on him, during which he was not pleasant to approach.

One evening when he was walking with a friend in Piccadilly, a girl coming from a side-street accosted him in German. Swithin, after staring at her in silence for some seconds, handed her a five-pound note, to the great amazement of his friend; nor could he himself have explained the meaning of this freak of generosity.

Of Rozsi he never heard again. . .

This, then, was the substance of what he remembered as he lay ill in bed. Stretching out his hand he pressed the bell. His valet appeared, crossing the room like a cat; a Swede, who had been with Swithin many years; a little man with a dried face and fierce moustache, morbidly sharp nerves, and a queer devotion to his master.

Swithin made a feeble gesture. 'Adolf,' he said, 'I'm very bad.'

'Yes, sir!'

'Why do you stand there like a cow?' asked Swithin; 'can't you see I'm very bad?'

'Yes, sir!' The valet's face twitched as though it masked the dance of obscure emotions.

'I shall feel better after dinner. What time is it?'

'Five o'clock.'

'I thought it was more. The afternoons are very long.'

'Yes, sir!'

Swithin sighed, as though he had expected the consolation of denial.

'Very likely I shall have a nap. Bring up hot water at halfpast six and shave me before dinner.'

The valet moved towards the door. Swithin raised himself.

'What did Mr James say to you?'

'He said you ought to have another doctor; two doctors, he said, better than one. He said, also, he would look in again on his way "home".'

Swithin grunted, 'Umph! What else did he say?'

'He said you didn't take care of yourself.'

Swithin glared.

'Has anybody else been to see me?'

The valet turned away his eyes. 'Mrs Thomas Forsyte came last Monday fortnight.'

'How long have I been ill?'

'Five weeks on Saturday.'

'Do you think I'm very bad?'

Adolf's face was covered suddenly with crow's-feet. 'You have no business to ask me question like that! I am not paid, sir, to answer question like that.'

Swithin said faintly: 'You're a peppery fool! Open a bottle of champagne!'

Adolf took a bottle of champagne from a cupboard and held nippers to it. He fixed his eyes on Swithin. 'The doctor said –'

'Open the bottle!'

'It is not –'

'Open the bottle – or I give you warning.'

Adolf moved the cork. He wiped a glass elaborately, filled it, and bore it scrupulously to the bedside. Suddenly twirling his moustaches, he wrung his hands, and burst out: 'It is poison.'

Swithin grinned faintly. 'You foreign fool!' he said. 'Get out!'

The valet vanished.

'He forgot himself!' thought Swithin. Slowly he raised the glass, slowly put it back, and sank gasping on his pillows. Almost at once he fell asleep.

He dreamed that he was at his club, sitting after dinner in the crowded smoking-room, with its bright walls and trefoils of light. It was there that he sat every evening, patient, solemn, lonely, and sometimes fell asleep, his square pale old face nodding to one side. He dreamed that he was gazing at the picture over the fireplace, of an old statesman with a high collar, supremely finished face, and sceptical eyebrows – the picture, smooth, and reticent as sealing-wax, of one who seemed for ever exhaling the narrow wisdom of final judgements. All round him, his fellow-members were chattering. Only he himself, the old sick member, was silent. If fellows only knew what it was like to sit by yourself and feel ill all the time! What they were saying he had heard a hundred times. They were talking of investments, of cigars, horses, actresses, machinery. What was that? A foreign patent for cleaning boilers? There was no such thing; boilers couldn't be cleaned, any fool knew that! If an Englishman couldn't clean a boiler, no foreigner could clean one. He appealed to the old statesman's eyes. But for once those eyes seemed hesitating, blurred, wanting in finality. They vanished. In their place were Rozsi's little deep-set eyes, with their wide and far-off look; and as he gazed they seemed to grow bright as steel, and to speak to him. Slowly the whole face grew to be there, floating on the dark background of the picture; it was pink, aloof, unfathomable, enticing, with its fluffy hair and quick lips, just as he had last seen it. 'Are you looking for something?' she seemed to say: 'I could show you.'

'I have everything safe enough,' answered Swithin, and in his sleep he groaned.

He felt the touch of fingers on his forehead. 'I'm dreaming,' he thought in his dream.

She had vanished; and far away, from behind the picture, came a sound of footsteps.

Aloud, in his sleep, Swithin muttered: 'I've missed it.' Again he heard the rustling of those light footsteps, and close in his ear a sound, like a sob. He awoke; the sob was his own. Great drops of perspiration stood on his forehead. 'What is it?' he thought; 'what have I lost?' Slowly his mind travelled over his investments; he could not think of any single one that was unsafe. What was it, then, that he had lost? Struggling on his pillows, he clutched the wine-glass. His lips touched the wine. 'This isn't the "Heidsieck"!' he thought angrily, and before the reality of that displeasure all the dim vision passed away. But as he bent to drink, something snapped, and, with a sigh, Swithin Forsyte died above the bubbles . . .

When James Forsyte came in again on his way home, the valet, trembling, took his hat and stick.

'How's your master?'

'My master is dead, sir!'

'Dead! He can't be! I left him safe an hour ago!'

On the bed Swithin's body was doubled like a sack; his hand still grasped the glass.

James Forsyte paused. 'Swithin!' he said, and with his hand to his ear he waited for an answer; but none came, and slowly in the glass a last bubble rose and burst.

December 1900

A STOIC

I

§ 1

Aequam memento rebus in arduis
Servare mentem. HORACE

IN the City of Liverpool, on a January day of 1905, the Board-room of 'The Island Navigation Company' rested, as it were, after the labours of the afternoon. The long table was still littered with the ink, pens, blotting-paper, and abandoned documents of six persons – a deserted battlefield of the brain. And, lonely, in his chairman's seat at the top end old Sylvanus Heythorp sat, with closed eyes, still and heavy as an image. One puffy, feeble hand, whose fingers quivered, rested on the arm of his chair; the thick white hair on his massive head glistened in the light from a green-shaded lamp. He was not asleep, for every now and then his sanguine cheeks filled, and a sound, half sigh, half grunt, escaped his thick lips between a white moustache and the tiny tuft of white hairs above his cleft chin. Sunk in the chair, that square thick trunk of a body in short black-braided coat seemed divested of all neck.

Young Gilbert Farney, secretary of 'The Island Navigation Company', entering his hushed Board-room, stepped briskly to the table, gathered some papers, and stood looking at his chairman. Not more than thirty-five, with the bright hues of the optimist in his hair, beard, cheeks, and eyes, he had a nose and lips which curled ironically. For, in his view, he *was* the Company; and its Board did but exist to chequer his importance. Five days in the week for seven hours a day he wrote, and thought, and wove the threads of its business, and this lot came down once a week for two or three hours, and taught their grandmother to suck eggs. But watching that red-checked, white-haired, somnolent figure, his smile was not so contemp-

tuous as might have been expected. For after all, the chairman
was a wonderful old boy. A man of go and insight could not
but respect him. Eighty! Half paralysed, over head and ears in
debt, having gone the pace all his life – or so they said! – till at
last that mine in Ecuador had done for him – before the secretary's day, of course, but he had heard of it. The old chap had
bought it up on spec' – '*de l'audace, toujours de l'audace,*' as
he was so fond of saying – paid for it half in cash and half in
promises, and then – the thing had turned out empty, and left
him with £20,000 worth of the old shares unredeemed. The old
boy had weathered it out without a bankruptcy so far. In-
domitable old buffer; and never fussy like the rest of them!
Young Farney, though a secretary, was capable of attachment;
and his eyes expressed a pitying affection. The Board meeting
had been long and 'snaggy' – a final settling of that Pillin
business. Rum go the chairman forcing it on them like this!
And with quiet satisfaction the secretary thought: 'And he
never would have got it through if I hadn't made up my mind
that it really is good business!' For to expand the Company was
to expand himself. Still, to buy four ships with the freight
market so depressed was a bit startling, and there would be
opposition at the general meeting. Never mind! He and the
chairman could put it through – put it through. And suddenly he
saw the old man looking at him.

Only from those eyes could one appreciate the strength of life
yet flowing underground in that well-nigh helpless carcase –
deep-coloured little blue wells, tiny, jovial, round windows.

A sigh travelled up through layers of flesh, and he said almost inaudibly:

'Have they come, Mr Farney?'

'Yes, sir. I've put them in the transfer office; said you'd be
with them in a minute; but I wasn't going to wake you.'

'Haven't been asleep. Help me up.'

Grasping the edge of the table with his trembling hands, the
old man pulled, and, with Farney heaving him behind, attained
his feet. He stood about five feet ten, and weighed fully fourteen stone; not corpulent, but very thick all through; his round
and massive head alone would have outweighed a baby. With eyes

shut, he seemed to be trying to get the better of his own weight, then he moved with the slowness of a barnacle towards the door. The secretary, watching him, thought: 'Marvellous old chap! How he gets about by himself is a miracle! And he can't retire, they say – lives on his fees!'

But the chairman was through the green baize door. At his tortoise gait he traversed the inner office, where the youthful clerks suspended their figuring – to grin behind his back – and entered the transfer office, where eight gentlemen were sitting. Seven rose, and one did not. Old Heythorp raised a saluting hand to the level of his chest and moving to an arm-chair, lowered himself into it.

'Well, gentlemen?'

One of the eight gentlemen got up again.

'Mr Heythorp, we've appointed Mr Brownbee to voice our views. Mr Brownbee!' And down he sat.

Mr Brownbee rose – a stoutish man some seventy years of age, with little grey side whiskers, and one of those utterly steady faces only to be seen in England, faces which convey the sense of business from father to son for generations; faces which make wars, and passion, and free thought seem equally incredible; faces which inspire confidence, and awaken in one a desire to get up and leave the room. Mr Brownbee rose, and said in a suave voice:

'Mr Heythorp, we here represent about £14,000. When we had the pleasure of meeting you last July, you will recollect that you held out a prospect of some more satisfactory arrangement by Christmas. We are now in January, and I am bound to say we none of us get younger.'

From the depths of old Heythorp a preliminary rumble came travelling, reached the surface, and materialized:

'Don't know about you – feel a boy, myself.'

The eight gentlemen looked at him. Was he going to try and put them off again? Mr Brownbee said with unruffled calm:

'I'm sure we're very glad to hear it. But to come to the point. We have felt, Mr Heythorp, and I'm sure you won't think it unreasonable, that – er – bankruptcy would be the most satisfactory solution. We have waited a long time, and we want to know definitely where we stand; for, to be quite frank, we don't see any prospect of improvement; indeed, we fear the opposite.'

'You think I'm going to join the majority.'

This plumping out of what was at the back of their minds produced in Mr Brownbee and his colleagues a sort of chemical disturbance. They coughed, moved their feet, and turned away their eyes, till the one who had not risen, a solicitor named Ventnor, said bluffly:

'Well, put it that way if you like.'

Old Heythorp's little deep eyes twinkled.

'My grandfather lived to be a hundred; my father ninety-six – both of them rips. I'm only eighty, gentlemen; blameless life compared with theirs.'

'Indeed,' Mr Brownbee said, 'we hope you have many years of this life before you.'

'More of this than of another.' And a silence fell, till old Heythorp added: 'You're getting a thousand a year out of my fees. Mistake to kill the goose that lays the golden eggs. I'll make it twelve hundred. If you force me to resign my directorships by bankruptcy, you won't get a rap, you know.'

Mr Brownbee cleared his throat:

'We think, Mr Heythorp, you should make it at least fifteen hundred. In that case we might perhaps consider –'

Old Heythorp shook his head.

'We can hadly accept your assertion that we should get nothing in the event of bankruptcy. We fancy you greatly underrate the possibilities. Fifteen hundred a year is the least you can do for us.'

'See you d—d first.'

Another silence followed, then Ventnor, the solicitor, said irascibly:

'We know where we are, then.'

Mr Brownbee added almost nervously:

'Are we to understand that twelve hundred a year is your – your last word?'

Old Heythorp nodded. 'Come again this day month, and I'll see what I can do for you'; and he shut his eyes.

Round Mr Brownbee six of the gentlemen gathered, speaking

in low voices; Mr Ventnor nursed a leg and glowered at old Heythorp, who sat with his eyes closed. Mr Brownbee went over and conferred with Mr Ventnor, then clearing his throat, he said:

'Well, sir, we have considered your proposal; we agree to accept it for the moment. We will come again, as you suggest, in a month's time. We hope that you will by then have seen your way to something more substantial, with a view to avoiding what we should all regret, but which I fear will otherwise become inevitable.'

Old Heythorp nodded. The eight gentlemen took their hats, and went out one by one, Mr Brownbee courteously bringing up the rear.

The old man, who could not get up without assistance, stayed musing in his chair. He had diddled 'em for the moment into giving him another month, and when that month was up – he would diddle 'em again! A month ought to make the Pillin business safe, with all that hung on it. That poor funky chap Joe Pillin! A gurgling chuckle escaped his red lips. What a shadow the fellow had looked, trotting in that evening just a month ago, behind his valet's announcement: 'Mr Pillin, sir.'

What a parchmenty, precise, threadpaper of a chap, with his bird's claw of a hand, and his muffled-up throat, and his quavery:

'How do you do, Sylvanus? I'm afraid you're not –'

'First rate. Sit down. Have some port.'

'Port! I never drink it. Poison to me! Poison!'

'Do you good!'

'Oh! I know, that's what you always say. You've a monstrous constitution, Sylvanus. If I drank port and smoked cigars and sat up till one o'clock, I should be in my grave tomorrow. I'm not the man I was. The fact is I've come to see if you can help me. I'm getting old; I'm growing nervous –'

'You always were as chickeny as an old hen, Joe.'

'Well, my nature's not like yours. To come to the point, I want to sell my ships and retire. I need rest. Freights are very depressed. I've got my family to think of.'

'Crack on, and go broke; buck you up like anything!'

'I'm quite serious, Sylvanus.'

'Never knew you anything else, Joe.'

A quavering cough, and out it had come:

'Now – in a word – won't your "Island Navigation Company" buy my ships?'

A pause, a twinkle, a puff of smoke. 'Make it worth my while!' He had said it in jest; and then, in a flash, the idea had come to him. Rosamund and her youngsters! What a chance to put something between them and destitution when he had joined the majority! And so he said: 'We don't want your silly ships.'

That claw of a hand waved in deprecation. 'They're very good ships – doing quite well. It's only my wretched health. If I were a strong man I shouldn't dream –'

'What d'you want for 'em?' Good Lord! how he jumped if you asked him a plain question. The chap was as nervous as a guinea-fowl!

'Here are the figures – for the last four years. I think you'll agree that I couldn't ask less than seventy thousand.'

Through the smoke of his cigar old Heythorp had digested those figures slowly, Joe Pillin feeling his teeth and sucking lozenges the while; then he said:

'Sixty thousand! And out of that you pay me ten per cent, if I get it through for you. Take it or leave it.'

'My dear Sylvanus, that's almost – cynical.'

'Too good a price – you'll never get it without me.'

'But a – but a commission! You could never disclose it!'

'Arrange that all right. Think it over. Freights'll go lower yet. Have some port.'

'No, no. Thank you. No! So you think freights will go lower?'

'Sure of it.'

'Well, I'll be going. I'm sure I don't know. It's – it's – I must think.'

'Think your hardest.'

'Yes, yes. Good-bye. I can't imagine how you still go on smoking those things and drinking port.'

'See you in your grave yet, Joe.' What a feeble smile the poor fellow had! Laugh – he couldn't! And, alone again, he had browsed, developing the idea which had come to him.

Though, to dwell in the heart of shipping, Sylvanus Heythorp had lived at Liverpool twenty years, he was from the Eastern Counties, of a family so old that it professed to despise the Conquest. Each of its generations occupied nearly twice as long as those of less tenacious men. Traditionally of Danish origin, its men folk had as a rule bright reddish-brown hair, red cheeks, large round heads, excellent teeth and poor morals. They had done their best for the population of any country in which they had settled, their offshoots swarmed. Born in the early twenties of the nineteenth century, Sylvanus Heythorp, after an education broken by escapades both at school and college, had fetched up in that simple London of the late forties, where claret, opera, and eight per cent for your money ruled a cheery roost. Made partner in his shipping firm well before he was thirty, he had sailed with a wet sheet and a flowing tide; dancers, claret, Clicquot, and piquet; a cab with a tiger; some travel – all that delicious early-Victorian consciousness of nothing save a golden time. It was all so full and mellow that he was forty before he had his only love affair of any depth – with the daughter of one of his own clerks, a *liaison* so awkward as to necessitate a sedulous concealment. The death of that girl, after three years, leaving him a natural son, had been the chief, perhaps the only real, sorrow of his life. Five years later he married. What for? God only knew! as he was in the habit of remarking. His wife had been a hard, worldly, well-connected woman, who presented him with two unnatural children, a girl and a boy, and grew harder, more worldly, less handsome, in the process. The migration to Liverpool, which took place when he was sixty and she forty-two, broke what she still had of heart, but she lingered on twelve years, finding solace in bridge, and being haughty towards Liverpool. Old Heythorp saw her to her rest without regret. He had felt no love for her whatever, and practically none for her two children – they were in his view colourless, pragmatical, very unexpected characters. His son Ernest – in the Admiralty – he thought a poor, careful stick. His daughter Adela, an excellent manager, delighting in

spiritual conversation and the society of tame men, rarely failed
to show him that she considered him a hopeless heathen. They
saw as little as need be of each other. She was provided for under
that settlement he had made on her mother fifteen years ago, well
before the not altogether unexpected crisis in his affairs. Very
different was the feeling he had bestowed on that son of his
'under the rose'. The boy, who had always gone by his mother's
name of Larne, had on her death been sent to some relations of
hers in Ireland, and there brought up. He had been called to
the Dublin bar, and married, young, a girl half Cornish and
half Irish; presently, having cost old Heythorp in all a pretty
penny, he had died impecunious, leaving his fair Rosamund at
thirty with a girl of eight and a boy of five. She had not spent
six months of widowhood before coming over from Dublin to
claim the old man's guardianship. A remarkably pretty woman,
like a full-blown rose, with greenish hazel eyes, she had turned
up one morning at the offices of 'The Island Navigation Company', accompanied by her two children – for he had never
divulged to them his private address. And since then they always
had been more or less on his hands, occupying a small house in
a suburb of Liverpool. He visited them there, but never asked
them to the house in Sefton Park, which was in fact his daughter's; so that his proper family and friends were unaware of
their existence.

Rosamund Larne was one of those precarious ladies who
make uncertain incomes by writing full-bodied storyettes. In the
most dismal circumstances she enjoyed a buoyancy bordering on
the indecent, which always amused old Heythorp's cynicism.
But of his grandchildren Phyllis and Jock (wild as colts) he had
become fond. And this chance of getting six thousand pounds
settled on them at a stroke had seemed to him nothing but
heaven-sent. As things were, if he 'went off' – and, of course,
he might at any moment – there wouldn't be a penny for them;
for he would 'cut up' a good fifteen thousand to the bad. He
was now giving them some three hundred a year out of his fees;
and dead directors unfortunately earned no fees! Six thousand
pounds at four and a half per cent, settled so that their mother
couldn't 'blue it', would give them a certain two hundred and

fifty pounds a year – better than beggary. And the more he thought the better he liked it, if only that shaky chap, Joe Pillin, didn't shy off when he'd bitten his nails short over it !

Four evenings later, the 'shaky chap' had again appeared at his house in Sefton Park.

'I've thought it over, Sylvanus. I don't like it.'

'No ; but you'll do it.'

'It's a sacrifice. Fifty-four thousand for four ships – it means a considerable reduction in my income.'

'It means security, my boy.'

'Well, there is that ; but you know, I really can't be party to a secret commission. If it came out, think of my name and goodness knows what.'

'It won't come out.'

'Yes, yes, so you say, but –'

'All you've got to do's to execute a settlement on some third parties that I'll name. I'm not going to take a penny of it myself. Get your own lawyer to draw it up and make him trustee. You can sign it when the purchase has gone through. I'll trust you, Joe. What stock have you got that gives four and a half per cent?'

'Midland –'

'That'll do. You needn't sell.'

'Yes, but who *are* these people ? '

'Woman and her children I want to do a good turn to.' What a face the fellow had made ! 'Afraid of being connected with a woman, Joe ? '

'Yes, you may laugh – I *am* afraid of being connected with someone else's woman. I don't like it – I don't like it at all. I've not led your life, Sylvanus.'

'Lucky for you ; you'd have been dead long ago. Tell your lawyer's it's an old flame of yours – you old dog ! '

'Yes, there it is at once, you see. I might be subject to blackmail.'

'Tell him to keep it dark, and just pay over the income, quarterly.'

'I don't like it, Sylvanus – I don't like it.'

'Then leave it, and be hanged to you. Have a cigar ? '

'You know I never smoke. Is there no other way ? '

'Yes. Sell stock in London, bank the proceeds there and bring me six thousand pounds in notes. I'll hold 'em till after the general meeting. If the thing doesn't go through, I'll hand 'em back to you.'

'No; I like that even less.'

'Rather I trusted *you*, eh!'

'No, not at all, Sylvanus, not at all. But it's all playing round the law.'

'There's no law to prevent you doing what you like with your money. What I do's nothing to you. And mind you, I'm taking nothing from it – not a mag. You assist the widowed and the fatherless – just your line, Joe!'

'What a fellow you are, Sylvanus; you don't seem capable of taking anything seriously.'

'Care killed the cat!'

Left alone after this second interview, he had thought: 'The beggar'll jump.'

And the beggar *had*. That settlement was drawn and only awaited signature. The Board today had decided on the purchase; and all that remained was to get it ratified at the general meeting. Let him but get that over, and this provision for his grandchildren made, and he would snap his fingers at Brownbee and his crew – the canting humbugs! 'Hope you have many years of this life before you!' As if they cared for anything but his money – *their* money rather! And becoming conscious of the length of his reverie, he grasped the arms of his chair, heaved at his own bulk, in an effort to rise, growing redder and redder in face and neck. It was one of the hundred things his doctor had told him not to do for fear of apoplexy, the humbug! Why didn't Farney or one of those young fellows come and help him up? To call out was undignified. But was he to sit there all night? Three times he failed, and after each failure sat motionless again, crimson and exhausted; the fourth time he succeeded, and slowly made for the office. Passing through, he stopped and said in his extinct voice:

'You young gentlemen had forgotten me.'

'Mr Farney said you didn't wish to be disturbed, sir.'

'Very good of him. Give me my hat and coat.'

'Yes, sir.'

'Thank you. What time is it?'

'Six o'clock, sir.'

'Tell Mr Farney to come and see me tomorrow at noon, about my speech for the general meeting.'

'Yes, sir.'

'Good night to you.'

'Good night, sir.'

At his tortoise gait he passed between the office stools to the door, opened it feebly, and slowly vanished.

Shutting the door behind him, a clerk said:

'Poor old chairman! He's on his last!'

Another answered:

'Gosh! He's a tough old hulk. He'll go down fightin'.'

§ 2

Issuing from the offices of 'The Island Navigation Company', Sylvanus Heythorp moved towards the corner whence he always took tram to Sefton Park. The crowded street had all that prosperous air of catching or missing something which characterizes the town where London and New York and Dublin meet. Old Heythorp had to cross to the far side, and he sallied forth without regard to traffic. That snail-like passage had in it a touch of the sublime; the old man seemed saying: 'Knock me down and be d—d to you – I'm not going to hurry.' His life was saved perhaps ten times a day by the British character at large, compounded of phlegm and a liking to take something under its protection. The tram conductors on that line were especially used to him, never failing to catch him under the arms and heave him like a sack of coals, while with trembling hands he pulled hard at the rail and strap.

'All right, sir?'

'Thank you.'

He moved into the body of the tram, where somebody would always get up from kindness and the fear that he might sit down on them; and there he stayed motionless, his little eyes tight closed. With his red face, tuft of white hairs above his square cleft block of shaven chin, and his big high-crowned bowler hat, which yet seemed too petty for his head with its thick hair – he looked like some kind of an idol dug up and decked out in gear a size too small.

One of those voices of young men from public schools and exchanges where things are bought and sold, said:

'How de do, Mr Heythorp?'

Old Heythorp opened his eyes. That sleek cub, Joe Pillin's son! What a young pup – with his round eyes, and his round cheeks, and his little moustache, his fur coat, his spats, his diamond pin!

'How's your father?' he said.

'Thanks, rather below par, worryin' about his ships. Suppose you haven't any news for him, sir?'

Old Heythorp nodded. The young man was one of his pet abominations, embodying all the complacent, little-headed mediocrity of this new generation; natty fellows all turned out of the same mould, sippers and tasters, chaps without drive or capacity, without even vices; and he did not intend to gratify the cub's curiosity.

'Come to my house,' he said; 'I'll give you a note for him.'

'Tha–anks; I'd like to cheer the old man up.'

The old man! Cheeky brat! And closing his eyes he relapsed into immobility. The tram wound and ground its upward way, and he mused. When he was that cub's age – twenty-eight or whatever it might be – he had done most things; been up Vesuvius, driven four-in-hand, lost his last penny on the Derby and won it back on the Oaks, known all the dancers and operatic stars of the day, fought a duel with a Yankee at Dieppe and winged him for saying through his confounded nose that Old England was played out; been a controlling voice already in his shipping firm; drunk five other of the best men in London under the table; broken his neck steeplechasing; shot a burglar in the legs; been nearly drowned, for a bet; killed snipe in Chelsea; been to Court for his sins; stared a ghost out of countenance; and travelled with a lady of Spain. If this young pup had done the last, it would be all he had; and yet, no doubt, he would call himself a 'spark.'

The conductor touched his arm.

''Ere you are, sir.'

'Thank you.'

He lowered himself to the ground, and moved in the bluish darkness towards the gate of his daughter's house. Bob Pillin walked beside him, thinking: 'Poor old josser, he *is* gettin' a back number!' And he said: 'I should have thought you ought to drive, sir. My old guv'nor would knock up at once if he went about at night like this.'

The answer rumbled out into the misty air:

'Your father's got no chest; never had.'

Bob Pillin gave vent to one of those fat cackles which come so readily from a certain type of man; and old Heythorp thought: 'Laughing at his father! Parrot!'

They had reached the porch.

A woman with dark hair and a thin, straight face and figure was arranging some flowers in the hall. She turned and said:

'You really ought not to be so late, Father! It's wicked at this time of year. Who is it – Oh! Mr Pillin, how do you do? Have you had tea? Won't you come to the drawing-room; or do you want to see my father?'

'Tha–anks! I believe your father –' And he thought: 'By Jove! the old chap *is* a caution!' For old Heythorp was crossing the hall without having paid the faintest attention to his daughter. Murmuring again:

'Tha–anks awfully; he wants to give me something,' he followed. Miss Heythorp was not his style at all; he had a kind of dread of that thin woman who looked as if she could never be unbuttoned. They said she was a great churchgoer and all that sort of thing.

In his sanctum old Heythorp had moved to his writing-table and was evidently anxious to sit down.

'Shall I give you a hand, sir?'

Receiving a shake of the head, Bob Pillin stood by the fire and watched. The old 'sport' liked to paddle his own canoe. Fancy having to lower yourself into a chair like that! When an old Johnny got to such a state it was really a mercy when he snuffed out, and made way for younger men. How his

Companies could go on putting up with such a fossil for chairman was a marvel! The fossil rumbled and said in that almost inaudible voice:

'I suppose you're beginning to look forward to your father's shoes?'

Bob Pillin's mouth opened. The voice went on:

'Dibs and no responsibility. Tell him from me to drink port – add five years to his life.'

To this unwarranted attack Bob Pillin made no answer save a laugh; he perceived that a manservant had entered the room.

'A Mrs Larne, sir. Will you see her?'

At this announcement the old man seemed to try and start; then he nodded, and held out the note he had written. Bob Pillin received it together with the impression of a murmur which sounded like: 'Scratch a poll, Poll!' and passing the fine figure of a woman in a fur coat, who seemed to warm the air as she went by, he was in the hall again before he perceived that he had left his hat.

A young and pretty girl was standing on the bearskin before the fire looking at him with round-eyed innocence. He thought: 'This is better; I mustn't disturb them for my hat'; and approaching the fire, said:

'Jolly cold, isn't it?'

The girl smiled: 'Yes – jolly.'

He noticed that she had a large bunch of violets at her breast, a lot of fair hair, a short straight nose, and round blue-grey eyes very frank and open. 'Er –' he said, 'I've left my hat in there.'

'What larks!' And at her little clear laugh something moved within Bob Pillin.

'You know this house well?'

She shook her head. 'But it's rather scrummy, isn't it?'

Bob Pillin, who had never yet thought so, answered:

'Quite O.K.'

The girl threw up her head to laugh again. 'O.K.? What's that?'

Bob Pillin saw her white round throat, and thought: 'She *is* a ripper!' And he said with a certain desperation:

'My name's Pillin. Yours is Larne, isn't it? Are you a relation here?'

'He's our Guardy. Isn't he a chook?'

That rumbling whisper like 'Scratch a poll, Poll!' recurring to Bob Pillin, he said with reservation:

'You know him better than I do.'

'Oh! Aren't you his grandson, or something?'

Bob Pillin did not cross himself.

'Lord! No! My dad's an old friend of his; that's all.'

'Is your dad like him?'

'Not much.'

'What a pity! It would have been lovely if they'd been Tweedles.'

Bob Pillin thought: 'This bit is something new. I wonder what her Christian name is.' And he said:

'What did your godfather and godmothers in your baptism –?'

The girl laughed; she seemed to laugh at everything.

'Phyllis.'

Could he say: 'Is my only joy'? Better keep it! But – for what? He wouldn't see her again if he didn't look out! And he said:

'I live at the last house in the park – the red one. D'you know it? Where do you?'

'Oh! a long way – 23, Millicent Villas. It's a poky little house. I hate it. We have awful larks, though.'

'Who are we?'

'Mother, and myself, and Jock – he's an awful boy. You can't conceive what an awful boy he is. He's got nearly red hair; I think he'll be just like Guardy when he gets old. He's *awful*!'

Bob Pillin murmured:

'I should like to see him.'

'Would you? I'll ask mother if you can. You won't want to again; he goes off all the time like a squib.' She threw back her head, and again Bob Pillin felt a little giddy. He collected himself, and drawled:

'Are you going in to see your Guardy?'

'No. Mother's got something special to say. We've never been here before, you see. Isn't he fun, though?'

'Fun!'

'I think he's the greatest lark: but he's awfully nice to me. Jock calls him the last of the Stoic'uns.'

A voice called from old Heythorp's den:

'Phyllis!' It had a particular ring, that voice, as if coming from beautifully formed red lips, of which the lower one must curve the least bit over; it had, too, a caressing vitality, and a kind of warm falsity.

The girl threw a laughing look back over her shoulder, and vanished through the door into the room.

Bob Pillin remained with his back to the fire and his puppy round eyes fixed on the air that her figure had last occupied. He was experiencing a sensation never felt before. Those travels with a lady of Spain, charitably conceded him by old Heythorp, had so far satisfied the emotional side of this young man; they had stopped short at Brighton and Scarborough, and been preserved from even the slightest intrusion of love. A calculated and hygienic career had caused no anxiety either to himself or his father; and this sudden swoop of something more than admiration gave him an uncomfortable choky feeling just above his high round collar, and in the temples a sort of buzzing – those first symptoms of chivalry. A man of the world does not, however, succumb without a struggle; and if his hat had not been out of reach, who knows whether he would not have left the house hurriedly, saying to himself: 'No, no, my boy; Millicent Villas is hardly your form, when your intentions are honourable'? For somehow that round and laughing face, bob of glistening hair, those wide-opened grey eyes, refused to awaken the beginnings of other intentions – such is the effect of youth and innocence on even the steadiest young men. With a kind of moral stammer, he was thinking: 'Can I – dare I offer to see them to their tram? Couldn't I even nip out and get the car round and send them home in it? No, I might miss them – better stick it out here! What a jolly laugh! What a ripping face – strawberries and cream, hay, and all that! Millicent Villas!' And he wrote it on his cuff.

The door was opening; he heard that warm vibrating voice:
'Come along, Phyllis!' – the girl's laugh so high and fresh:
'Right-o! Coming!' And with, perhaps, the first real tremor he
had ever known, he crossed to the front door. All the more
chivalrous to escort them to the tram without a hat! And suddenly he heard: 'I've got your hat, young man!' And her
mother's voice, warm, and simulating shock: 'Phyllis, you awful gairl! Did you ever see such an awful gairl, Mr –'

'Pillin, Mother.'

And then – he did not quite know how – insulated from the
January air by laughter and the scent of fur and violets, he was
between them walking to their tram. It was like an experience
out of the 'Arabian Nights', or something of that sort, an in-
toxication which made one say one was going their way, though
one would have to come all the way back in the same beastly
tram. Nothing so warming had ever happened to him as sitting
between them on that drive, so that he forgot the note in his
pocket, and his desire to relieve the anxiety of the 'old man', his
father. At the tram's terminus they all got out. There issued a
purr of invitation to come and see them sometime; a clear:
'Jock'll love to see you!' A low laugh: 'You awful gairl!' And
a flash of cunning zigzagged across his brain. Taking off his
hat, he said:

'Thanks awfully; rather!' and put his foot back on the step
of the tram. Thus did he delicately expose the depths of his
chivalry!

'Oh! you *said* you were going our way! What one-ers you
do tell! Oh!' The words were as music; the sight of those
eyes growing rounder, the most perfect he had ever seen; and
Mrs Larne's low laugh, so warm yet so preoccupied, and the
tips of the girl's fingers waving back above her head. He heaved
a sigh and knew no more till he was seated at his club before a
bottle of champagne Home! Not he! He wished to drink and
dream. 'The old man' would get his news all right tomorrow!

§ 3

The words: 'A Mrs Larne to see you, sir,' had been of a nature to astonish weaker nerves. What had brought her here? She knew she mustn't come! Old Heythorp had watched her entrance with cynical amusement. The way she whiffed herself at that young pup in passing, the way her eyes slid round! He had a very just appreciation of his son's widow; and a smile settled deep between his chin tuft and his moustache. She lifted his hand, kissed it, pressed it to her splendid bust, and said:

'So here I am at last, you see. Aren't you surprised?'

Old Heythorp shook his head.

'I really had to come and see you, Guardy; we haven't had a sight of you for such an age. And in this awful weather! How are you, dear old Guardy?'

'Never better.' And, watching her green-grey eyes, he added: 'Haven't a penny for you!'

Her face did not fall; she gave her feather-laugh.

'How dreadful of you to think I came for that! But I *am* in an awful fix, Guardy.'

'Never knew you not to be.'

'Just let me tell you, dear; it'll be some relief. I'm having the most terrible time.'

She sank into a low chair, disengaging an overpowering scent of violets, while melancholy struggled to subdue her face and body.

'The most awful fix. I expect to be sold up any moment. We may be on the streets tomorrow. I daren't tell the children; they're so happy, poor darlings. I shall be obliged to take Jock away from school. And Phyllis will have to stop her piano and dancing; it's an absolute crisis. And all due to those Midland Syndicate people. I've been counting on at least two hundred for my new story, and the wretches have refused it.'

With a tiny handkerchief she removed one tear from the corner of one eye. 'It *is* hard, Guardy; I worked my brain silly over that story.'

From old Heythorp came a mutter which sounded suspiciously like: 'Rats!'

Heaving a sigh, which conveyed nothing but the generosity of her breathing apparatus, Mrs Larne went on:

'You couldn't, I suppose, let me have just one hundred?'

'Not a bob.'

She sighed again, her eyes slid round the room; then in her warm voice she murmured:

'Guardy, you *were* my dear Philip's father, weren't you? I've never said anything; but *of course* you were. He was so like you, and so is Jock.'

Nothing moved in old Heythorp's face. No pagan image consulted with flowers and song and sacrifice could have returned less answer. Her dear Philip! She had led him the devil of a life, or he was a Dutchman! And what the deuce made her suddenly trot out the skeleton like this? But Mrs Larne's eyes were still wandering.

'What a lovely house! You know, I think you ought to help me, Guardy. Just imagine if your grandchildren were thrown out into the street!'

The old man grinned. He was not going to deny his relationship – it was her look-out, not his. But neither was he going to let her rush him.

'And they will be; you *couldn't* look on and see it. Do come to my rescue this once. You really might do something for them.'

With a rumbling sigh he answered:

'Wait. Can't give you a penny now. Poor as a church mouse.'

'Oh! Guardy!'

'Fact.'

Mrs Larne heaved one of her most buoyant sighs. She certainly did not believe him.

'Well!' she said; 'you'll be sorry when we come round one night and sing for pennies under your window. Wouldn't you like to see Phyllis? I left her in the hall . She's growing such a sweet gairl. Guardy – just fifty!'

'Not a rap.'

Mrs Larne threw up her hands. 'Well! You'll repent it. I'm at my last gasp.' She sighed profoundly, and the perfume of violets escaped in a cloud. Then, getting up, she went to the door and called: 'Phyllis!'

When the girl entered old Heythorp felt the nearest approach to a flutter of the heart for many years. She had put her hair up! She was like a spring day in January; such a relief from that scented humbug, her mother. Pleasant the touch of her lips on his forehead, the sound of her clear voice, the sight of her slim movements, the feeling that she did him credit – clean-run stock, she and that young scamp Jock – better than the holy woman, his daughter Adela, would produce if anyone were ever fool enough to marry her, or that pragmatical fellow, his son Ernest.

And when they were gone he reflected with added zest on the six thousand pounds he was getting for them out of Joe Pillin and his ships. He would have to pitch it strong in his speech at the general meeting. With freights so low, there was bound to be opposition. No dash nowadays; nothing but flabby caution! They were a scrim-shanking lot on the Board – he had had to pull them round one by one – the deuce of a tug getting this thing through! And yet, the business was sound enough. Those ships would earn money, properly handled – good money!

His valet, coming in to prepare him for dinner, found him asleep. He had for the old man as much admiration as may be felt for one who cannot put his own trousers on. He would say to the housemaid Molly: 'He's a game old blighter – must have been a rare one in his day. Cocks his hat at you, even now, I see!' To which the girl, Irish and pretty, would reply: 'Well, an' sure I don't mind, if it gives um a pleasure. 'Tis better anyway than the sad eye I get from herself.'

At dinner, old Heythorp always sat at one end of the rose-wood table and his daughter at the other. It was the eminent moment of the day. With napkin tucked high into his waist-coat, he gave himself to the meal with passion. His palate was undimmed, his digestion unimpaired. He could still eat as much as two men, and drink more than one. And while he savoured each mouthful he never spoke if he could help it. The holy woman had nothing to say that he cared to hear, and he nothing to say that she cared to listen to. She had a horror, too, of what she called 'the pleasures of the table' – those lusts of the flesh! She was always longing to dock his grub, he knew. Would

see her further first! What other pleasures were there at his age?
Let her wait till *she* was eighty. But she never would be; too
thin and holy!

This evening, however, with the advent of the partridge she
did speak.

'Who were your visitors, Father?'

Trust her for nosing anything out! Fixing his little blue
eyes on her, he mumbled with a very full mouth: 'Ladies.'

'So I saw; what ladies?'

He had a longing to say: 'Part of one of my families under
the rose.' As a fact it was the best part of the only one, but the
temptation to multiply exceedingly was almost overpowering.
He checked himself, however, and went on eating partridge,
his secret irritation crimsoning his cheeks; and he watched her
eyes, those cold precise and round grey eyes, noting it, and knew
she was thinking: 'He eats too much.'

She said: 'Sorry I'm not considered fit to be told. You ought
not to be drinking hock.'

Old Heythorp took up the long green glass, drained it, and
repressing fumes and emotion went on with his partridge. His
daughter pursed her lips, took a sip of water, and said:

'I know their name is Larne, but it conveyed nothing to me;
perhaps it's just as well.'

The old man, mastering a spasm, said with a grin:

'My daughter-in-law and my granddaughter.'

'What? Ernest married – Oh! nonsense!'

He chuckled, and shook his head.

'Then do you mean to say, Father, that you were married before you married my mother?'

'No.'

The expression on her face was as good as a play!

She said with a sort of disgust: 'Not married! I see. I suppose those people are hanging round your neck, then; no wonder you're always in difficulties. Are there any more of them?'

Again the old man suppressed that spasm, and the veins in
his neck and forehead swelled alarmingly. If he had spoken he
would infallibly have choked. He ceased eating, and putting his
hands on the table tried to raise himself. He could not, and

subsiding in his chair sat glaring at the stiff, quiet figure of his daughter.

'Don't be silly, Father, and make a scene before Meller. Finish your dinner.'

He did not answer. He was not going to sit there to be dragooned and insulted! His helplessness had never so weighed on him before. It was like a revelation. A log – that had to put up with anything! A log! And, waiting for his valet to return, he cunningly took up his fork.

In that saintly voice of hers she said:

'I suppose you don't realize that it's a shock to me. I don't know what Ernest will think –'

'Ernest be d—d.'

'I do wish, Father, you wouldn't swear.'

Old Heythorp's rage found vent in a sort of rumble. How the devil had he gone on all these years in the same house with that woman, dining with her day after day! But the servant had come back now, and putting down his fork he said:

'Help me up!'

The man paused, thunderstruck, with the *soufflé* balanced. To leave dinner unfinished – it was a portent!

'Help me up!'

'Mr Heythorp's not very well, Meller; take his other arm.'

The old man shook off her hand.

'I'm very well. Help me up. Dine in my own room in future.'

Raised to his feet, he walked slowly out; but in his sanctum he did not sit down, obsessed by this first overwhelming realization of his helplessness. He stood swaying a little, holding on to the table, till the servant, having finished serving dinner, brought in his port.

'Are you waiting to sit down, sir?'

He shook his head. Hang it, he could do that for himself, anyway. He must think of something to fortify his position against that woman. And he said:

'Send me Molly!'

'Yes, sir.' The man put down the port and went.

Old Heythorp filled his glass, drank, and filled again. He took a cigar from the box and lighted it. The girl came in, a grey-eyed, dark-haired damsel, and stood with her hands folded, her head a little to one side, her lips a little parted. The old man said :

'You're a human being.'

'I would hope so, sirr.'

'I'm going to ask you something as a human being – not a servant – see?'

'No, sirr; but I will be glad to do annything you like.'

'Then put your nose in here every now and then, to see if I want anything. Meller goes out sometimes. Don't say anything; just put your nose in.'

'Oh! an' I will; 'tis a pleasure 'twill be to do ut.'

He nodded, and when she had gone lowered himself into his chair with a sense of appeasement. Pretty girl! Comfort to see a pretty face – not a pale, peeky thing like Adela's. His anger burned up anew. So she counted on his helplessness, had begun to count on that, had she? She should see that there was life in the old dog yet! And his sacrifice of the uneaten *soufflé*, the still less eaten mushrooms, the peppermint sweet with which he usually concluded dinner, seemed to consecrate that purpose. They all thought he was a hulk, without a shot left in the locker! He had seen a couple of them at the Board that afternoon shrugging at each other, as though saying: 'Look at him!' And young Farney pitying him. Pity, forsooth! And that coarse-grained solicitor chap at the creditors' meeting curling his lips as much as to say: 'One foot in the grave!' He had seen the clerks dowsing the glim of their grins; and that young pup Bob Pillin screwing up his supercilious mug over his dog-collar. He knew that scented humbug Rosamund was getting scared that he'd drop off before she'd squeezed him dry. And his valet was always looking him up and down queerly. As to that holy woman –! Not quite so fast! Not quite so fast! And filling his glass for the fourth time, he slowly sucked down the dark red fluid, with the 'old boots' flavour which his soul loved, and, drawing deep at his cigar, closed his eyes.

2

§ 1

The room in the hotel where the general meetings of 'The Island Navigation Company' were held was nearly full when the secretary came through the door which as yet divided the shareholders from their directors. Having surveyed their empty chairs, their ink and papers, and nodded to a shareholder or two, he stood, watch in hand, contemplating the congregation. A thicker attendance than he had ever seen! Due, no doubt, to the lower dividend, and this Pillin business. And his tongue curled. For if he had a natural contempt for his Board, with the exception of the chairman, he had a still more natural contempt for his shareholders. Amusing spectacle when you come to think of it, a general meeting! Unique! Eighty or a hundred men, and five women, assembled through sheer devotion to their money. Was any other function in the world so singlehearted? Church was nothing to it – so many motives were mingled there with devotion to one's soul. A well-educated young man – reader of Anatole France, and other writers – he enjoyed ironic speculation. What earthly good did they think they got by coming here? Half-past two! He put his watch back into his pocket, and passed into the Board-room.

There, the fumes of lunch and of a short preliminary meeting made cosy the February atmosphere. By the fire four directors were conversing rather restlessly; the fifth was combing his beard; the chairman sat with eyes closed; the red lips moving rhythmically in the sucking of a lozenge, the slips of his speech ready in his hand. The secretary said in his cheerful voice: 'Time, sir.'

Old Heythorp swallowed, lifted his arms, rose with help, and walked through to his place at the centre of the table. The five directors followed. And, standing at the chairman's right, the secretary read the minutes, forming the words precisely with his curling tongue. Then, assisting the chairman to his feet, he watched those rows of faces, and thought: 'Mistake to let them see he can't get up without help. He ought to have let me read his speech – I wrote it.'

The chairman began to speak:

'It is my duty and my pleasure, ladies and gentlemen, for the nineteenth consecutive year to present to you the directors' report and the accounts for the past twelve months. You will all have had special notice of a measure of policy on which your Board has decided, and to which you will be asked today to give your adherence – to that I shall come at the end of my remarks . . .'

"Excuse me, sir; we can't hear a word down here.'

'Ah!' thought the secretary, 'I was expecting that.'

The chairman went on, undisturbed. But several shareholders now rose, and the same speaker said testily: 'We might as well go home. If the chairman's got no voice, can't somebody read for him?'

The chairman took a sip of water, and resumed. Almost all the last six rows were now on their feet, and amid a hubbub of murmurs the chairman held out to the secretary the slips of his speech, and fell heavily back into his chair.

The secretary re-read from the beginning; and as each sentence fell from his tongue, he thought: 'How good that is!' 'That's very clear!' 'A neat touch!' 'This is getting them.' It seemed to him a pity they could not know it was all his composition. When at last he came to the Pillin sale he paused for a second.

'I come now to the measure of policy to which I made allusion at the beginning of my speech. Your Board has decided to expand your enterprise by purchasing the entire fleet of Pillin & Co. Ltd. By this transaction we become the owners of the four steamships *Smyrna*, *Damascus*, *Tyre*, and *Sidon,* vessels in prime condition with a total freight-carrying capacity of fifteen thousand tons, at the low inclusive price of sixty thousand pounds. Gentlemen, "*Vestigia nulla retrorsum!*"' – it was the chairman's phrase, his bit of the speech, and the secretary did it more than justice. 'Times are bad, but your Board is emphatically of the opinion that they are touching bottom; and this, in their view, is the psychological moment for a forward

71

stroke. They confidently recommend your adoption of their policy and the ratification of this purchase, which they believe will, in the not far distant future, substantially increase the profits of the Company.' The secretary sat down with reluctance. The speech should have continued with a number of appealing sentences which he had carefully prepared, but the chairman had cut them out with the simple comment: 'They ought to be glad of the chance.' It was, in his view, an error.

The director who had combed his beard now rose – a man of presence, who might be trusted to say nothing long and suavely. While he was speaking the secretary was busy noting whence opposition was likely to come. The majority were sitting owl-like – a good sign; but some dozen were studying their copies of the report, and three at least were making notes – Westgate, for instance, who wanted to get on the Board, and was sure to make himself unpleasant – the time-honoured method of vinegar; and Batterson, who also desired to come on, and might be trusted to support the Board – the time-honoured method of oil; while, if one knew anything of human nature, the fellow who had complained that he might as well go home would have something uncomfortable to say. The director finished his remarks, combed his beard with his fingers, and sat down.

A momentary pause ensued. Then Messieurs Westgate and Batterson rose together. Seeing the chairman nod towards the latter, the secretary thought: 'Mistake! He should have humoured Westgate by giving him precedence.' But that was the worst of the old man, he had no notion of the *suaviter in modo!* Mr Batterson – thus unchained – would like, if he might be so allowed, to congratulate the Board on having piloted their ship so smoothly through the troublous waters of the past year. With their worthy chairman still at the helm, he had no doubt that in spite of the still low – he would not say falling – barometer, and the – er – unseasonable climacteric, they might rely on weathering the – er – he would not say storm. He would confess that the present dividend of four per cent was not one which satisfied every aspiration ('Hear, hear!'), but speaking for himself, and he hoped for others – and here Mr Batterson looked round – he recognized that in all the circumstances it was as much as they had the right – er – to expect. But following the bold but to *his* mind prudent development which the Board proposed to make, he thought that they might reasonably, if not sanguinely, anticipate a more golden future. ('No, no!') A shareholder said, 'No, no!' That might seem to indicate a certain lack of confidence in the special proposal before the meeting. ('Yes!') From that lack of confidence he would like at once to dissociate himself. Their chairman, a man of foresight and acumen, and valour proved on many a field and – er – sea, would not have committed himself to this policy without good reason. In his opinion they were in safe hands, and he was glad to register his support of the measure proposed. The chairman had well said in his speech: '*Vestigia nulla retrorsum!*' Shareholders would agree with him that there could be no better motto for Englishmen. Ahem!

Mr Batterson sat down. And Mr Westgate rose: He wanted – he said – to know more, much more, about this proposition, which to his mind was of a very dubious wisdom ... 'Ah!' thought the secretary, 'I told the old boy he must tell them more' ... To whom, for instance, had the proposal first been made? To him! – the chairman said. Good! But why were Pillins selling, if freights were to go up, as they were told?

'Matter of opinion.'

'Quite so; and in my opinion they are going lower, and Pillins were right to sell. It follows that we are wrong to buy.' ('Hear, hear!' 'No, no!') 'Pillins are shrewd people. What does the chairman say? Nerves! Does he mean to tell us that this sale was the result of nerves?'

The chairman nodded.

'That appears to me a somewhat fantastic theory; but I will leave that and confine myself to asking the grounds on which the chairman bases his confidence; in fact, what it is which is actuating the Board in pressing on us at such a time what I have no hesitation in stigmatizing as a rash proposal. In a word, I want light as well as leading in this matter.'

Mr Westgate sat down.

What would the chairman do now? The situation was

distinctly awkward – seeing his helplessness and the luke-warm-
ness of the Board behind him. And the secretary felt more
strongly than ever the absurdity of his being an underling, he
who in a few well-chosen words could so easily have twisted
the meeting round his thumb. Suddenly he heard the long,
rumbling sigh which preluded the chairman's speeches.

'Has any other gentleman anything to say before I move the
adoption of the report?'

Phew! That would put their backs up. Yes, sure enough it
had brought that fellow, who had said he might as well go
home, to his feet! Now for something nasty!

'Mr Westgate requires answering. I don't like this business.
I don't impute anything to anybody; but it looks to me as if
there were something behind it which the shareholders ought
to be told. Not only that; but, to speak frankly, I'm not satisfied to be ridden over roughshod in this fashion by one who,
whatever he may have been in the past, is obviously not now
in the prime of his faculties.'

With a gasp the secretary thought: 'I knew that was a plain-
spoken man!'

He heard again the rumbling beside him. The chairman had
gone crimson, his mouth was pursed, his little eyes were very
blue.

'Help me up,' he said.

The secretary helped him, and waited, rather breathless.

The chairman took a sip of water, and his voice, unexpectedly
loud, broke an ominous hush:

'Never been so insulted in my life. My best services have
been at your disposal for nineteen years; you know what measure of success this Company has attained. I am the oldest man
here, and my experience of shipping is, I hope, a little greater
than that of the two gentlemen who spoke last. I have done my
best for you, ladies and gentlemen, and we shall see whether
you are going to endorse an indictment of my judgement and of
my honour, if I am to take the last speaker seriously. This purchase is for your good. "There is a tide in the affairs of men" –
and I for one am not content, never have been, to stagnate. If
that is what you want, however, by all means give your support

to these gentlemen and have done with it. I tell you freights will go up before the end of the year; the purchase is a sound one, more than a sound one – I, at any rate, stand or fall by it. Refuse to ratify it, if you like; if you do, I shall resign.'

He sank back into his seat. The secretary, stealing a glance, thought with a sort of enthusiasm: 'Bravo! Who'd have thought he could rally his voice like that? A good touch, too, that about his honour! I believe he's knocked them. It's still dicky, though, if that fellow at the back gets up again; the old chap can't work that stop a second time.' Ah! here was 'old Apple-pie' on his hind legs. That was all right!

'I do not hesitate to say that I am an old friend of the chairman; we are, many of us, old friends of the chairman, and it has been painful to me, and I doubt not to others, to hear an attack made on him. If he is old in body, he is young in mental vigour and courage. I wish we were all as young. We ought to stand by him; I say, we ought to stand by him.' ('Hear, hear! Hear, hear!') And the secretary thought: 'That's done it!' And he felt a sudden odd emotion, watching the chairman bobbing his body, like a wooden toy, at old Appleby; and old Appleby bobbing back. Then, seeing a shareholder close to the door get up, thought: 'Who's that? I know his face – Ah! yes; Ventnor, the solicitor – he's one of the chairman's creditors that are coming again this afternoon. What now?'

'I can't agree that we ought to let sentiment interfere with our judgement in this matter. The question is simply: How are our pockets going to be affected? I came here with some misgivings, but the attitude of the chairman has been such as to remove them; and I shall support the proposition.' The secretary thought: 'That's all right – only he said it rather queerly – rather queerly.'

Then, after a long silence, the chairman, without rising, said:

'I move the adoption of the report and accounts.'

'I second that.'

'Those in favour signify the same in the usual way. Contrary? Carried.' The secretary noted the dissentients, six in number, and that Mr Westgate did not vote.

A quarter of an hour later he stood in the body of the

emptying room supplying names to one of the gentlemen of the Press. The passionless fellow said: 'Haythorp, with an "a"; oh! an "e"; he seems an old man. Thank you. I may have the slips? Would you like to see a proof? With an "a" you said – oh! an "e". Good afternoon!' And the secretary thought: 'Those fellows, what *does* go on inside them? Fancy not knowing the old chairman by now! ...'

§ 2

Back in the proper office of 'The Island Navigation Company' old Heythorp sat smoking a cigar and smiling like a purring cat. He was dreaming a little of his triumph, sifting with his old brain, still subtle, the wheat from the chaff of the demurrers: Westgate – nothing in that – professional discontent till they silenced him with a place on the Board – but not while *he* held the reins! That chap at the back – an ill-conditioned fellow! 'Something behind!' Suspicious brute! There *was* something – but – hang it! they might think themselves lucky to get four ships at that price, and all due to him! It was on the last speaker that his mind dwelt with a doubt. That fellow Ventnor, to whom he owed money – there had been something just a little queer about his tone – as much as to say, 'I smell a rat.' Well one would see that at the creditors' meeting in half an hour.

'Mr Pillin, sir.'

'Show him in!'

In a fur coat which seemed to extinguish his thin form, Joe Pillin entered. It was snowing, and the cold had nipped and yellowed his meagre face between its slight grey whiskering. He said thinly:

'How are you, Sylvanus? Aren't you perished in this cold?'

'Warm as a toast. Sit down. Take off your coat.'

'Oh! I should be lost without it. You must have a fire inside you. So – so it's gone through?'

Old Heythorp nodded; and Joe Pillin, wandering like a spirit, scrutinized the shut door. He came back to the table, and said in a low voice:

'It's a great sacrifice.'

Old Heythorp smiled.

'Have you signed the deed poll?'

Producing a parchment from his pocket Joe Pillin unfolded it with caution to disclose his signature, and said:

'I don't like it – it's irrevocable.'

A chuckle escaped old Heythorp.

'As death.'

Joe Pillin's voice passed up into the treble clef.

'I can't bear irrevocable things. I consider you stampeded me, playing on my nerves.'

Examining the signatures old Heythorp murmured:

'Tell your lawyer to lock it up. He must think you a sad dog, Joe.'

"Ah! Suppose on my death it comes to the knowledge of my wife!'

'She won't be able to make it hotter for you than you'll be already.'

Joe Pillin replaced the deed within his coat, emitting a queer thin noise. He simply could not bear joking on such subjects.

'Well,' he said, 'you've got your way; you always do. Who is this Mrs Larne? You oughtn't to keep me in the dark. It seems my boy met her at your house. You told me she didn't come there.'

Old Heythorp said with relish:

'Her husband was my son by a woman I was fond of before I married; her children are my grandchildren. You've provided for them. Best thing you ever did.'

'I don't know – I don't know. I'm sorry you told me. It makes it all the more doubtful. As soon as the transfer's complete, I shall get away abroad. This cold's killing me. I wish you'd give me your recipe for keeping warm.'

'Get a new inside.'

Joe Pillin regarded his old friend with a sort of yearning. 'And yet,' he said, 'I suppose, with your full-blooded habit, your life hangs by a thread, doesn't it?'

'A stout one, my boy!'

'Well, good-bye, Sylvanus. You're a Job's comforter; I must be getting home.' He put on his hat, and, lost in his fur coat, passed out into the corridor. On the stairs he met a man who said:

'How do you do, Mr Pillin? I know your son. Been seeing the chairman? I see your sale's gone through all right. I hope that'll do us some good, but I suppose you think the other way?'

Peering at him from under his hat, Joe Pillin said:

'Mr Ventnor, I think? Thank you! It's very cold, isn't it?' And, with that cautious remark, he passed on down.

Alone again, old Heythorp thought: 'By George! What a wavering, quavering, thread-paper of a fellow! What misery life must be to a chap like that! He walks in fear – he wallows in it. Poor devil!' And a curious feeling swelled in his heart, of elation, of lightness such as he had not known for years. Those two young things were safe now from penury – safe! After dealing with those infernal creditors of his he would go round and have a look at the children. With a hundred and twenty a year the boy could go into the Army – best place for a young scamp like that. The girl would go off like hot cakes, of course, but she needn't take the first calf that came along. As for their mother, she must look after herself; nothing under two thousand a year would keep *her* out of debt. But trust her for wheedling and bluffing her way out of any scrape! Watching his cigar-smoke curl and disperse he was consicious of the strain he had been under these last six weeks, aware suddenly of how greatly he had baulked at thought of today's general meeting. Yes! It might have turned out nasty. He knew well enough the forces on the Board, and off, who would be only too glad to shelve him. If he were shelved here his other two Companies would be sure to follow suit, and bang would go every penny of his income – he would be a pauper dependent on that holy woman. Well! Safe now for another year if he could stave off these sharks once more. It might be a harder job this time, but he was in luck – in luck, and it must hold. And taking a luxurious pull at his cigar, he rang the handbell.

'Bring 'em in here, Mr Farney. And let me have a cup of China tea as strong as you can make it.'

'Yes, sir. Will you see the proof of the press report, or will you leave it to me?'

'To you.'

'Yes, sir. It was a good meeting, wasn't it?'

Old Heythorp nodded.

'Wonderful how your voice came back just at the right moment. I was afraid things were going to be difficult. The insult did it, I think. It was a monstrous thing to say. I could have punched his head.'

Again old Heythorp nodded; and, looking into the secretary's fine blue eyes, he repeated: 'Bring 'em in.'

The lonely minute before the entrance of his creditors passed in the thought: 'So that's how it struck him! Short shrift I should get if it came out.'

The gentlemen, who numbered ten this time, bowed to their debtor, evidently wondering why the deuce they troubled to be polite to an old man who kept them out of their money. Then, the secretary reappearing with a cup of China tea, they watched while their debtor drank it. The feat was tremulous. Would he get through without spilling it all down his front, or choking? To those unaccustomed to his private life it was slightly miraculous. He put the cup down empty, tremblingly removed some yellow drops from the little white tuft below his lip, re-lit his cigar, and said:

'No use beating about the bush, gentlemen; I can offer you fourteen hundred a year so long as I live and hold my directorships, and not a penny more. If you can't accept that, you must make me bankrupt and get about sixpence in the pound. My qualifying shares will fetch a couple of thousand at market price. I own nothing else. The house I live in, and everything in it, barring my clothes, my wine, and my cigars, belong to my daughter under a settlement fifteen years old. My solicitors and bankers will give you every information. That's the position in a nutshell.'

In spite of business habits the surprise of the ten gentlemen was only partially concealed. A man who owed them so much would naturally say he owned nothing, but would he refer them to his solicitors and bankers unless he were telling the truth? Then Mr Ventnor said:

'Will you submit your pass books?'

'No, but I'll authorize my bankers to give you a full statement of my receipts for the last five years – longer, if you like.'

The strategic stroke of placing the ten gentlemen round the Board table had made it impossible for them to consult freely without being overheard, but the low-voiced transference of thought travelling round was summed up at last by Mr Brownbee.

'We think, Mr Heythorp, that your fees and dividends should enable you to set aside for us a larger sum. Sixteen hundred, in fact, is what we think you should give us yearly. Representing, as we do, sixteen thousand pounds, the prospect is not cheering, but we hope you have some good years before you yet. We understand your income to be two thousand pounds.'

Old Heythorp shook his head. 'Nineteen hundred and thirty pounds in a good year. Must eat and drink; must have a man to look after me – not as active as I was. Can't do on less than five hundred pounds. Fourteen hundred's all I can give you, gentlemen; it's an advance of two hundred pounds. That's my last word.'

The silence was broken by Mr Ventnor.

'And it's my last word that I'm not satisfied. If these other gentlemen accept your proposition I shall be forced to consider what I can do on my own account.'

The old man stared at him, and answered:

'Oh! you will, sir; we shall see.'

The others had risen and were gathered in a knot at the end of the table; old Heythorp and Mr Ventnor alone remained seated. The old man's lower lip projected till the white hairs below stood out like bristles. 'You ugly dog,' he was thinking, 'you think you've got something up your sleeve. Well, do your worst!' The 'ugly dog' rose abruptly and joined the others. And old Heythorp closed his eyes, sitting perfectly still, with his cigar, which had gone out, sticking up between his teeth. Mr Brownbee turning to voice the decision come to, cleared his throat.

'Mr Heythorp,' he said, 'if your bankers and solicitors bear out your statements, we shall accept your offer *faute de mieux*, in consideration of your –' but meeting the old man's eyes, which said so very plainly: 'Blow your consideration!' he ended with a stammer: 'Perhaps you will kindly furnish us with the authorization you spoke of?'

Old Heythorp nodded, and Mr Brownbee, with a little bow, clasped his hat to his breast and moved towards the door. The nine gentlemen followed. Mr Ventnor, bringing up the rear, turned and looked back. But the old man's eyes were already closed again.

The moment his creditors were gone, old Heythorp sounded the hand-bell.

'Help me up, Mr Farney. That Ventnor — what's his holding?'

'Quite small. Only ten shares, I think.'

'Ah! What time is it?'

'Quarter to four, sir.'

'Get me a taxi.'

After visiting his bank and his solicitors he struggled once more into his cab and caused it to be driven towards Millicent Villas. A kind of sleepy triumph permeated his whole being, bumped and shaken by the cab's rapid progress. So! He was free of those sharks now so long as he could hold on to his Companies; and he would still have a hundred a year or more to spare for Rosamund and her youngsters. He could live on four hundred, or even three-fifty, without losing his independence, for there would be no standing life in that holy woman's house unless he could pay his own scot! A good day's work! The best for many a long month!

The cab stopped before the villa.

§ 3

There are rooms which refuse to give away their owners, and rooms which seem to say: 'They really are like this.' Of such was Rosamund Larne's — a sort of permanent confession, seeming to remark to anyone who entered: 'Her taste? Well, you can see — cheerful and exuberant; her habits — yes, she sits here all the morning in a dressing-gown, smoking cigarettes and dropping ink; kindly observe my carpet. Notice the piano — it has a look of coming and going, according to the exchequer. This very deep-cushioned sofa is permanent, however; the water-colours on the walls are safe, too – they're by herself. Mark the scent of mimosa – she likes flowers, and likes them strong. No clock, of course. Examine the bureau – she is obviously always ringing for 'the drumstick', and saying: 'Where's this, Ellen, and where's that? You naughty gairl, you've been tidying.' Cast an eye on that pile of manuscript – she has evidently a genius for composition; it flows off her pen – like Shakespeare, she never blots a line. See how she's had the electric light put in, instead of that horrid gas; but try and turn either of them on – you can't; last quarter isn't paid, of course; and she uses an old lamp, you can tell that by the ceiling. The dog over there, who will not answer to the name of 'Carmen', a Pekinese spaniel like a little Djin, all prominent eyes rolling their blacks, and no nose between – yes, Carmen looks as if she didn't know what was coming next; she's right – it's a pet-and-slap-again life! Consider, too, the fittings of the tea-tray, rather soiled, though not quite tin, but I say unto you that no millionaire's in all its glory ever had a liqueur bottle on it.'

When old Heythorp entered this room, which extended from back to front of the little house, preceded by the announcement 'Mr Æsop,' it was resonant with a very clatter-bodandigo of noises, from Phyllis playing the Machiche; from the boy Jock on the hearth-rug, emitting at short intervals the most piercing notes from an ocarina; from Mrs Larne on the sofa, talking with her trailing volubility to Bob Pillin; from Bob Pillin muttering: 'Ye – es! Qui – ite! Ye – es!' and gazing at Phyllis over his collar. And, on the window-sill, as far as she could get from all this noise, the little dog Carmen was rolling her eyes. At sight of their visitor Jock blew one rending screech, and bolting behind the sofa, placed his chin on its top, so that nothing but his round pink unmoving face was visible, and the dog Carmen tried to climb the blind cord.

Encircled from behind by the arms of Phyllis, and preceded by the gracious perfumed bulk of Mrs Larne, old Heythorp was escorted to the sofa. It was low, and when he had plumped down on to it, the boy Jock emitted a hollow groan. Bob Pillin was the first to break the silence.

'How are you, sir? I hope it's gone through.'

Old Heythorp nodded. His eyes were fixed on the liqueur, and Mrs Larne murmured:

'Guardy, you *must* try our new liqueur. Jock, you awful boy, get up and bring Guardy a glass.'

The boy Jock approached the tea-table, took up a glass, put it to his eye and filled it rapidly.

'You horrible boy, you could see that glass has been used.'

In a high round voice rather like an angel's, Jock answered:

'All right, Mother; I'll get rid of it,' and rapidly swallowing the yellow liqueur, took up another glass.

Mrs Larne laughed.

'What *am* I to do with him?'

A loud shriek prevented a response. Phyllis, who had taken her brother by the ear to lead him to the door, let him go to clasp her injured self. Bob Pillin went hastening towards her; and following the young man with her chin, Mrs Larne, said smiling:

'Aren't those children awful? He's such a nice fellow. We like him so much, Guardy.'

The old man grinned. So she was making up to that young pup! Rosamund Larne, watching him, murmured:

'Oh! Guardy, you're as bad as Jock. He takes after you terribly. Look at the shape of his head. Jock, come here!' The innocent boy approached; with his girlish complexion, his flowery blue eyes, his perfect mouth, he stood before his mother like a large cherub. And suddenly he blew his ocarina in a dreadful manner. Mrs Larne launched a box at his ears, and receiving the wind of it he fell prone.

'That's the way he behaves. Be off with you, you awful boy. I want to talk to Guardy.'

The boy withdrew on his stomach, and sat against the wall cross-legged, fixing his innocent round eyes on old Heythorp. Mrs Larne sighed.

'Things are worse and worse, Guardy. I'm at my wits' end

to tide over this quarter. You wouldn't advance me a hundred on my new story? I'm sure to get two for it in the end.'

The old man shook his head.

'I've done something for you and the children,' he said. 'You'll get notice of it in a day or two; ask no questions.'

'Oh! Guardy! Oh! you dear!' And her gaze rested on Bob Pillin, leaning over the piano, where Phyllis again sat.

Old Heythorp snorted. 'What are you cultivating that young gaby for? She mustn't be grabbed up by any fool who comes along.'

Mrs Larne murmured at once:

'Of course, the dear gairl is *much* too young. Phyllis, come and talk to Guardy!'

When the girl was installed beside him on the sofa, and he had felt that little thrill of warmth the proximity of youth can bring, he said:

'Been a good girl?'

She shook her head.

'Can't, when Jock's not at school. Mother can't pay for him this term.'

Hearing his name, the boy Jock blew his ocarina till Mrs Larne drove him from the room, and Phyllis went on:

'He's more awful than anything you can think of. Was my dad at all like him, Guardy? Mother's always so mysterious about him. I suppose you knew him well.'

Old Heythorp, incapable of confusion, answered stolidly:

'Not very.'

'Who was *his* father? *I* don't believe even mother knows.'

'Man about town in my day.'

'Oh! your day must have been jolly. Did you wear peg-top trousers, and dundrearies?'

Old Heythorp nodded.

'What larks! And I suppose you had lots of adventures with opera dancers and gambling. The young men are all so good now.' Her eyes rested on Bob Pillin. 'That young man's a perfect stick of goodness.'

Old Heythorp grunted.

'You wouldn't know how good he was,' Phyllis went on

musingly, 'unless you'd sat next him in a tunnel. The other day he had his waist squeezed and he simply sat still and did nothing. And then when the tunnel ended, it was Jock after all, not me. His face was – Oh! ah! ha! ha! Ah! ha!' She threw back her head, displaying all her white, round throat. Then edging near, she whispered:

'He likes to pretend, of course, that he's fearfully lively. He's promised to take mother and me to the theatre and supper afterwards. Won't it be scrummy! Only, I haven't anything to go in.'

Old Heythorp said: 'What do you want? Irish poplin?'

Her mouth opened wide: 'Oh! Guardy! Soft white satin!'

'How many yards'll go round you?'

'I should think about twelve. We could make it ourselves. You *are* a chook!'

A scent of hair, like hay, enveloped him, her lips bobbed against his nose, and there came a feeling in his heart as when he rolled the first sip of a special wine against his palate. This little house was a rumpty-too affair, her mother was a humbug, the boy a cheeky young rascal, but there was a warmth here he never felt in that big house which had been his wife's and was now his holy daughter's. And once more he rejoiced at his day's work, and the success of his breach of trust, which put some little ground beneath these young feet, in a hard and unscrupulous world. Phyllis whispered in his ear:

'Guardy, do look; he *will* stare at me like that. Isn't it awful – like a boiled rabbit?'

Bob Pillin, attentive to Mrs Larne, was gazing with all his might over her shoulder at the girl. The young man was moonstruck, that was clear! There was something almost touching in the stare of those puppy dog's eyes. And he thought: 'Young beggar – wish I were his age!' The utter injustice of having an old and helpless body, when your desire for enjoyment was as great as ever! They said a man was as old as he felt! Fools! A man was as old as his legs and arms, and not a day younger. He heard the girl beside him utter a discomfortable sound, and saw her face cloud as if tears were not far off; she jumped up, and going to the window, lifted the little dog and buried her face in its brown and white fur. Old Heythorp thought: 'She sees that her humbugging mother is using her as a decoy.' But she had come back, and the little dog, rolling its eyes horribly at the strange figure on the sofa, in a desperate effort to escape succeeded in reaching her shoulder, where it stayed perched like a cat, held by one paw and trying to back away into space. Old Heythorp said abruptly:

'Are you very fond of your mother?'

'Of course I am, Guardy. I adore her.'

'H'm! Listen to me. When you come of age or marry, you'll have a hundred and twenty a year of your own that you can't get rid of. Don't ever be persuaded into doing what you don't want. And remember: Your mother's a sieve, no good giving her money; keep what you'll get for yourself – it's only a pittance, and you'll want it all – every penny.'

Phyllis's eyes had opened very wide; so that he wondered if she had taken in his words.

'Oh! Isn't money horrible, Guardy?'

'The want of it.'

'No, it's beastly altogether. If only we were like birds. Or if one could put out a plate overnight, and have just enough in the morning to use during the day.'

Old Heythorp sighed.

'There's only one thing in life that matters – independence. Lose that, and you lose everything. That's the value of money. Help me up.'

Phyllis stretched out her hands, and the little dog, running down her back, resumed its perch on the window-sill, close to the blind cord.

Once on his feet, old Heythorp said:

'Give me a kiss. You'll have your satin tomorrow.'

Then looking at Bob Pillin, he remarked:

'Going my way? I'll give you a lift.'

The young man, giving Phyllis one appealing look, answered dully: 'Tha–anks!' and they went out together to the taxi. In that draughtless vehicle they sat, full of who knows what contempt of age for youth, and youth for age; the old man resenting this young pup's aspiration to his granddaughter; the young man annoyed that this old image had dragged

him away before he wished to go. Old Heythorp said at last:
'Well?'

Thus expected to say something, Bob Pillin muttered:

'Glad your meetin' went off well, sir. You scored a triumph, I should think.'

'Why?'

'Oh! I don't know. I thought you had a good bit of opposition contend with.'

Old Heythorp looked at him.

'Your grandmother!' he said; then, with his habitual instincts of attack, added: 'You make the most of your opportunities, I see.'

At this rude assault Bob Pillin's red-cheeked face assumed a certain dignity. 'I don't know what you mean, sir. Mrs Larne is very kind to me.'

'No doubt. But don't try to pick the flowers.'

Thoroughly upset, Bob Pillin preserved a dogged silence. This fortnight, since he had first met Phyllis in old Heythorp's hall, had been the most singular of his existence up to now. He would never have believed that a fellow could be so quickly and completely bowled, could succumb without a kick, without even wanting to kick. To one with his philosophy of having a good time and never committing himself too far, it was in the nature of 'a fair knock-out', and yet so pleasurable, except for the wear and tear about one's chances. If only he knew how far the old boy really counted in the matter! To say: 'My intentions are strictly honourable' would be old-fashioned; besides – the old fellow might have no right to hear it. They called him Guardy, but without knowing more he did not want to admit the old curmudgeon's right to interfere.

'Are you a relation of theirs, sir?'

Old Heythorp nodded.

Bob Pillin went on with desperation:

'I should like to know what your objection to me is.'

The old man turned his head so far as he was able; a grim smile bristled the hairs about his lips, and twinkled in his eyes. What did he object to? Why – everything! Object to! That sleek head, those puppy-dog eyes, fattish red cheeks, high collars, pearl pin, spats, and drawl – pah! the imbecility, the smugness of his mug; no go, no devil in any of his sort, in any of these fish-veined, coddled-up young bloods, nothing but playing for safety! And he wheezed out:

'Milk and water masquerading as port wine.'

Bob Pillin frowned.

It was almost too much for the composure even of a man of the world. That this paralytic old fellow should express contempt for his virility was really the last thing in jests. Luckily he could not take it seriously. But suddenly he thought: 'What if he really has the power to stop my going there, and means to turn them against me!' And his heart quailed.

'Awfully sorry, sir,' he said, 'if you don't think I'm wild enough. Anything I can do for you in that line –'

The old man grunted; and realizing that he had been quite witty, Bob Pillin went on:

'I know I'm not in debt, no entanglements, got a decent income, pretty good expectations and all that; but I can soon put that all right if I'm not fit without.'

It was perhaps his first attempt at irony, and he could not help thinking how good it was.

But old Heythorp preserved a deadly silence. He looked like a stuffed man, a regular Aunt Sally sitting there, with the fixed red in his cheeks, his stivered hair, square block of a body, and no neck that you could see – only wanting the pipe in his mouth! Could there really be danger from such an old idol? The idol spoke:

'I'll give you a word of advice. Don't hang round there, or you'll burn your fingers. Remember me to your father. Good night!'

The taxi had stopped before the house in Sefton Park. An insensate impulse to remain seated and argue the point fought in Bob Pillin with an impulse to leap out, shake his fist in at the window, and walk off. He merely said, however:

'Thanks for the lift. Good night!' And, getting out deliberately, he walked off.

Old Heythorp, waiting for the driver to help him up, thought:

'Fatter, but no more guts than his father!'

In his sanctum he sank at once into his chair. It was wonderfully still there every day at this hour; just the click of the coals, just the faintest ruffle from the wind in the trees of the park. And it was cosily warm, only the fire lightening the darkness. A drowsy beatitude pervaded the old man. A good day's work! A triumph – that young pup had said. Yes! Something of a triumph! He had held on, and won. And dinner to look forward to, yet. A nap – a nap! And soon, rhythmic, soft, sonorous, his breathing rose, with now and then that pathetic twitching of the old who dream.

3

§ 1

When Bob Pillin emerged from the little front garden of 23, Millicent Villas ten days later, his sentiments were ravelled, and he could not get hold of an end to pull straight the stuff of his mind.

He had found Mrs Larne and Phyllis in the sitting-room, and Phyllis had been crying; he was sure she had been crying; and that memory still infected the sentiments evoked by later happenings. Old Heythorp had said: 'You'll burn your fingers.' The process had begun. Having sent her daughter away on a pretext really a bit too thin, Mrs Larne had installed him beside her scented bulk on the sofa, and poured into his ear such a tale of monetary woe and entanglement, such a mass of present difficulties and rosy prospects, that his brain still whirled, and only one thing emerged clearly – that she wanted fifty pounds, which she would repay him on quarter-day; for their Guardy had made a settlement by which, until the dear children came of age, she would have sixty pounds every quarter. It was only a question of a few weeks; he might ask Messrs Scriven and Coles; they would tell him the security was quite safe. He certainly might ask Messrs Scriven and Coles – they happened to be his father's solicitors; but it hardly seemed to touch the point. Bob Pillin had a certain shrewd caution, and the point was whether he was going to begin to lend money to a woman who, he could see, might borrow up to seventy times seven on the strength of his infatuation for her daughter. That was rather too strong! Yet, if he didn't – she might take a sudden dislike to him, and where would he be then? Besides, would not a loan make his position stronger? And then – such is the effect of love even on the younger generation – that thought seemed to him unworthy. If he lent at all, it should be from chivalry – ulterior motives might go hang! And the memory of the tear-marks on Phyllis's pretty pale-pink cheeks; and her petulantly mournful: 'Oh! young man, isn't money beastly!' scraped his heart, and ravished his judgement. All the same, fifty pounds was fifty pounds, and goodness knew how much more; and what did he know of Mrs Larne, after all, except that she was a relative of old Heythorp's and wrote stories – told them too, if he was not mistaken? Perhaps it would be better to see Scrivens'. But again that absurd nobility assaulted him. Phyllis! Phyllis! Besides, were not settlements always drawn so that they refused to form security for anything? Thus, hampered and troubled, he hailed a cab. He was dining with the Ventnors on the Cheshire side, and would be late if he didn't get home sharp to dress.

Driving, white-tied and waistcoated, in his father's car, he thought with a certain contumely of the younger Ventnor girl, whom he had been wont to consider pretty before he knew Phyllis. And seated next her at dinner, he quite enjoyed his new sense of superiority to her charms, and the ease with which he could chaff and be agreeable. And all the time he suffered from the suppressed longing which scarcely ever left him now, to think and talk of Phyllis. Ventnor's fizz was good and plentiful, his old Madeira absolutely first chop, and the only other man present a teetotal curate, who withdrew with the ladies to talk his parish shop. Favoured by these circumstances, and the perception that Ventnor was an agreeable fellow, Bob Pillin yielded to his secret itch to get near the subject of his affections.

'Do you happen,' he said airily, 'to know a Mrs Larne – relative of old Heythorp's – rather a handsome woman – she writes stories.'

Mr Ventnor shook his head. A closer scrutiny than Bob Pillin's would have seen that he also moved his ears.

'Of old Heythorp's? Didn't know he had any, except his daughter, and that son of his in the Admiralty.'

Bob Pillin felt the glow of his secret hobby spreading within him.

'She is, though – lives rather out of town; got a son and daughter. I thought you might know her stories – clever woman.'

Mr Ventnor smiled.

'Ah!' he said enigmatically, 'these lady novelists! Does she make any money by them?'

Bob Pillin knew that to make money by writing meant success, but that not to make money by writing was artistic, and implied that you had private means, which perhaps was even more distinguished. And he said:

'Oh! she has private means, I know.'

Mr Ventnor reached for the Madeira.

'So she's a relative of old Heythorp's,' he said. 'He's a very old friend of your father's. He ought to go bankrupt, you know.'

To Bob Pillin, glowing with passion and Madeira, the idea of bankruptcy seemed discreditable in connection with a relative of Phyllis. Besides, the old boy was far from that! Had he not just made this settlement on Mrs Larne? And he said:

'I think you're mistaken. That's of the past.'

Mr Ventnor smiled.

'Will you bet?' he said.

Bob Pillin also smiled. 'I should be bettin' on a certainty.'

Mr Ventnor passed his hand over his whiskered face. 'Don't you believe it; he hasn't a mag to his name. Fill your glass.'

Bob Pillin said, with a certain resentment:

'Well, I happen to know he's just made a settlement of five or six thousand pounds. Don't know if you call that being bankrupt.'

'What! On this Mrs Larne?'

Confused, uncertain whether he had said something derogatory or indiscreet, or something which added distinction to Phyllis, Bob Pillin hesitated, then gave a nod.

Mr Ventnor rose and extended his short legs before the fire.

'No, my boy,' he said. 'No!'

Unaccustomed to flat contradiction, Bob Pillin reddened.

'I'll bet you a tenner. Ask Scrivens'.'

Mr Ventnor ejaculated:

'Scrivens' – but they're not –' then, staring rather hard, he added: 'I won't bet. You may be right. Scrivens' are your father's solicitors too, aren't they? Always been sorry he didn't come to me. Shall we join the ladies?' And to the drawing-room he preceded a young man more uncertain in his mind than on his feet . . .

Charles Ventnor was not one to let you see that more was going on within than met the eye. But there was a good deal going on that evening, and after his conversation with young Bob he had occasion more than once to turn away and rub his hands together. When, after that second creditors' meeting, he had walked down the stairway which led to the offices of 'The Island Navigation Company', he had been deep in thought. Short, squarely built, rather stout, with moustache and large mutton-chop whiskers of a red-brown, and a faint floridity in face and dress, he impressed at first sight only by a certain truly British vulgarity. One felt that here was a hail-fellow-well-met man who liked lunch and dinner, went to Scarborough for his summer holidays, sat on his wife, took his daughters out in a boat and was never sick. One felt that he went to church every Sunday morning, looked upwards as he moved through life, disliked the unsuccessful, and expanded with his second glass of wine. But then a clear look into his well-clothed face and red-brown eyes would give the feeling: 'There's something fulvous here; he might be a bit too foxy.' A third look brought the thought: 'He's certainly a bully.' He was not a large creditor of old Heythorp. With interest on the original, he calculated his claim at three hundred pounds – unredeemed shares in that old Ecuador mine. But he had waited for his money eight years, and could never imagine how it came about that he had been induced to wait so long. There had been, of course, for one who liked 'big pots', a certain glamour about the personality of old Heythorp, still a bit of a swell in shipping circles, and a bit of

an aristocrat in Liverpool. But during the last year Charles
Ventnor had realized that the old chap's star had definitely set—
when that happens, of course, there is no more glamour, and
the time has come to get your money. Weakness in oneself and
others is despicable! Besides, he had food for thought, and de-
scending the stairs he chewed it. He smelt a rat – creatures for
which both by nature and profession he had a nose. Through
Bob Pillin, on whom he sometimes dwelt in connection with
his younger daughter, he knew that old Pillin and old Heythorp had been friends for thirty years and more. That, to an
astute mind, suggested something behind this sale. The thought
had already occurred to him when he read his copy of the report. A commission would be a breach of trust, of course, but
there were ways of doing things; the old chap was devilish hard
pressed, and human nature was human nature! His lawyerish
mind habitually put two and two together. The old fellow had
deliberately appointed to meet his creditors again just after the
general meeting which would decide the purchase – had said he
might do something for them then. Had that no significance?

In these circumstances Charles Ventnor had come to the meeting with eyes wide open and mouth tight closed. And he had
watched. It was certainly remarkable that such an old and feeble
man, with no neck at all, who looked indeed as if he might go
off with apoplexy any moment, should actually say that he
'stood or fell' by this purchase, knowing that if he fell he would
be a beggar. Why should the old chap be so keen on getting it
through? It would do him personally no good, unless – Exactly!
He had left the meeting, therefore, secretly confident that old
Heythorp had got something out of this transaction which
would enable him to make a substantial proposal to his creditors. So that when the old man had declared that he was going
to make none, something had turned sour in his heart, and he
had said to himself: 'All right, you old rascal! You don't know
C. V.' The cavalier manner of that beggarly old rip, the defiant
look of his deep little eyes, had put a polish on the rancour of
one who prided himself on letting no man get the better of him.
All that evening, seated on one side of the fire, while Mrs Ventnor sat on the other, and the younger daughter played Gounod's

Serenade on the violin – he cogitated. And now and again he smiled, but not too much. He did not see his way as yet, but had little doubt that before long he would. It would not be hard to knock that chipped old idol off his perch. There was already a healthy feeling among the shareholders that he was past work and should be scrapped. The old chap should find that Charles V. was not to be defied; that when he got his teeth into a thing, he did not let it go. By hook or crook he would have the old man off his Boards, or his debt out of him as the price of leaving him alone. His life or his money – and the old fellow should determine which. With the memory of that defiance fresh within him, he almost hoped it might come to be the first, and turning to Mrs Ventnor, he said abruptly:

'Have a little dinner Friday week, and ask young Pillin and the curate.' He specified the curate, a teetotaller, because he had two daughters, and males and females must be paired, but he intended to pack him off after dinner to the drawing-room to discuss parish matters while he and Bob Pillin sat over their wine. What he expected to get out of the young man he did not as yet know.

On the day of the dinner, before departing for the office, he had gone to his cellar. Would three bottles of Perrier Jouet do the trick, or must he add one of the old Madeira? He decided to be on the safe side. A bottle or so of champagne went very little way with him personally, and young Pillin might be another.

The Madeira having done its work by turning the conversation into such an admirable channel, he had cut it short for fear young Pillin might drink the lot or get wind of the rat. And when his guests were gone, and his family had retired, he stood staring into the fire, putting together the pieces of the puzzle. Five or six thousand pounds – six would be ten per cent on sixty! Exactly! Scrivens' – young Pillin had said! But Crow & Donkin, not Scriven & Coles, were old Heythorp's solicitors. What could that mean, save that the old man wanted to cover the tracks of a secret commission, and had handled the matter through solicitors who did not know the state of his affairs! But why Pillin's solicitors? With this sale just going through, it must look deuced fishy to them too. Was it all a mare's nest, after all? In such circumstances he himself would have taken the matter to a London firm who knew nothing of anybody. Puzzled, therefore, and rather disheartened, feeling too that touch of liver which was wont to follow his old Madeira, he went up to bed and woke his wife to ask her why the dickens they couldn't always have soup like that!

Next day he continued to brood over his puzzle, and no fresh light came; but having a matter on which his firm and Scrivens' were in touch, he decided to go over in person, and see if he could surprise something out of them. Feeling, from experience, that any really delicate matter would only be entrusted to the most responsible member of the firm, he had asked to see Scriven himself, and just as he had taken his hat to go, he said casually:

'By the way, you do some business for old Mr Heythorp don't you?'

Scriven, raising his eyebrows a little, muttered: 'Er – no,' in exactly the tone Mr Ventnor himself used when he wished to imply that though he didn't as a fact do business, he probably soon would. He knew therefore that the answer was a true one. And nonplussed, he hazarded:

'Oh! I thought you did, in regard to a Mrs Larne.'

This time he had certainly drawn blood of sorts, for down came Scriven's eyebrows, and he said:

'Mrs Larne – we know a Mrs Larne, but not in that connection. Why?'

'Oh! Young Pillin told me –'

'Young Pillin? Why, it's his –!' A little pause, and then: 'Old Mr Heythorp's solicitors are Crow & Donkin, I believe.'

Mr Ventnor held out his hand. 'Yes, yes,' he said; 'goodbye. Glad to have got that matter settled up,' and out he went, and down the street, important, smiling. By George! He had got it! 'It's his father' – Scriven had been going to say. What a plant! Exactly! Oh! neat! Old Pillin had made the settlement direct; and the solicitors were in the dark; that disposed of his difficulty about *them*. No money had passed between old Pillin and old Heythorp – not a penny. Oh! neat! But not neat enough

for Charles Ventnor, who had that nose for rats. Then his smile
died, and with a little chill he perceived that it was all based
on supposition – not quite good enough to go on! What then?
Somehow he must see this Mrs Larne, or better – old Pillin himself. The point to ascertain was whether she had any connection
of her own with Pillin. Clearly young Pillin didn't know of it;
for, according to him, old Heythorp had made the settlement.
By Jove! That old rascal was deep – all the more satisfaction
in proving that he was not as deep as C. V. To unmask the old
cheat was already beginning to seem in the nature of a public
service. But on what pretext could he visit Pillin? A subscription to the Windeatt almshouses! That would make him talk in
self-defence and he would take care not to press the request to
the actual point of getting a subscription. He caused himself to
be driven to the Pillin residence in Sefton Park. Ushered into a
room on the ground floor, heated in American fashion, Mr
Ventnor unbuttoned his coat. A man of sanguine constitution,
he found this hot-house atmosphere a little trying. And having
sympathetically obtained Joe Pillin's reluctant refusal – Quite
so! One could not indefinitely extend one's subscriptions even
for the best of causes! – he said gently:

'By the way, you know Mrs Larne, don't you?'

The effect of that simple shot surpassed his highest hopes.
Joe Pillin's face, never highly coloured, turned a sort of grey;
he opened his thin lips, shut them quickly, as birds do, and
something seemed to pass with difficulty down his scraggy
throat. The hollows, which nerve exhaustion delves in the
cheeks of men whose cheek-bones are not high, increased alarmingly. For a moment he looked deathly; then, moistening his
lips, he said:

'Larne – Larne? No, I don't seem –'

Mr Ventnor, who had taken care to be drawing on his gloves,
murmured:

'Oh! I thought – your son knows her; a relation of old Heythorp's,' and he looked up.

Joe Pillin had his handkerchief to his mouth; he coughed
feebly, then with more and more vigour:

'I'm in very poor health,' he said, at last. 'I'm getting abroad at once. This cold's killing me. What name did you say?' And he remained with his handkerchief against his teeth.

Mr Ventnor repeated:

'Larne. Writes stories.'

Joe Pillin muttered into his handkerchief:

'Ah! H'm! No – I – no! My son knows all sorts of people. I shall have to try Mentone. Are you going? Good-bye! Good-bye! I'm sorry; ah! ha! My cough – ah! ha h'h'm! Very distressing. Ye-hes! My cough! ah! ha h'h'm! Most distressing. Ye-hes!'

Out in the drive Mr Ventnor took a deep breath of the frosty air. Not much doubt now! The two names had worked like charms. This weakly old fellow would make a pretty witness, would simply crumple under cross-examination. What a contrast to that hoary old sinner Heythorp, whose brazenness nothing could affect. The rat was as large as life! And the only point was how to make the best use of it. Then – for his experience was wide – the possibility dawned on him, that after all, this Mrs Larne might only have been old Pillin's mistress – or be his natural daughter, or have some other blackmailing hold on him. Any such connection would account for his agitation, for his denying her, for his son's ignorance. Only it wouldn't account for young Pillin's saying that old Heythorp had made the settlement. He could only have got that from the woman herself. Still, to make absolutely sure, he had better try and see her. But how? It would never do to ask Bob Pillin for an introduction, after this interview with his father. He would have to go on his own and chance it. Wrote stories did she? Perhaps a newspaper would know her address; or the Directory would give it – not a common name! And, hot on the scent, he drove to a post office. Yes, there it was, right enough! 'Larne, Mrs R. – 23, Millicent Villas.' And thinking to himself: 'No time like the present,' he turned in that direction. The job was delicate. He must be careful not to do anything which might compromise his power of making public use of his knowledge. Yes – ticklish! What he did now must have a proper legal bottom. Still, anyway you looked at it, he had a *right* to investigate a fraud on himself as a shareholder of 'The Island Navigation Company', and a fraud on himself as a creditor of old Heythorp. Quite! But suppose this Mrs Larne was really entangled with old Pillin, and the settlement a mere reward of virtue, easy or otherwise. Well! in that case there'd be no secret commission to make public, and he needn't go further. So that, in either event, he would be all right. Only – how to introduce himself? He might pretend he was a newspaper man wanting a story. No, that wouldn't do! He must not represent that he was what he was not, in case he had afterwards to justify his actions publicly, always a difficult thing, if you were not careful! At that moment there came into his mind a question Bob Pillin had asked the other night. 'By the way, you can't borrow on a settlement, can you? Isn't there generally some clause against it?' Had this woman been trying to borrow from him on that settlement? But at this moment he reached the house, and got out of his cab still undecided as to how he was going to work the oracle. Impudence, constitutional and professional, sustained him in saying to the little maid:

'Mrs Larne at home? Say Mr Charles Ventnor, will you?'

His quick brown eyes took in the apparel of the passage which served for hall – the deep blue paper on the walls, lilac-patterned curtains over the doors, the well-known print of a nude young woman looking over her shoulder, and he thought: 'H'm! Distinctly tasty!' They noted, too, a small brown-and-white dog cowering in terror at the very end of the passage, and he murmured affably: 'Fluffy! Come here, Fluffy!' till Carmen's teeth chattered in her head.

'Will you come in, sir?'

Mr Ventnor ran his hand over his whiskers, and, entering a room, was impressed at once by its air of domesticity. On a sofa a handsome woman and a pretty young girl were surrounded by sewing apparatus and some white material. The girl looked up, but the elder lady rose.

Mr Ventnor said easily:

'You know my young friend, Mr Robert Pillin, I think.'

The lady, whose bulk and bloom struck him to the point of admiration, murmured in a full sweet drawl:

'Oh! Ye–es. Are you from Messrs Scrivens'?'

With the swift reflection: 'As I thought!' Mr Ventnor answered:

'Er – not exactly. I *am* a solicitor though; came just to ask about a certain settlement that Mr Pillin tells me you're entitled under.'

'Phyllis dear!'

Seeing the girl about to rise from underneath the white stuff, Mr Ventnor said quickly:

'Pray don't disturb yourself – just a formality!' It had struck him at once that the lady would have to speak the truth in the presence of this third party, and he went on: 'Quite recent, I think. This'll be your first interest – on six thousand pounds? Is that right?' And at the limpid assent of that rich, sweet voice, he thought: 'Fine woman; what eyes!'

'Thank you; that's quite enough. I can go to Scrivens' for any detail. Nice young fellow, Bob Pillin, isn't he?' He saw the girl's chin tilt, and Mrs Larne's full mouth curling in a smile.

'Delightful young man; we're very fond of him.'

And he proceeded:

'I'm quite an old friend of his; have you known him long?'

'Oh! no. How long, Phyllis, since we met him at Guardy's? About a month. But he's so unaffected – quite at home with us. A *nice* fellow.'

Mr Ventnor murmured:

'Very different from his father, isn't he?'

'Is he! We don't know his father; he's a shipowner, I think.'

Mr Ventnor rubbed his hands: 'Ye – es,' he said, 'just giving up – a warm man. Young Pillin's a lucky fellow – only son. So you met him at old Mr Heythorp's. I know him too – relation of yours, I believe.'

'Our dear Guardy – such a wonderful man.'

Mr. Ventnor echoed: 'Wonderful – regular old Roman.'

'Oh! but he's so *kind*!' Mrs Larne lifted the white stuff: 'Look what he's given this naughty gairl!'

Mr Ventnor murmured: 'Charming! Charming! Bob Pillin said, I think, that Mr Heythorp was your settlor.'

One of those little clouds which visit the brows of women

who have owed money in their time passed swiftly athwart Mrs Larne's eyes. For a moment they seemed saying: 'Don't you want to know too much?' Then they slid from under it.

'Won't you sit down?' she said. 'You must forgive our being at work.'

Mr Ventnor, who had need of sorting his impressions, shook his head.

'Thank you; I must be getting on. Then Messrs Scriven can – a mere formality! Good-bye! Good-bye, Miss Larne. I'm sure the dress will be most becoming.'

And with memories of a too clear look from the girl's eyes, of a warm firm pressure from the woman's hand, Mr Ventnor backed towards the door and passed away just in time to avoid hearing in two voices:

'What a nice lawyer!'

'What a horrid man!'

Back in his cab, he continued to rub his hands. No, she *didn't* know old Pillin! That was certain; not from her words, but from her face. She wanted to know him, or about him, anyway. She was trying to hook young Bob for that sprig of a girl – it was clear as mud. H'm! it would astonish his young friend to hear that he had called. Well, let it! And a curious mixture of emotions beset Mr Ventnor. He saw the whole thing now so plainly, and really could not refrain from a certain admiration. The law had been properly diddled! There was nothing to prevent a man from settling money on a woman he had never seen; and so old Pillin's settlement could probably not be upset. But old Heythorp could. It was neat, though, oh! neat! And that was a fine woman – remarkably! He had a sort of feeling that if only the settlement had been in danger, it might have been worth while to have made a bargain – a woman like that could have made it worth while! And he believed her quite capable of entertaining the proposition! Her eye! Pity – quite a pity! Mrs Ventnor was not a wife who satisfied every aspiration. But alas! the settlement *was* safe. This baulking of the sentiment of love, whipped up, if anything, the longing for justice in Mr Ventnor. That old chap should feel his teeth now. As a piece of investigation it was not so bad – not so bad at all!

He had had a bit of luck, of course – no, not luck – just that knack of doing the right thing at the right moment which marks a real genius for affairs.

But getting into his train to return to Mrs Ventnor, he thought: 'A woman like that would have been –!' And he sighed.

§ 2

With a neatly written cheque for fifty pounds in his pocket Bob Pillin turned in at 23, Millicent Villas on the afternoon after Mr Ventnor's visit. Chivalry had won the day. And he rang the bell with an elation which astonished him, for he knew he was doing a soft thing.

'Mrs Larne is out, sir; Miss Phyllis is at home.'

His heart leaped.

'Oh – h! I'm sorry. I wonder if she'd see me?'

The little maid answered:

'I think she's been washin' 'er 'air, sir, but it may be dry by now. I'll see.'

Bob Pillin stood stock still beneath the young woman on the wall. He could scarcely breathe. If her hair were not dry – how awful! Suddenly he heard floating down a clear but smothered: 'Oh! Gefoozleme!' and other words which he could not catch. The little maid came running down.

'Miss Phyllis says, sir, she'll be with you in a jiffy. And I was to tell you that Master Jock is loose, sir.'

Bob Pillin answered 'Tha – anks,' and passed into the drawing-room. He went to the bureau, took an envelope, enclosed the cheque, and addressing it: 'Mrs Larne,' replaced it in his pocket. Then he crossed over to the mirror. Never till this last month had he really doubted his own face; but now he wanted for it things he had never wanted. It had too much flesh and colour. It did not reflect his passion. This was a handicap. With a narrow white piping round his waistcoat opening, and a buttonhole of tuberoses, he had tried to repair its deficiencies. But do what he would, he was never easy about himself nowadays, never up to that pitch which could make him confident in her presence. And until this month to lack confidence had never been his wont. A clear, high, mocking voice said:

'Oh – h! Conceited young man!'

And spinning round he saw Phyllis in the doorway. Her light brown hair was fluffed out on her shoulders, so that he felt a kind of fainting-sweet sensation, and murmured inarticulately:

'Oh! I say – how jolly!'

'Lawks! It's awful! Have you come to see mother?'

Balanced between fear and daring, conscious of a scent of hay and verbena and camomile, Bob Pillin stammered:

'Ye–es. I – I'm glad she's not in, though.'

Her laugh seemed to him terribly unfeeling.

'Oh! oh! Don't be foolish. Sit down. Isn't washing one's head awful?'

Bob Pillin answered feebly:

'Of course, I haven't much experience.'

Her mouth opened.

'Oh! You *are* – aren't you?'

And he thought desperately: 'Dare I – oughtn't I – couldn't I somehow take her hand or put my arm round her, or something?' Instead, he sat very rigid at his end of the sofa, while she sat lax and lissom at the other, and one of those crises of paralysis which beset would-be lovers fixed him to the soul.

Sometimes during this last month memories of a past existence, when chaff and even kisses came readily to the lips, and girls were fair game, would make him think: 'Is she really such an innocent? Doesn't she really want me to kiss her?' Alas! such intrusions lasted but a moment before a blast of awe and chivalry withered them, and a strange and tragic delicacy – like nothing he had ever known – resumed its sway. And suddenly he heard her say:

'Why do you know such awful men?'

'What? I don't know any *awful* men.'

'Oh yes, you do; one came here yesterday; he had whiskers, and he was awful.'

'Whiskers?' His soul revolted in disclaimer, 'I believe I only know one man with whiskers – a lawyer.'

'Yes – that was him; a perfectly horrid man. Mother didn't mind him, but *I* thought he was a beast.'

'Ventnor! Came here? How d'you mean?'

'He did; about some business of yours, too.' Her face had clouded over. Bob Pillin had of late been harassed by the stillborn beginning of a poem:

> I rode upon my way and saw
> A maid who watched me from the door.

It never grew longer, and was prompted by the feeling that her face was like an April day. The cloud which came on it now was like an April cloud, as if a bright shower of rain must follow. Brushing aside the two distressful lines, he said:

'Look here, Miss Larne – Phyllis – look here!'

'All right, I'm looking!'

'What does it mean – how did he come? What did he say?'

She shook her head, and her hair quivered; the scent of camomile, verbena, hay, was wafted; then looking at her lap, she muttered:

'I wish you wouldn't – I wish mother wouldn't – I hate it. Oh! Money! Beastly – beastly!' and a tearful sigh shivered itself into Bob Pillin's reddening ears.

'I say – don't! And do tell me, because –'

'Oh! you *know*.'

'I don't – I don't know anything at all. I never –'

Phyllis looked up at him. 'Don't tell fibs; you know mother's borrowing money from you, and it's hateful!'

A desire to lie roundly, a sense of the cheque in his pocket, a feeling of injustice, the emotion of pity, and a confused and black astonishment about Ventnor, caused Bob Pillin to stammer:

'Well, I'm d—d!' and to miss the look which Phyllis gave him through her lashes – a look saying:

'Ah! that's better!'

'I *am* d—d! Look here! D'you mean to say that Ventnor came here about my lending money? I never said a word to him –'

'There you see – you *are* lending!'

He clutched his hair.

'We've got to have this out,' he added.

'Not by the roots! Oh! you do look funny. I've never seen you with your hair untidy. Oh! oh!'

Bob Pillin rose and paced the room. In the midst of his emotion he could not help seeing himself sidelong in the mirror; and on pretext of holding his head in both his hands, tried earnestly to restore his hair. Then coming to a halt he said:

'Suppose I *am* lending money to your mother, what does it matter? It's only till quarter-day. Anybody might want money.'

Phyllis did not raise her face.

'Why are you lending it?'

'Because – because – why shouldn't I?' and diving suddenly, he seized her hands.

She wrenched them free; and with the emotion of despair, Bob Pillin took out the envelope.

'If you like,' he said, 'I'll tear this up. I don't want to lend it, if you don't want me to; but I thought – I thought –' It was for her alone he had been going to lend this money!

Phyllis murmured through her hair:

'Yes! You thought that *I* – that's what's so hateful!'

Apprehension pierced his mind.

'Oh? I never – I swear I never –'

'Yes, you did; you thought I wanted you to lend it.'

She jumped up, and brushed past him into the window.

So she thought she was being used as a decoy! That was awful – especially since it was true. He knew well enough that Mrs Larne was working his admiration for her daughter for all that it was worth. And he said with simple fervour:

'What rot!' It produced no effect, and at his wits' end, he almost shouted: 'Look, Phyllis! If you don't want me to – here goes!' Phyllis turned. Tearing the envelope across he threw the bits into the fire. 'There it is,' he said.

Her eyes grew round; she said in an awed voice: 'Oh!'

In a sort of agony of honesty he said:

'It was only a cheque. Now you've got your way.'

Staring at the fire she answered slowly:

'I expect you'd better go before mother comes.'

Bob Pillin's mouth fell ajar; he secretly agreed, but the idea of sacrificing a moment alone with her was intolerable, and he said hardily:

'No, I shall stick it!'

Phyllis sneezed.

'My hair isn't a bit dry,' and she sat down on the fender with her back to the fire.

A certain spirituality had come into Bob Pillin's face. If only he could get that wheeze off: 'Phyllis is my only joy!' or even: 'Phyllis – do you – won't you – mayn't I?' But nothing came – nothing.

And suddenly she said:

'Oh! don't breathe so loud; it's awful!'

'Breathe? I wasn't!'

'You were; just like Carmen when she's dreaming.'

He had walked three steps towards the door, before he thought: 'What does it matter? I can stand anything from her'; and walked the three steps back again.

She said softly:

'Poor young man!'

He answered gloomily:

'I suppose you realize that this may be the last time you'll see me?'

'Why? I thought you were going to take us to the theatre.'

'I don't know whether your mother will – after –'

Phyllis gave a little clear laugh.

'You don't know mother. Nothing makes any difference to her.'

And Bob Pillin muttered:

'I see.' He did not, but it was of no consequence. Then the thought of Ventnor again ousted all others. What on earth – how on earth! He searched his mind for what he could possibly have said the other night. Surely he had not asked him to do anything; certainly not given him their address. There was something very odd about it that had jolly well got to be cleared up! And he said:

'Are you sure the name of that johnny who came here yesterday was Ventnor?'

Phyllis nodded.

'And he was short, and had whiskers?'

'Yes; red, and red eyes.'

He murmured reluctantly:

'It must be him. Jolly good cheek; I simply can't understand. I shall go and see him. How on earth did he know your address?'

'I expect you gave it him.'

'I did not. I won't have you thinking me a squirt.'

Phyllis jumped up. 'Oh! Lawks! Here's mother!' Mrs Larne was coming up the garden. Bob Pillin made for the door. 'Good-bye,' he said; 'I'm going.' But Mrs Larne was already in the hall. Enveloping him in fur and her rich personality, she drew him with her into the drawing-room, where the back window was open and Phyllis gone.

'I hope,' she said, 'those naughty children have been making you comfortable. That nice lawyer of yours came yesterday. He seemed quite satisfied.'

Very red above his collar, Bob Pillin stammered:

'I never told him to; he isn't my lawyer. I don't know what it means.'

Mrs Larne smiled. 'My dear boy, it's all right. You needn't be so squeamish. I want it to be quite on a business footing.'

Restraining a fearful inclination to blurt out: 'It's not going to be on any footing!' Bob Pillin mumbled: 'I must go; I'm late.'

'And when will you be able –?'

'Oh! I'll – I'll send – I'll write. Good-bye!' And suddenly he found that Mrs Larne had him by the lapel of his coat. The scent of violets and fur was overpowering, and the thought flashed through him: 'I believe she only wanted to take money off old Joseph in the Bible. I can't leave my coat in her hands! What shall I do?'

Mrs Larne was murmuring:

'It would be *so* sweet of you if you could manage it today'; and her hand slid over his chest. 'Oh! You *have* brought your cheque-book – what a nice boy!'

Bob Pillin took it out in desperation, and, sitting down at the bureau, wrote a cheque similar to that which he had torn and burned. A warm kiss lighted on his eyebrow, his head was pressed for a moment to a furry bosom; a hand took the cheque; a voice said: 'How delightful!' and a sigh immersed him in a bath of perfume. Backing to the door, he gasped:

'Don't mention it; and – and *don't tell Phyllis, please*. Goodbye!'

Once through the garden gate, he thought: 'By gum! I've done it now. That Phyllis should know about it at all! That beast Ventnor!'

His face grew almost grim. He would go and see what that meant anyway!

§3

Mr Ventnor had not left his office when his young friend's card was brought to him. Tempted for a moment to deny his own presence, he thought: 'No! What's the good? Bound to see him sometime!' If he had not exactly courage, he had that particular blend of self-confidence and insensibility which must needs distinguish those who follow the law; nor did he ever forget that he was in the right.

'Show him in!' he said.

He would be quite bland, but young Pillin might whistle for an explanation; he was still tormented, too, by the memory of rich curves and moving lips, and the possibilities of better acquaintanceship.

While shaking the young man's hand his quick and fulvous eye detected at once the discomposure behind that mask of cheek and collar, and relapsing into one of those swivel chairs which give one an advantage over men more statically seated, he said:

'You look pretty bobbish. Anything I can do for you?'

Bob Pillin, in the fixed chair of the consulter, nursed his bowler on his knee.

'Well, yes, there is. I've just been to see Mrs Larne.'

Mr Ventnor did not flinch.

'Ah! Nice woman; pretty daughter, too!' And into those words he put a certain meaning. He never waited to be bullied. Bob Pillin felt the pressure of his blood increasing.

'Look here, Ventnor,' he said, 'I want an explanation.'

'What of?'

'Why, of your going there, and using my name, and God knows what.'

Mr Ventnor gave his chair two little twiddles before he said:

'Well, you won't get it.'

Bob Pillin remained for a moment taken aback; then he muttered resolutely:

'It's not the conduct of a gentleman.'

Every man has his illusions, and no man likes them disturbed. The gingery tint underlying Mr Ventnor's colouring overlaid it; even the whites of his eyes grew red.

'Oh!' he said; 'indeed! You mind your own business, will you?'

'It is my business – very much so. You made use of my name, and I don't choose –'

'The devil you don't! Now, I tell you what –' Mr Ventnor leaned forward – 'you'd better hold your tongue, and not exasperate me. I'm a good-tempered man, but I won't stand your impudence.'

Clenching his bowler hat, and only kept in his seat by that sense of something behind, Bob Pillin ejaculated:

'Impudence! That's good – after what you did! Look here, why did you? It's so extraordinary!'

Mr Ventnor answered:

'Oh! is it? You wait a bit, my friend!'

Still more moved by the mystery of this affair, Bob Pillin could only mutter:

'I never gave you their address; we were only talking about old Heythorp.'

And at the smile which spread between Mr Ventnor's whiskers, he jumped up, crying:

'It's not the thing, and you're not going to put me off, I insist on an explanation.'

Mr Ventnor leaned back, crossing his stout legs, joining the tips of his thick fingers. In this attitude he was always self-possessed.

'You do – do you?'

'Yes. You must have had some reason.'

Mr Ventnor gazed up at him.

'I'll give you a piece of advice, young cock, and charge you nothing for it, too: Ask no questions, and you'll be told no lies. And here's another: Go away before you forget yourself again.'

The natural stolidity of Bob Pillin's face was only just proof against this speech. He said thickly:

'If you go there again and use my name, I'll – Well, it's lucky for you you're not my age. Anyway I'll relieve you of my acquaintanceship in future. Good evening!' and he went to the door. Mr Ventnor had risen.

'Very well,' he said loudly. 'Good riddance! You wait and see which boot the leg is on!'

But Bob Pillin was gone, leaving the lawyer with a very red face, a very angry heart, and a vague sense of disorder in his speech. Not only Bob Pillin, but his tender aspirations had all left him; he no longer dallied with the memory of Mrs Larne, but like a man and a Briton thought only of how to get his own back and punish evildoers. The atrocious words of his young friend, 'It's not the conduct of a gentleman,' festered in the heart of one who was made gentle not merely by nature but by Act of Parliament, and he registered a solemn vow to wipe the insult out, if not with blood, with verjuice. It was his duty, and they should d—d well see him do it!

4

§ 1

Sylvanus Heythorp seldom went to bed before one or rose before eleven. The latter habit alone kept his valet from handing in the resignation which the former habit prompted almost every night.

Propped on his pillows in a crimson dressing-gown, and freshly shaved, he looked more Roman than he ever did, except in his bath. Having disposed of coffee, he was wont to read his letters, and *The Morning Post*, for he had always been a Tory, and could not stomach paying a halfpenny for his news. Not that there were many letters – when a man has reached the age of eighty, who should write to him except to ask for money?

It was Valentine's Day. Through his bedroom window he could see the trees of the park, where the birds were in song, though he could not hear them. He had never been interested in Nature – full-blooded men with short necks seldom are.

This morning indeed there *were* two letters, and he opened that which smelt of something. Inside was a thing like a Christmas card, save that the naked babe had in his hands a bow and arrow, and words coming out of his mouth: 'To be your Valentine.' There was also a little pink note with one blue forget-me-not printed at the top. It ran:

Dearest Guardy,
I'm sorry this is such a mangy little valentine; I couldn't go out to get it because I've got a beastly cold, so I asked Jock, and the pig bought this. The satin is simply scrumptious. If you don't come and see me in it some time soon, I shall come and show it to you. I wish I had a moustache because my top lip feels just like a matchbox, but it's rather ripping having breakfast in bed. Mr Pillin's taking us to the theatre the day after tomorrow evening. Isn't it nummy! I'm going to have rum and honey for my cold.

Good-bye,
Your Phyllis.

So this that quivered in his thick fingers, too insensitive to feel it, was a valentine for *him*! Forty years ago that young thing's grandmother had given him his last. It made him out a very old chap! Forty years ago! Had that been himself living then? And himself, who, as a youth, came on the town in 'forty-five? Not a thought, not a feeling the same! They said you changed your body every seven years. The mind with it, too, perhaps! Well, he had come to the last of his bodies, now! And that holy woman had been urging him to take it to Bath, with her face as long as a tea-tray, and some gammon from that doctor of his. Too full a habit – dock his port – no alcohol – might go off in a coma any night! Knock off – not he! Rather die any day than turn teetotaller! When a man had nothing left in life except his dinner, his bottle, his cigar, and the dreams they gave him – these doctors forsooth must want to cut them off! No, no! *Carpe diem!* while you lived, get something out of it. And now that he had made all the provision he could for those youngsters, his life was no good to anyone but himself; and the sooner he went off the better, if he ceased to enjoy what there was left, or lost the power to say: 'I'll do this and that, and you be jiggered!' Keep a stiff lip until you crashed, and then go clean! He sounded the bell beside him twice – for Molly, not his man. And when the girl came in, and stood, pretty in her print frock, her fluffy over-fine dark hair escaping from under her cap, he gazed at her in silence.

'Yes, sirr?'

'Want to look at you, that's all.'

'Oh! an' I'm not tidy, sirr.'

'Never mind. Had your valentine?'

'No, sirr; who would send me one, then?'

'Haven't you a young man?'

'Well, I might. But he's over in my country.'

'What d'you think of this?'

He held out the little boy.

The girl took the card and scrutinized it reverently; she said in a detached voice:

'Indeed, an' ut's pretty, too.'

'Would you like it?'

'Oh! if 'tis not taking ut from you.'

Old Heythorp shook his head, and pointed to the dressing-table.

'Over there – you'll find a sovereign. Little present for a good girl.'

She uttered a deep sigh. 'Oh! sirr, 'tis too much; 'tis kingly.'

'Take it.'

She took it, and came back, her hands clasping the sovereign and the valentine, in an attitude as of prayer.

The old man's gaze rested on her with satisfaction.

'I like pretty faces – can't bear sour ones. Tell Meller to get my bath ready.'

When she had gone he took up the other letter – some law-yer's writing – and opening it with the usual difficulty read:

February 13th, 1905

Sir,

Certain facts having come to my knowledge, I deem it my duty to call a special meeting of the shareholders of 'The Island Navigation Coy.', to consider circumstances in connection with the purchase of Mr Joseph Pillin's fleet. And I give you notice that at this meeting your conduct will be called in question.

I am Sir,

Yours faithfully,

Charles Ventnor.

Sylvanus Heythorp, Esq.

Having read this missive, old Heythorp remained some minutes without stirring. Ventnor! That solicitor chap who had made himself unpleasant at the creditors' meetings!

There are men whom a really bad bit of news at once stampedes out of all power of coherent thought and action, and men who at first simply do not take it in. Old Heythorp took it in fast enough; coming from a lawyer it was about as nasty as it could be. But, at once, with stoic wariness his old brain began casting round. What did this fellow really know? And what exactly could he do? One thing was certain; even if he knew everything, he couldn't upset that settlement. The youngsters were all right. The old man grasped the fact that only his own position was at stake. But this was enough in all conscience; a name which had been before the public fifty-odd years – income, independence, more perhaps. It would take little, seeing his age and feebleness, to make his Companies throw him over. But what had the fellow got hold of? How decide whether or no to take notice; to let him do his worst, or to try and get into touch with him? And what was the fellow's motive? He held ten shares! That would never make a man take all this trouble, and over a purchase which was really first-rate business for the Company. Yes! His conscience was quite clean. He had not betrayed his Company – on the contrary, had done it a good turn, got them four sound ships at a low price – against much opposition. That he might have done the Company a better turn, and got the ships at fifty-four thousand, did not trouble him – the six thousand was a deuced sight better employed; and he had not pocketed a penny piece himself! But the fellow's motive? Spite?

Looked like it. Spite, because he had been disappointed of his money, and defied into the bargain! H'm! If that were so, he might still be got to blow cold again. His eyes lighted on the pink note with the blue forget-me-not. It marked as it were the high-water mark of what was left to him of life; and this other letter in his hand – by Jove! – low-water mark! And with a deep and rumbling sigh he thought: 'No, I'm not going to be beaten by this fellow.'

'Your bath is ready, sir.'

Crumpling the two letters into the pocket of his dressing-gown, he said:

'Help me up: and telephone to Mr Farney to be good enough to come round . . .'

An hour later when the secretary entered, his chairman was sitting by the fire perusing the articles of association. And, waiting for him to look up, watching the articles shaking in that thick, feeble hand, the secretary had one of those moments of philosophy not too frequent with his kind. Some said the only happy time of life was when you had no passions, nothing to hope and live for. But did you really ever reach such a stage? The old chairman, for instance, still had his passion for getting his own way, still had his prestige, and set a lot of store by it! And he said:

'Good morning sir; I hope you're all right in this east wind. The purchase is completed.'

'Best thing the Company ever did. Have you heard from a shareholder called Ventnor? You know the man I mean.'

'No, sir. I haven't.'

'Well! You may get a letter that'll make you open your eyes. An impudent scoundrel! Just write at my dictation.'

Charles Ventnor, Esq.   *February 14th, 1905*

Sir, – I have your letter of yesterday's date, the contents of which I am at a loss to understand. My solicitors will be instructed to take the necessary measures.

'Phew! What's all this about?' the secretary thought.

Yours truly . . . I'll sign.

And the shaky letters closed the page:

Sylvanus Heythorp.

'Post that as you go.'

'Anything else I can do for you, sir?'

'Nothing, except to let me know if you hear from this fellow.'

When the secretary had gone the old man thought: 'So! The ruffian hasn't called the meeting yet. That'll bring him round here fast enough if it's his money he wants – blackmailing scoundrel!'

'Mr Pillin, sir; and will you wait lunch, or will you have it in the dining-room?'

'In the dining-room.'

At the sight of that death's-head of a fellow, old Heythorp felt a sort of pity. He looked bad enough already – and this news would make him look worse. Joe Pillin glanced round at the two closed doors.

'How are you, Sylvanus? I'm very poorly.' He came closer, and lowered his voice: 'Why did you get me to make that settlement? I must have been mad. I've had a man called Ventnor – I didn't like his manner. He asked me if I knew a Mrs Larne.'

'Ha! What did you say?'

'What could I say? I *don't* know her. But why did he ask?'

'Smells a rat.'

Joe Pillin grasped the edge of the table with both hands.

'Oh!' he murmured. 'Oh! don't say that!'

Old Heythorp held out to him the crumpled letter.

When he had read it Joe Pillin sat down abruptly before the fire.

'Pull yourself together, Joe; they can't touch you, and they can't upset either the purchase or the settlement. They can upset me, that's all.'

Joe Pillin answered, with trembling lips:

'How you can sit there, and look the same as ever! Are you sure they can't touch me?'

Old Heythorp nodded grimly.

'They talk of an Act, but they haven't passed it yet. They might prove a breach of trust against me. But I'll diddle them. Keep your pecker up, and get off abroad.'

'Yes, yes. I must. I'm very bad. I was going tomorrow. But

I don't know, I'm sure, with this hanging over me. My son knowing her makes it worse. He knows this man Ventnor too. And I daren't say anything to Bob. What are you thinking of, Sylvanus? You look very funny.'

Old Heythorp seemed to rouse himself from a sort of coma.

'I want my lunch,' he said. 'Will you stop and have some?'

Joe Pillin stammered out:

'Lunch! I don't know when I shall eat again. What are you going to do, Sylvanus?'

'Bluff the beggar out of it.'

'But suppose you can't?'

'Buy him off. He's one of my creditors.'

Joe Pillin stared at him afresh. 'You always had such nerve,' he said yearningly. 'Do you ever wake up between two and four? I do – and everything's black.'

'Put a good stiff nightcap on, my boy, before going to bed.'

'Yes; I sometimes wish I was less temperate. But I couldn't stand it. I'm told your doctor forbids you alcohol.'

'He does. That's why I drink it.'

Joe Pillin, brooding over the fire, said: 'This meeting – d'you think they mean to have it? D'you think this man really knows? If my name gets into the newspapers –' but encountering his old friend's deep little eyes, he stopped. 'So you advise me to get off tomorrow, then?'

Old Heythorp nodded.

'Your lunch is served, sir.'

Joe Pillin started violently, and rose.

'Well, good-bye, Sylvanus – good-bye! I don't suppose I shall be back till the summer, if I ever come back!' He sank his voice: 'I shall rely on you. You won't let them, will you?'

Old Heythorp lifted his hand, and Joe Pillin put into that swollen shaking paw his pale and spindly fingers. 'I wish I had your pluck,' he said sadly. 'Good-bye, Sylvanus,' and turning, he passed out.

Old Heythorp thought: 'Poor shaky chap. All to pieces at the first shot!' And, going to his lunch, ate more heavily than usual.

§ 2

Mr Ventnor, on reaching his office and opening his letters, found, as he had anticipated, one from 'that old rascal.' Its contents excited in him the need to know his own mind. Fortunately this was not complicated by a sense of dignity – he only had to consider the position with an eye on not being made to *look* a fool. The point was simply whether he set more store by his money than by his desire for – er – justice. If not, he had merely to convene the special meeting, and lay before it the plain fact that Mr Joseph Pillin, selling his ships for sixty thousand pounds, had just made a settlement of six thousand pounds on a lady whom he did not know, a daughter, ward, or what-not – of the purchasing Company's chairman, who had said, moreover, at the general meeting, that he stood or fell by the transaction; he had merely to do this, and demand that an explanation be required from the old man of such a startling coincidence. Convinced that no explanation would hold water, he felt sure that his action would be at once followed by the collapse, if nothing more, of that old image, and the infliction of a nasty slur on old Pillin and his hopeful son. On the other hand, three hundred pounds was money; and if old Heythorp were to say to him: 'What do you want to make this fuss for? – here's what I owe you!' could a man of business and the world let his sense of justice – however he might itch to have it satisfied – stand in the way of what was after all also his sense of justice? – for this money had been owing to him for the deuce of a long time. In this dilemma, the words: 'My solicitors will be instructed' were of notable service in helping him to form a decision, for he had a certain dislike of other solicitors, and an intimate knowledge of the law of libel and slander; if by any remote chance there should be a slip between the cup and the lip, Charles Ventnor might be in the soup – a position which he deprecated both by nature and profession. High thinking, therefore, decided him at last to answer thus:

February 15th, 1905

Sir,

I have received your note. I think it may be fair, before taking further steps in this matter, to ask you for a personal explanation of the circumstances to which I alluded. I therefore propose with your permission to call on you at your private residence at five o'clock tomorrow afternoon.

Yours faithfully,

Charles Ventnor.

Sylvanus Heythorp, Esq.

Having sent this missive, and arranged in his mind the damning, if circumstantial, evidence he had accumulated, he awaited the hour with confidence, for his nature was not lacking in the cock-surety of a Briton. All the same, he dressed himself particularly well that morning, putting on a blue and white striped waistcoat which, with a cream-coloured tie, set off his fulvous whiskers and full blue eyes; and he lunched, if anything, more fully than his wont, eating a stronger cheese and taking a glass of special Club ale. He took care to be late, too, to show the old fellow that his coming at all was in the nature of an act of grace. A strong scent of hyacinths greeted him in the hall; and Mr Ventnor, who was an amateur of flowers, stopped to put his nose into a fine bloom and think uncontrollably of Mrs Larne. Pity! The things one had to give up in life – fine women – one thing and another. Pity! The thought inspired in him a timely anger; and he followed the servant, intending to stand no nonsense from this paralytic old rascal.

The room he entered was lighted by a bright fire, and a single electric lamp with an orange shade on a table covered by a black satin cloth. There were heavily gleaming oil paintings on the walls, a heavy old brass chandelier without candles, heavy dark red curtains, and an indefinable scent of burnt acorns, coffee, cigars, and old man. He became conscious of a candescent spot on the far side of the hearth, where the light fell on old Heythorp's thick white hair.

'Mr Ventnor, sir.'

The candescent spot moved. A voice said: 'Sit down.'

Mr Ventnor sat in an armchair on the opposite side of the

fire; and, finding a kind of somnolence creeping over him, pinched himself. He wanted all his wits about him.

The old man was speaking in that extinct voice of his, and Mr Ventnor said rather pettishly:

'Beg pardon, I don't get you.'

Old Heythorp's voice swelled with sudden force:

'Your letters are Greek to me.'

'Oh! Indeed! I think we can soon make them into plain English!'

'Sooner the better.'

Mr Ventnor passed through a moment of indecision. Should he lay his cards on the table. It was not his habit, and the proceeding was sometimes attended with risk. The knowledge, however, that he could always take them up again, seeing there was no third person here to testify that he had laid them down, decided him, and he said:

'Well, Mr Heythorp, the long and short of the matter is this: Our friend Mr Pillin paid you a commission of ten per cent on the sale of his ships. Oh! yes. He settled the money, not on you, but on your relative Mrs Larne and her children. This, as you know, is a breach of trust on your part.'

The old man's voice: 'Where did you get hold of that cock-and-bull story?' brought him to his feet before the fire.

'It won't do, Mr Heythorp. My witnesses are Mr Pillin, Mrs Larne, and Mr Scriven.'

'What have you come here for, then – blackmail?'

Mr Ventnor straightened his waistcoat; a rush of conscious virtue had dyed his face.

'Oh! you take that tone,' he said, 'do you? You think you can ride roughshod over everything? Well, you're very much mistaken. I advise you to keep a civil tongue and consider your position, or I'll make a beggar of you. I'm not sure this isn't a case for a prosecution!'

'Gammon!'

The choler in Charles Ventnor kept him silent for a moment; then he burst out:

'Neither gammon nor spinach. You owe me three hundred pounds, you've owed it me for years, and you have the impudence to take this attitude with me, have you? Now, I never bluster; I say what I mean. You just listen to me. Either you pay me what you owe me at once, or I call this meeting and make what I know public. You'll very soon find out where you are. And a good thing, too, for a more unscrupulous – unscrupulous –' he paused for breath.

Occupied with his own emotion, he had not observed the change in old Heythorp's face. The imperial on that lower lip was bristling, the crimson of those cheeks had spread to the roots of his white hair. He grasped the arms of his chair, trying to rise; his swollen hands trembled; a little saliva escaped one corner of his lips. And the words came out as if shaken by his teeth:

'So – so – you – you bully me!'

Conscious that the interview had suddenly passed from the phase of negotiation, Mr Ventnor looked hard at his opponent. He saw nothing but a decrepit, passionate, crimson-faced old man at bay, and all the instincts of one with everything on his side boiled up in him. The miserable old turkey-cock – the apoplectic image! And he said:

'And you'll do no good for yourself by getting into a passion. At your age, and in your condition, I recommend a little prudence. Now just take my terms quietly, or you know what'll happen. I'm not to be intimidated by any of your airs.' And seeing that the old man's rage was such that he simply could not speak, he took the opportunity of going on: 'I don't care two straws which you do – I'm out to show you who's master. If you think in your dotage you can domineer any longer – well, you'll find two can play at that game. Come, now, which are you going to do?'

The old man had sunk back in his chair, and only his little deep-blue eyes seemed living. Then he moved one hand, and Mr Ventnor saw that he was fumbling to reach the button of an electric bell at the end of a cord. 'I'll show him,' he thought, and stepping forward, he put it out of reach.

Thus frustrated, the old man remained motionless, staring up. The word 'blackmail' resumed its buzzing in Mr Ventnor's ears. The impudence – the consummate impudence of it from this fraudulent old ruffian with one foot in bankruptcy and one foot in the grave, if not in the dock.

'Yes,' he said, 'it's never too late to learn; and for once you've come up against someone a leetle bit too much for you. Haven't you now? You'd better cry *"Peccavi."*'

Then, in the deathly silence of the room, the moral force of his position, and the collapse as it seemed of his opponent, awakening a faint compunction, he took a turn over the Turkey carpet to readjust his mind.

'You're an old man, and I don't want to be too hard on you. I'm only showing you that you can't play fast and loose as if you were God Almighty any longer. You've had your own way too many years. And now you can't have it, see!' Then, as the old man again moved forward in his chair, he added: 'Now, don't get into a passion again; calm yourself, because I warn you – this is your last chance. I'm a man of my word; and what I say, I do.'

By a violent and unsuspected effort the old man jerked himself up and reached the bell. Mr Ventnor heard it ring, and said sharply:

'Mind you, it's nothing to me which you do. I came for your own good. Please yourself. Well?'

He was answered by the click of the door and the old man's husky voice:

'Show this hound out! And then come back!'

Mr Ventnor had presence of mind enough not to shake his fist. Muttering: 'Very well, Mr Heythorp! Ah! *Very* well!' he moved with dignity to the door. The careful shepherding of the servant renewed the fire of his anger. Hound! He had been called a hound!

§ 3

After seeing Mr Ventnor off the premises the man Meller returned to his master, whose face looked very odd – ''all patchy-like,' as he put it in the servants' hall, as though the blood driven to his head had mottled for good the snowy whiteness of the forehead. He received the unexpected order:

'Get me a hot bath ready, and put some pine stuff in it.'

When the old man was seated there, the valet asked:

'How long shall I give you, sir?'

'Twenty minutes.'

'Very good, sir.'

Lying in that steaming brown fragrant liquid, old Heythorp heaved a stertorous sigh. By losing his temper with that ill-conditioned cur he had cooked his goose. It was done to a turn; and he was a ruined man. If only – oh! if only he could have seized the fellow by the neck and pitched him out of the room! To have lived to be so spoken to; to have been unable to lift hand or foot, hardly even his voice – he would sooner have been dead! Yes – sooner have been dead! A dumb and measureless commotion was still at work in the recesses of that thick old body, silver-brown in the dark water, whose steam he drew deep into his wheezing lungs, as though for spiritual relief. To be beaten by a cur like that! To have a common cad of a pettifogging lawyer drag him down and kick him about; tumble a name which had stood high, in the dust! The fellow had the power to make him a byword and a beggar! It was incredible! But it was a fact. And tomorrow he would begin to do it – perhaps had begun already. His tree had come down with a crash! Eighty years – eighty good years! He regretted none of them – regretted nothing; least of all this breach of trust which had provided for his grandchildren – one of the best things he had ever done. The fellow was a cowardly hound, too! The way he had snatched the bell-pull out of his reach – despicable cur! And a chap like that was to put 'paid' to the account of Sylvanus Heythorp, to 'scratch' him out of life – so near the end of everything, the very end! His hand raised above the surface fell back on his stomach through the dark water, and a bubble or two rose. Not so fast – not so fast! He had but to slip down a foot, let the water close over his head, and 'Good-bye' to Master Ventnor's triumph! Dead men could not be kicked off the Boards of Companies. Dead men could not be beggared, deprived of their independence. He smiled and stirred a little in the bath till the water reached the white hairs on his lower lip. It smelt nice! And he took a long sniff. He had had a good life, a good life! And with the thought that he had it in his power at any moment to put Master Ventnor's nose out of joint – to beat the beggar after all, a sense of assuagement and well-being crept over him. His blood ran more evenly again. He closed his eyes. They talked about an after-life – people like that holy woman. Gammon! You went to sleep – a long sleep; no dreams. A nap after dinner! Dinner! His tongue sought his palate! Yes! he could eat a good dinner! That dog hadn't put him off his stroke! The best dinner he had ever eaten was the one he gave to Jack Herring, Chichester, Thornworthy, Nick Treffry and Jolyon Forsyte, at Pole's. Good Lord! In 'sixty – yes – 'sixty-five? Just before he fell in love with Alice Larne – ten years before he came to Liverpool. That *was* a dinner! Cost twenty-four pounds for the six of them – and Forsyte an absurdly moderate fellow. Only Nick Treffry and himself had been three-bottle men! Dead! Every jack man of them. And suddenly he thought: 'My name's a good one – I was never down before – never beaten!'

A voice above the steam said:

'The twenty minutes is up, sir.'

'All right; I'll get out. Evening clothes.'

And Meller, taking out dress suit and shirt, thought: 'Now, what does the old bloomer want dressin' up again for; why can't he go to bed and have his dinner there? When a man's like a baby, the cradle's the place for him . . .'

An hour later, at the scene of his encounter with Mr Ventnor, where the table was already laid for dinner, old Heythorp stood and gazed. The curtains had been drawn back, the window thrown open to air the room, and he could see out there the shapes of the dark trees and a sky grape-coloured, in the mild, moist night. It smelt good. A sensuous feeling stirred in him, warm from his bath, clothed from head to foot in fresh garments. Deuce of a time since he had dined in full fig! He would have liked a woman dining opposite – but not the holy woman; no, by George! – would have liked to see light falling on a woman's shoulders once again, and a pair of bright eyes! He crossed, snail-like, towards the fire. There that bullying fellow had stood with his back to it – confound his impudence! – as if the place belonged to him. And suddenly he had a vision of his three secretaries' faces – especially young Farney's – as they would look when the pack got him by the throat and pulled him down. His co-directors, too! Old Heythorp! How are the mighty fallen! And that hound jubilant!

His valet passed the room to shut the window and draw the curtains. This chap too! The day he could no longer pay his wages, and had lost the power to say 'Shan't want your services any more' – when he could no longer even pay his doctor for doing his best to kill him off! Power, interest, independence, all – gone! To be dressed and undressed, given pap, like a baby in arms, served as they chose to serve him, and wished out of the way – broken, dishonoured! By money alone an old man had his being! Meat, drink, movement, breath! When all his money was gone the holy woman would let him know it fast enough. They would all let him know it; or if they didn't, it would be out of pity! He had never been pitied yet – thank God! And he said:

'Get me up a bottle of Perrier Jouet. What's the menu?'

'Germaine soup, sir; filly de sole; sweetbread; cutlet soubees, rum souffly.'

'Tell her to give me a *hors-d'œuvre*, and put on a savoury.'

'Yes, sir.'

When the man had gone, he thought: 'I should have liked an oyster – too late now!' and going over to his bureau he fumblingly pulled out the top drawer. There was little in it – just a few papers, business papers on his Companies, and a schedule of his debts; not even a copy of his will – he had not made one, nothing to leave! Letters he had never kept. Half a dozen bills, a few receipts, and the little pink note with the blue forget-me-not. That was the lot! An old tree gives up bearing leaves, and its roots dry up, before it comes down in a wind; an old man's world slowly falls away from him till he stands alone in the night. Looking at the pink note, he thought: 'Suppose I'd married Alice – a man never had a better mistress!' He fumbled the drawer to; but still he strayed feebly about the room, with a curious shrinking from sitting down, legacy from the quarter of an hour he had been compelled to sit while that hound worried at his throat. He was opposite one of the pictures now. It gleamed, dark and oily, limning a Scots Grey who had mounted a wounded Russian on his horse, and was bringing him back prisoner from the Balaclava charge. A very old friend – bought in 'fifty-nine. It had hung in his chambers in the albany – hung with him ever since. With whom would it hang when he was gone? For that holy woman would scrap it to a certainty, and stick up some Crucifixion or other, some new-fangled high art thing! She could even do that now if she liked – for she owned it, owned every mortal stick in the room, to the very glass he would drink his champagne from; all made over under the settlement fifteen years ago, before his last big gamble went wrong. *'De l'audace, toujours de l'audace!'* The gamble which had brought him down till his throat at last was at the mercy of a bullying hound. The pitcher and the well! At the mercy –! The sound of a popping cork dragged him from reverie. He moved to his seat, back to the window, and sat down to his dinner. By George! They had got him an oyster! And he said:

'I've forgotten my teeth!'

While the man was gone for them, he swallowed the oysters, methodically touching them one by one with cayenne, Chili vinegar, and lemon. Ummm! Not quite what they used to be at Pimm's in the best days, but not bad – not bad! Then seeing the little blue bowl lying before him, he looked up and said:

'My compliments to cook on the oysters. Give me the champagne.' And he lifted his trembling teeth. Thank God, he could still put 'em in for himself! The creaming goldenish fluid from the napkined bottle slowly reached the brim of his glass, which had a hollow stem; raising it to his lips, very red between the white hairs above and below, he drank with a gurgling noise, and put the glass down – empty. Nectar! And just cold enough!

'I frapped in the least bit, sir.'

'Quite right. What's that smell of flowers?'

'It's from those 'yacinths on the sideboard, sir. They come from Mrs Larne, this afternoon.'

'Put 'em on the table. Where's my daughter?'

'She's had dinner, sir; goin' to a ball, I think.'

'A ball!'

'Charity ball, I fancy, sir.'

'Ummm! Give me a touch of the old sherry with the soup.'

'Yes, sir. I shall have to open a bottle.'

'Very well, then, do!'

On his way to the cellar the man confided to Molly, who was carrying the soup:

'The Guv'nor's going it tonight! What he'll be like tomorrow I dunno.'

The girl answered softly:

'Poor old man, let um have his pleasure.' And, in the hall, with the soup tureen against her bosom, she hummed above the steam, and thought of the ribbons on her new chemises, bought out of the sovereign he had given her.

And old Heythorp, digesting his oysters, snuffed the scent of the hyacinths, and thought of the St Germain, his favourite soup. It wouldn't be first-rate, at this time of year – should be made with little young home-grown peas. Paris was the place for it. Ah! The French were the fellows for eating, and – looking things in the face! Not hypocrites – not ashamed of their reason or their senses!

The soup came in. He sipped it, bending forward as far as he could, his napkin tucked in over his shirt-front like a bib. He got the bouquet of that sherry to a T – his sense of smell was very keen tonight; rare old stuff it was – more than a year since he had tasted it – but no one drank sherry nowadays, hadn't the constitution for it! The fish came up, and went down; and with the sweetbread he took his second glass of champagne. Always the best, that second glass – the stomach well warmed, and the palate not yet dulled. Umm! So that fellow thought he had him beaten, did he? And he said suddenly:

'The fur coat in the wardrobe, I've no use for it. You can take it away tonight.'

With tempered gratitude the valet answered:

'Thank you, sir; much obliged, I'm sure.' So the old buffer had found out there was moth in it!

'Have I worried you much?'

'No, sir; not at all, sir – that is, no more than reason.'

'Afraid I have. Very sorry – can't help it. You'll find that, when you get like me.'

'Yes, sir; I've always admired your pluck, sir.'

'Um! Very good of you to say so.'

'Always think of you keepin' the flag flyin', sir.'

Old Heythorp bent his body from the waist.

'Much obliged to you.'

'Not at all, sir. Cook's done a little spinach in cream with the soubees.'

'Ah! Tell her from me it's a capital dinner, so far.'

'Thank you, sir.'

Alone again, old Heythorp sat unmoving, his brain just narcotically touched. 'The flag flyin' – the flag flyin'!' He raised his glass and sucked. He had an appetite now, and finished the three cutlets, and all the sauce and spinach. Pity! he could have managed a snipe – fresh shot! A desire to delay, to lengthen dinner, was strong upon him; there were but the *soufflé* and the savoury to come. He would have enjoyed, too, someone to talk to. He had always been fond of good company – been good company himself, or so they said – not that he had had a chance of late. Even at the Boards they avoided talking to him, he had noticed for a long time. Well! that wouldn't trouble him again – he had sat through his last Board, no doubt. They shouldn't kick him off, though; he wouldn't give them that pleasure – had seen the beggars hankering after his chairman's shoes too long. The *soufflé* was before him now, and lifting his glass, he said:

'Fill up.'

'These are the special glasses, sir; only four to the bottle.'

'Fill up.'

The servant filled, screwing up his mouth.

Old Heythorp drank, and put the glass down empty with a sigh. He had been faithful to his principles, finished the bottle before touching the sweet – a good bottle – of a good brand! And now for the *soufflé*! Delicious, flipped down with the old sherry! So that holy woman was going to a ball, was she! How deuced funny! Who would dance with a dry stick like that, all eaten up with a piety which was just sexual disappointment? Ah! yes, lots of women like that – had often noticed 'em – pitied 'em too, until you had to do with them and they made you as unhappy as themselves, and were tyrants into the bargain. And he asked:

'What's the savoury?'

'Cheese remmykin, sir.'

His favourite.

'I'll have my port with it – the 'sixty-eight.'

The man stood gazing with evident stupefaction. He had not expected this. The old man's face was very flushed, but that might be the bath. He said feebly:

'Are you sure you ought, sir?'

'No, but I'm going to.'

'Would you mind if I spoke to Miss Heythorp, sir?'

'If you do, you can leave my service.'

'Well, sir, I don't accept the responsibility.'

'Who asked you to?'

'No, sir.'

'Well, get it, then; and don't be an ass.'

'Yes, sir.' If the old man were not humoured he would have a fit, perhaps!

And the old man sat quietly staring at the hyacinths. He felt happy, his whole being lined and warmed and drowsed – and there was more to come! What had the holy folk to give you compared with the comfort of a good dinner? Could they make you dream, and see life rosy for a little? No, they could only give you promissory notes which would never be cashed. A man had nothing but his pluck – they only tried to undermine it, and make him squeal for help. He could see his precious doctor throwing up his hands: 'Port after a bottle of champagne – you'll die of it!' And a very good death too – none better. A sound broke the silence of the closed-up room. Music? His daughter playing the piano overhead. Singing too! What a trickle of a voice! Jenny Lind! The Swedish nightingale – he had never missed the nights when she was singing – Jenny Lind!

'It's very hot, sir. Shall I take it out of the case?'

Ah! The ramequin!

'Touch of butter, and the cayenne!'

'Yes, sir.'

He ate it slowly, savouring each mouthful; had never tasted

a better. With cheese – port! He drank one glass, and said:
'Help me to my chair.'

And settled there before the fire with decanter and glass and
hand-bell on the little low table by his side, he murmured:

'Bring coffee, and my cigar, in twenty minutes.'

Tonight he would do justice to his wine, not smoking till he
had finished. As old Horace said:

> *Aequam memento rebus in arduis*
> *Servare mentem.*

And, raising his glass, he sipped slowly, spilling a drop or two,
shutting his eyes.

The faint silvery squealing of the holy woman in the room
above, the scent of hyacinths, the drowse of the fire, on which a
cedar log had just been laid, the feeling of the port soaking
down into the crannies of his being, made up a momentary
Paradise. Then the music stopped; and no sound rose but the
tiny groans of the log trying to resist the fire. Dreamily he
thought: 'Life wears you out, wears you out. Logs on a fire!'
And he filled his glass again. That fellow had been careless;
there were dregs at the bottom of the decanter and he had got
down to them! Then, as the last drop from his tilted glass
trickled into the white hairs on his chin, he heard the coffee
tray put down, and taking his cigar he put it to his ear, rolling
it in his thick fingers. In prime condition! And drawing a first
whiff, he said:

'Open the bottle of the old brandy in the sideboard.'

'Brandy, sir? I really daren't, sir.'

'Are you my servant or not?'

'Yes, sir, but –'

A minute of silence, then the man went hastily to the sideboard, took out the bottle, and drew the cork. The tide of crimson in the old man's face had frightened him.

'Leave it there.'

The unfortunate valet placed the bottle on the little table. 'I'll
have to tell her,' he thought; 'but if I take away the port decanter and the glass, it won't look so bad.' And, carrying them,
he left the room.

Slowly the old man drank his coffee, and the liqueur of brandy. The whole gamut! And watching his cigar-smoke wreathing blue in the orange glow, he smiled. The last night to call his soul his own, the last night of his independence. Send in his resignations tomorrow – not wait to be kicked off! Not give that fellow a chance!

A voice which seemed to come from far off, said:

'Father! You're drinking brandy! How *can* you – you know it's simple poison to you!' A figure in white, scarcely actual, loomed up close. He took the bottle to fill up his liqueur glass, in defiance; but a hand in a long white glove, with another dangling from its wrist, pulled it away, shook it at him, and replaced it in the sideboard. And, just as when Mr Ventnor stood there accusing him, a swelling and churning in his throat prevented him from speech; his lips moved, but only a little froth came forth.

His daughter had approached again. She stood quite close, in white satin, thin-faced, sallow, with eyebrows raised, and her dark hair frizzed – yes! frizzed – the holy woman! With all his might he tried to say: 'So you bully me, do you – you bully me *tonight*!' but only the word 'so' and a sort of whispering came forth. He heard her speaking. 'It's no good your getting angry, Father. After champagne – it's wicked!' Then her form receded in a sort of rustling white mist; she was gone; and he heard the spluttering and growling of her taxi, bearing her to the ball. So! She tyrannized and bullied, even before she had him at her mercy, did she? She should see! Anger had brightened his eyes; the room came clear again. And slowly raising himself he sounded the bell twice, for the girl, not for that fellow Meller, who was in the plot. As soon as the pretty black and white-aproned figure stood before him, he said:

'Help me up!'

Twice her soft pulling was not enough, and he sank back. The third time he struggled to his feet.

'Thank you; that'll do.' Then, waiting till she was gone, he crossed the room, fumbled open the sideboard door, and took out the bottle. Reaching over the polished oak, he grasped a sherry glass; and holding the bottle with both hands, tipped the liquor into it, put it to his lips and sucked. Drop by drop it passed over his palate – mild, very old, old as himself, coloured like sunlight, fragrant. To the last drop he drank it, then hugging the bottle to his shirt-front, he moved snail-like to his chair, and fell back into its depths.

For some minutes he remained there motionless, the bottle clasped to his chest, thinking: 'This is not the attitude of a gentleman. I must put it down on the table – on the table'; but a thick cloud was between him and everything. It was with his hands he would have to put the bottle on the table! But he could not find his hands, could not feel them. His mind see-sawed in strophe and antistrophe: 'You can't move!' – 'I will move!' 'You're beaten' – 'I'm not beat.' 'Give up' – 'I won't.' That struggle to find his hands seemed to last for ever – he *must* find them! After that – go down – all standing – after that! Everything round him was red. Then the red cloud cleared just a little, and he could hear the clock – 'tick – tick – tick'; a faint sensation spread from his shoulders down to his wrists, down his palms; and yes – he could feel the bottle! He re-doubled his struggle to get forward in his chair; to get forward to put the bottle down. It was not dignified like this! One arm he could move now; but he could not grip the bottle nearly tight enough to put it down. Working his whole body forward, inch by inch, he shifted himself up in the chair till he could lean sideways, and the bottle, slipping down his chest, dropped slanting to the edge of the low stool-table. Then with all his might he screwed his trunk and arms an inch further, and the bottle stood. He had done it – done it! His lips twitched into a smile; his body sagged back to its old position. He had done it! And he closed his eyes . . .

At half-past eleven the girl Molly, opening the door, looked at him and said softly: 'Sirr! there's some ladies, and a gentleman!' But he did not answer. And, still holding the door, she whispered out into the hall:

'He's asleep, miss.'

A voice whispered back:

'Oh! Just let me go in, I won't wake him unless he does. But I do want to show him my dress.'

The girl moved aside; and on tiptoe Phyllis passed in. She walked to where, between the lamp-glow and the fire-glow, she was lighted up. White satin – her first low-cut dress – the flush of her first supper party – a gardenia at her breast, another in her fingers! Oh! what a pity he was asleep! How red he looked! How funnily old men breathed! And mysteriously, as a child might, she whispered:

'Guardy!'

No answer! And pouting, she stood twiddling the gardenia. Then suddenly she thought: 'I'll put it in his buttonhole! When he wakes up and sees it, how he'll jump!'

And stealing close, she bent and slipped it in. Two faces looked at her from round the door; she heard Bob Pillin's smothered chuckle; her mother's rich and feathery laugh. Oh! How red his forehead was! She touched it with her lips; skipped back, twirled round, danced silently a second, blew a kiss, and like quicksilver was gone.

And the whispering, the chuckling, and one little out-pealing laugh rose in the hall.

But the old man slept. Nor until Meller came at his usual hour of half-past twelve, was it known that he would never wake.

1916

A PORTRAIT

❧❦❧

I⊤ is at the age of eighty that I picture him, without the vestige of a stoop, rather above middle height, of very well-proportioned figure, whose flatness of back and easy movements were the admiration of all who saw them. His iron-grey eyes had lost none of their colour, they were set-in deep, so that their upper lids were invisible, and had a peculiar questioning directness, apt to change suddenly into twinkles. His head was of fine shape – one did not suspect that it required a specially made hat, being a size larger than almost any other head; it was framed in very silky silvery hair, brushed in an arch across his forehead, and falling in becoming curves over the tips of his ears; and he wore always a full white beard and moutaches, which concealed a jaw and chin of great determination cleft by a dimple. His nose had been broken in his early boyhood; it was the nose of a thinker, broad and of noticeable shape. The colour of his cheeks was a fine dry brown; his brow very capacious, both wide and high, and endowed with a singular serenity. But it was the balance and poise of his head which commanded so much attention. In a theatre, church, concert-hall, there was never any head so fine as his, for the silvery hair and beard lent to its massiveness a curious grace and delicacy.

The owner of that head could not but be endowed with force, sagacity, humour, and the sense of justice. It expressed, indeed, his essential quality – equanimity; for there were two men in him – he of the chin and jaw, a man of action and tenacity, and he of the nose and brow, the man of speculation and impersonality; yet these two were so curiously balanced and blended that there was no harsh ungraceful conflict. And what made this equanimity so memorable was the fact that both his power of action and his power of speculation were of high quality. He was not a commonplace person content with a little of both. He wanted and had wanted throughout life, if one may judge by records, a good deal of both, ever demanding with one half of him strong and continuous action, and with the other half, high and clean thought and behaviour. The desire for the best both in material and spiritual things remained with him through life. He felt things deeply; and but for his strange balance, and a yearning for inward peace which never seems to have deserted him, his ship might well have gone down in tragedy.

To those who had watched that journey, his voyage through life seemed favourable, always on the top of the weather. He had worked hard, and he had played hard, but never too hard. And though one might often see him irritated, I think no one ever saw him bored. He perceived a joke quicker than most of us; he was never eccentric, yet fundamentally independent of other people's opinions, and perhaps a little unconscious that there were better men than he. Not that he was conceited, for of this quality, so closely allied to stupidity and humbug, he had about as much as the babe unborn. He was, indeed, a natural foe to anaemia in any of its forms, just as he was instinctively hostile to gross bull-beef men and women. The words, 'a bullying chap,' were used by him as crushing dispraise. I can recall him now in his chair after dinner, listening to one who, puffing his cigarette, is letting himself go on a stream of robustious, rather swaggering, complacencies; with what a comprehending straight look he regards the speaker, not scornful, not sarcastic, but simply, as it were, saying: 'No, my young buck, for all your fine full-blooded talk, and all your red face, you are what I see you to be, and you will do what I tell you to do!' Such men had no chance with him when it came to the tug of war; he laid his will on them as if they had been children.

He was that rather rare thing, a pure-blooded Englishman; having no strain of Scotch, Welsh, Irish, or foreign blood in his pedigree for four hundred years at least. He sprang from a long line of farmers intermarrying with their kind in the most southern corner of Devonshire, and it is probable that Norse and British blood were combined in him in a high state of equality. Even in the actual situation of his place of origin, the principle of balance had been maintained, for the old farmhouse from which his grandfather had emerged had been perched close to the cliff. Thus, to the making of him had gone land and sea, the Norseman and the Celt.

Articled to the Law at the age of sixteen by his father, a Plymouth merchant, whose small ancient ships traded to the Mediterranean in fruits, leather, and wines, he had come to London, and at the earliest possible date (as was the habit with men in those times) had been entered on the rolls as a solicitor. Often has he told me of the dinner he gave in honour of that event. 'I was a thread-paper, then,' he would say (indeed, he never became fat), – 'We began with a barrel of oysters.' About that and other festivities of his youth there was all the rich and rollicking flavour of the days of Pickwick. He was practically dependent on his own exertions from the time he began to practise his profession, and it was characteristic of him that he never seems to have been hard pressed for money. The inherent sanity and moderation of his instincts preserved him, one imagines, from the financial ups and downs of most young men, for there was no niggardliness in him, and a certain breadth of conception characterized his money affairs throughout life. It was rather by the laws of gravity, therefore, whereby money judiciously employed attracts money, and the fact that he lived in that moneymaker's Golden Age, the nineteenth century, that he had long been (at the age of eighty) a wealthy man. Money was to him the symbol of a well-spent, well-ordered life, provocative of warmth in his heart because he loved his children, and was careful of them to a fault. He did not marry till he was forty-five, but his feeling for the future of his family manifested itself with the birth of his first child. Selecting a fair and high locality, not too far away from London, he set himself at once to make a country place, where the little things should have fresh air, new milk, and all the fruits of the earth, home-grown around them. Quite wonderful was the forethought he lavished on that house and little estate stretching down the side of a hill, with its walled gardens, pasture, corn-land and coppice. All was solid, and of the best, from the low four-square red brick house with its concrete terrace and French windows, to the cow-houses down by the coppice. From the oak trees, hundreds of years old, on the lawns, to the peach trees just planted along the south sunny walls. But here, too, there was no display for the sake of it, and no extravagance. Everything was at hand, from home-baked bread, to mushrooms wild and tame; from the stables with their squat clock-tower, to pigsties; from roses that won all the local prizes, to bluebells; but nothing redundant or pretentious.

The place was an endless pleasure to him, who to the last preserved his power of taking interest, not only in great, but in little things. Each small triumph over difficulty – the securing of hot water in such a quarter, the better lighting of another, the rescue of the nectarines from wasps, the quality of his Alderney cows, the encouragement of rooks – afforded him as much simple and sincere satisfaction as every little victory he achieved in his profession, or in the life of the Companies which he directed. But with all his shrewd practical sense, and almost naïve pleasure in material advantage, he combined a very real spiritual life of his own. Nor was there anything ascetic in that inner life. It was mellow as the music of Mozart, his most beloved composer; Art and Nature, both had their part in it. He was, for instance, very fond of opera, but only when it could be called 'grand'; and it grieved him that opera was no longer what it had been, yet was it secretly a grave satisfaction that he had known those classical glories denied to the present generation. He loved indeed almost all classical music, but (besides Mozart) especially Beethoven, Gluck, and Meyerbeer, whom he insisted (no less than Herbert Spencer) on considering a great composer. Wagner he tried very hard to appreciate and, after visiting Bayreuth, even persuaded himself that he had succeeded, though he never ceased to point out the great difference that existed between this person and Mozart. He loved the Old Masters of painting, having for favourites amongst the Italians: Rafael, Correggio, Titian, Tintoretto; and amongst Englishmen Reynolds and Romney. On the other hand, he regarded Hogarth and Rubens as coarse, but Vandyke he very much admired, because of his beautiful painting of hands, the hall-mark, he would maintain, of an artist's quality. I cannot remember his feeling about Rembrandt, but Turner he certainly distrusted as extravagant. Botticelli and the earlier masters he had not as yet quite learned to relish; and Impressionism, including Whistler, never really made conquest of his taste, though he always resolutely kept his mind open to what was modern – feeling himself young at heart.

Once on a spring day, getting over a stile, I remember him saying:

'Eighty! I can't believe it. Seems very queer. I don't feel it. Eighty!' And, pointing to a blackbird that was singing, he added: 'That takes the years off you!' His love of Nature was very intimate, simple, and unconscious. I can see him standing by the pond of a summer evening watching the great flocks of starlings, that visited those fields; or, with his head a little to one side, listening rapturously to a skylark. He would contemplate, too, with a sort of serene passion, sunset effects, and every kind of view.

But his greatest joy in life had been his long summer holidays, in Italy or among the Alps, and his memory was a perfect storehouse of peaks, passes, and arrivals at Italian inns. He had been a great walker, and, as an old man, was still very active. I can remember him on horseback at the age of sixty, though he had never been a sportsman – not being in the way of hunting, having insufficient patience for fishing, and preferring to spend such time as he might have had for shooting, in communing with his beloved mountains. His love for all kinds of beauty, indeed, was strangely potent; and perhaps the more natural and deep for its innocence of all tradition and formal culture. He got it, I think, from his mother, of whom he always spoke with reverence as 'the most beautiful woman in the Three Towns.' Yes, his love of beauty was a sensuous, warm glow pervading the whole of him, secretly separating him from the majority of his associates. A pretty face, a beautiful figure, a mellow tune, the sight of dancing, a blackbird's song, the moon behind a poplar tree, starry nights, sweet scents, and the language of Shakespeare – all these moved him deeply, the more perhaps because he had never learned to express his feelings. His attempts at literature indeed were strangely naïve and stilted; his verse, in the comic vein, rather good; but all, as it were, like his period, ashamed to express any intimate feeling except in classical language. Yet his literary tastes were catholic; Milton was his favourite poet, Byron he also admired; Browning he did not care for; his favourite novelist was George Eliot, and, curiously enough – in later life – Turgenev. I well remember when the translated volumes of that author were coming out, how he would ask for another of those yellow books. He did not know why he liked them, with all those 'crack-jaw' Russian names; but assuredly it was because they were written by one who worshipped beauty.

The works of Dickens and Thackeray he read with appreciation, on the whole, finding the first perhaps a little too grotesque, and the second a little too satiric. Scott, Trollope, Marryat Blackmore, Hardy, and Mark Twain also pleased him; but Meredith he thought too 'misty'.

A great theatre-goer all his life, he was very lukewarm towards modern actors, comparing them adversely with those constellations of the past, Edmund and Charles Kean, Charlie Mathews, Farren, Power, 'little Robson', and Helen Faucit. He was, however, a great lover of Kate Vaughan's dancing; an illustration of the equanimity of one who had formed his taste on Taglioni.

Irving he would only accept in *Louis XI, The Bells,* and, I think, *Charles I,* and for his mannerisms he had a great aversion. There was something of the old grand manner about his theatre habits. He attended with the very best and thinnest lavender kid gloves on his hands, which he would hold up rather high and clap together at the end of an act which pleased him; even, on memorable occasions, adding the word 'Bravo'. He never went out before the end of a play, however vehemently he might call it 'poor stuff', which, to be quite honest, he did about nine times out of ten. And he was ever ready to try again, having a sort of touching confidence in an art which had betrayed him so often. His opera hats were notable, usually of such age as to have lost shape, and surely the largest in London. Indeed, his dress was less varied than that of any man I have ever seen; but always neat and well-cut, for he went habitually to the best shops, and without eccentricity of any kind. He carried a repeating gold watch and thin round gold chain which passed, smooth and sinuous as a little snake, through a small black seal with a bird on it; and he never abandoned very well-made side-spring boots with cork soles, greatly resenting the way other boots dirtied his hands, which were thin and brown with long polished nails, and blue veins outstanding. For reading only, he wore tortoise-shelled eyeglasses, which he would perch low down on the bridge of his nose, so that he could look over them, for his eyes were very long-sighted. He was extremely fastidious in his linen, and all personal matters, yet impatient of being mollycoddled, or in any way over-valeted. Even on the finest days, he carried an umbrella, the ferrule of which, from his habit of stumping it on the pavement, had a worn and harassed look, and was rarely more than half present.

Having been a Conservative Liberal in politics till well past sixty, it was not until Disraeli's time that he became a Liberal Conservative. This was curious, for he always spoke doubtfully of 'Dizzy', and even breathed the word 'humbug' in connection with him. Probably he was offended by what he termed 'the extravagance' in Dizzy's rival. For the Duke of Devonshire and Lord Salisbury he had respect without enthusiasm; and conceived for John Bright a great admiration as soon as he was dead. But on the whole the politician who had most attracted him had been Palmerston, because – if memory serves – he had in such admirable degree the faculty of 'astonishing their weak nerves'. For, though never a Jingo, and in later days both cautious and sane in his Imperialism, he had all a Briton's essential deep-rooted distrust of the foreigner. He felt that they were not quite safe, not quite sound, and must from time to time be made to feel this. Born two years after the battle of Waterloo, he had inherited a certain high pride of island birth. And yet in one case, where he was for years in close contact with a foreigner he conceived for him so grave a respect, that it was quite amusing to watch the discomfiture of his traditional distrust. It was often a matter of wonder amongst those who knew him that a man of his ability and judgement had never even sought to make his mark in public affairs. Of the several reasons for this, the chief was, undoubtedly, the extraordinary balance of his temperament. To attain pre-eminence in any definite department of life would have warped and stunted too many of his instincts, removed too many of his interests; and so he never specialized in anything. He was quite unambitious, always taking the lead in whatever field he happened to be, by virtue of his great capacity and will-power, but never pushing himself, and apparently without any life-aim, but that of leading a sane, moderate, and harmonious existence.

And it is for this that he remains written on the national page, as the type of a lost and golden time, when life to each man seemed worth living for its own sake, without thought of its meaning as a whole, or much speculation as to its end. There was something classical, measured, and mellow in his march down the years, as if he had been god-mothered by Harmony. And yet, though he said his prayers and went to church, he could not fairly have been called a religious man; for at the time when he formed his religious habits, 'religion' had as yet received no shocks, and reigned triumphant over an unconscious nation whose spirit was sleeping; and when 'religion', disturbed to its foundations, began to die, and people all round him were just becoming religious enough to renounce the beliefs they no longer held, he was too old to change, and continued to employ the mechanism of a creed which had never really been vital to him. He was in essence pagan: All was right with his world! His love was absorbed by Nature, and his wonder by the Great Starry Scheme he felt all around. This was God to him; for it was ever in the presence of the stars that he was most moved to a sense of divine order. Looking up at those tremulous cold companions he seemed more reverent, and awed, than ever he was in the face of creeds or his fellow man. Whether stirred by the sheer beauty of Night, or by its dark immensity swarming with those glittering worlds, he would stand silent, and then, perhaps, say wistfully: 'What little bits of things we are! Poor little wretches!' Yes, it was then that he really worshipped, adoring the great wonders of Eternity. No one ever heard him talk with conviction of a future life. He was far too self-reliant to accept what he was told, save by his own inner voice; and that did not speak to him with certainty. In fact, as he grew old, to be uncertain of all such high things was part of his real religion; it seemed to him, I think, impertinent to pretend to intimate knowledge of what was so much bigger than himself. But neither his conventional creed, nor that awed uncertainty which was his real religion were ever out of hand; they jogged smoothly on in double harness, driven and guided by a supremer power – his reverence for Life. He abhorred fanaticism. In this he truly mirrored the spirit of that great peacefully expanding river, the Victorian Era, which began when he came of age. And yet, in speaking before him of deep or abstract things, it was not safe to reckon without his criticism, which would sometimes make powerfully shrewd deductions out of the sheer logical insight of a nature neither fundamentally concerned with other worlds, nor brought up to the ways of discussion. He was pre-eminently the son of a time between two ages – a past age of old, unquestioning faith in authority; a future age of new faith, already born but not yet grown. Still sheltering in the shade of the old tree which was severed at the roots and toppling, he never, I think, clearly saw – though he may have had glimpses – that men, like children whose mother has departed from their home, were slowly being forced to trust in, and be good to, themselves and to one another, and so to form out of their necessity, desperately, unconsciously, their new great belief in Humanity. Yes, he was the son of a *time between two ages* – the product of an era without real faith – an individualist to the core.

His attitude towards the poor, for instance, was essentially that of man to man. Save that he could not tolerate imposters (one of his favourite words), and saw through them with almost startling rapidity, he was compassionate to any who had fallen on evil fortune, and especially to those who had been in any way connected with him. But in these almonary transactions he was always particularly secretive, as if rather doubting their sagacity, and the wisdom of allowing them to become known – himself making up and despatching the parcels of old clothes, and rather surreptitiously producing such coins and writing such cheques as were necessary. But 'the poor', in bulk, were always to him the concern of the Poor Law pure and simple, and in no sense of the individual citizen. It was the same with malefactors, he might pity as well as condemn them, but the idea that the society to which he and they belonged was in any way responsible for them, would never have occurred to him. His sense of justice, like that of his period, was fundamentally based on the notion that every man had started with equal, or at all events, with quite sufficient opportunities, and must be judged as if he had. But, indeed, it was not the custom in his day to concern oneself with problems outside one's own class. Within that class, and in all matters domestic, no man was ever born with a nicer sense of justice. It was never overridden by his affections; very seldom, and that with a certain charming *naïveté*, by his interests. This sense of justice, however, in no way prevented him from being loved; for, in spite of a temper apt to take fire, flare up, and quickly die down again, he was one of the most lovable of men. There was not an ounce of dourness or asperity in his composition. His laughter was of a most infectious kind, singularly spontaneous and delightful, resembling the laughter of a child. The change which a joke wrought in the aspect of his large, dignified, and rather noble face, was disconcerting. It became wrinkled, or, as it were, crumpled; and such a twinkling overcame his eyes as was frequently only to be extinguished by moisture. 'That's rich!' was his favourite expression to describe what had tickled him; for he had preserved the use of Devonshire expressions, bringing them forth from an intimate pet drawer of memory, and lingering over them with real gusto. He still loved, too, such Devonshire dishes of his boyhood as 'junket' and 'toad in the hole'; and one of his favourite memories was that of the meals snatched at the old coaching inn at Exeter, while they changed the horses of the Plymouth to London coach. Twenty-four hours at ten miles an hour, without ever a break! Glorious drive! Glorious the joints of beef, the cherry brandy! Glorious the old stage coachman, a 'monstrous fat chap' who at that time ruled the road!

In the City, where his office was situate, he was wont, though at all times a very moderate eater, to frequent substantial, old-fashioned hostelries such as Roche's, Pim's, or Birch's in preference to newer and more pretentious places of refreshment. He had a remarkable palate too, and though he drank very little, was, in his prime, considered as fine a judge of wine as any in London. Of tea he was particularly fond, and always consumed the very best Indian, made with extreme care, maintaining that the Chinese variety was only fit for persons of no taste.

He had little liking for his profession, believing it to be beneath him, and that Heaven had intended him for an advocate; in which he was probably right, for his masterful acumen could not have failed to assure him a foremost position at the Bar. And in him, I think, it is certain that a great Judge was lost to the State. Despite this contempt for what he called the 'pettifogging' character of his occupation, he always inspired profound respect in his clients; and among the shareholders of his Companies, of which he directed several, his integrity and judgement stood so high that he was enabled to pursue successfully a line of policy often too comprehensive and far-seeing for the temper of the times. The reposeful dignity, and courage, of his head and figure when facing an awkward General Meeting could hardly have been exceeded. He sat, as it were, remote from its gusty temper, quietly determining its course.

Truly memorable were his conflicts with the only other man of his calibre on those Boards, and I cannot remember that he was ever beaten. He was at once the quicker tempered and more cautious. And if he had not the other's stoicism and iron nerve, he saw further into the matter in hand, was more unremitting in his effort, equally tenacious of purpose, and more magnetic. In fact, he had a way with him.

But, after all said, it was in his dealings with children that the best and sweetest side of his personality was manifested. With them he became completely tender, inexhaustibly interested in their interests, absurdly patient, and as careful as a mother. No child ever resisted him, or even dreamed of doing so. From the first moment they loved his white hair and beard, his 'feathers' as one little thing called them. They liked the touch of his thin hand, which was never wet or cold; and, holding to it, were always ready to walk with him – wandering with complete unanimity, not knowing quite where or for what reason. How often have I not watched him starting out on that high adventure with his grandson, his face turned gravely down towards a smaller face turned not quite so gravely up; and heard their voices tremendously concerned with all the things they might be going to do together! How often have I not seen them coming back tired as cats, but still concerned about what was next going to happen! And children were always willing to play cricket with him because he bowled to them very slowly, pitching up what he called 'three-quarter' balls, and himself always getting 'out' almost before he went in. For, though he became in his later years a great connoisseur of cricket, spending many days at Lord's or the Oval, choosing out play of the very highest class, and quite impatient of the Eton and Harrow Match, he still performed in a somewhat rococo fashion, as of a man taught in the late twenties of the last century, and having occasion to revive that knowledge about 1895. He bent his back knee, and played with a perfectly crooked bat, to the end that when he did hit the ball, which was not too often, it invariably climbed the air. There was, too, about his batting, a certain vein of recklessness or bravado, somewhat out of keeping with his general character, so that, as has been said, he was never in too long. And when he got out he would pitch the bat down as if he were annoyed, which would hugely please his grandson, showing of course that he had been trying his very best, as indeed, he generally had. But his bowling was extremely impressive, being effected with very bent knees, and a general air of first putting the ball to the eye, as if he were playing bowls; in this way he would go on and on giving the boy 'an innings', and getting much too hot. In fielding he never could remember on the spur of the moment whether it was his knees or his feet that he ought to close; and this, in combination with a habit of bending rather cautiously, because he was liable to lumbago, detracted somewhat from his brilliance; but when the ball was once in his hands, it was most exciting – impossible to tell whether he would throw it at the running batsman, the wicket, or the bowler, according as the game appeared to him at the moment to be double wicket, single wicket, or rounders. He had lived in days when games were not the be-all and end-all of existence, and had never acquired a proper seriousness in such matters. Those who passed from cricket with him to cricket in the cold wide world found a change for which at first they were unable to account. But even more fascinating to children than his way of playing cricket was his perfect identification with whatever might be the matter in hand. The examination of a shell, the listening to the voice of the sea imprisoned in it, the making of a cocked hat out of *The Times* newspaper, the doing up of little buttons, the feeding of pigeons with crumbs, the holding fast of a tiny leg while walking beside a pony, all these things absorbed him completely, so that no visible trace was left of the man whose judgement on affairs was admirable and profound. Nor, whatever the provocation, could he ever bring himself to point the moral of anything to a child, having that utter toleration of their foibles which only comes from a natural and perfectly unconscious love of being with them. His face, habitually tranquil, wore in their presence a mellow look of almost devil-may-care serenity.

Their sayings, too, he treasured, as though they were pearls. First poems, such as:

> I sorr a worm,
>   It was half-ly dead;
> I took a great spud,
>   And speared through his head

were to him of singular fair promise. Their diagnoses of character, moreover, especially after visiting a circus, filled him with pure rapture, and he would frequently repeat this one:

'Father, is Uncle a clever man?'

'H'm! well – yes, certainly.'

'I never seen no specimens. He can't balance a pole on his nose, for instance.'

To the declining benison of their prayers, from their 'darling father and mother', to 'all poor people who are in distress', he loved to listen, not so much for the sentiments expressed, as because, in their little nightgowns, they looked so sweet, and were so roundabout in their way of getting to work.

Yes, children were of all living things his chosen friends, and they knew it.

But in his long life he made singularly few fast friendships with grown-up people, and, as far as I know, no enemies. For there was in him, despite his geniality, a very strong vein of fastidiousness, and such essential deep love of domination, that he found, perhaps, few men of his own age and standing to whom he did not feel natively superior. His most real and life-long friendship was for a certain very big man with a profound hatred of humbug and a streak of 'the desperate character' in him. They held each other in the highest esteem, or, as they would probably have put it, swore by one another; the one grumbling at, but reverencing, the other's high and resolute equanimity; the other deploring and admiring the one's deep and generous recklessness. The expressions: 'Just like John, the careful fellow!' 'Just like Sil, reckless beggar!' were always on their lips, for like all their generation they were sparing of en-comium; and great, indeed, must have been their emotion be-fore they would show their feelings. Dear as they were to each other's hearts, they never talked together of spiritual things, they never spoke in generalities, but gravely smoking their cigars, discussed their acquaintances, investments, wine, their neph-ews and grandchildren, and the affairs of the State – condemn-ing the advertising fashion in which everything was now done. Once in a way they would tell a story – but they knew each other's stories too well; once in a way quote a line of Byron, Shakespeare, or Milton; or whistle to each other, inharmon-iously, a bar or two from some song that Grisi, Mario, or Jenny Lind had sung. Once in a way memories of the heyday of their youth, those far-off golden hours, stealing over them, they would sit silent, with their grave steady eyes following the little rings of bluish smoke... Yes, for all their lack of demonstra-tion, they loved each other well.

I seem still to see the subject of this portrait standing at his friend's funeral one bleak November day, the pale autumn sun-light falling on the silver of his uncovered head a little bowed, and on his grave face, for once so sad. I hear the tones of his voice, still full and steady; and from the soul in his eyes, look-ing, as it were, through and through those forms of death to some deep conclusion of his own, I know how big and sane and sweet he was.

His breed is dying now, it has nearly gone. But as I remember him with that great quiet forehead, with his tenderness, and his glance which travelled to the heart of what it rested on, I despair of seeing his like again. For, with him there seems to me to have passed away a principle, a golden rule of life, nay, more, a spirit – the soul of Balance. It has stolen away, as in the early morning the stars steal out of the sky. *He* knew its tranquil secret, and where he is, there must it still be hovering.

1908

THE GREY ANGEL

⊰⊹⊱

HER predilection for things French came from childish recollections of schooldays in Paris and a hasty removal thence by her father during the revolution of '48; of later travels as a little maiden, by diligence, to Pau and the then undiscovered Pyrenees, to Montpellier, and a Nice as yet unspoiled. Unto her seventy-eighth year, her French accent had remained unruffled, her soul in love with French gloves and dresses; and her face had the pale, unwrinkled, slightly aquiline perfection of the French marquise type – it may, perhaps, be doubted whether any French marquise ever looked the part so perfectly.

How it came about that she had settled down in a southern French town, in the summer of 1914, only her roving spirit knew. She had been a widow ten years, which she had passed in the quest of perfection; all her life she had been haunted by that instinct, half-smothered in ministering to her husband, children, and establishments in London and the country. Now, in loneliness, the intrinsic independence of her soul was able to assert itself, and from hotel to hotel she had wandered in England, Wales, Switzerland, France, till she had found what seemingly arrested her. Was it the age of that oldest of Western cities, that little mother of Western civilization, which captured her fancy? Or did a curious perversity turn her from more obvious abodes; or, again, was she kept there by the charm of a certain church which she would enter every day to steep herself in mellow darkness, the scent of incense, the drone of incantations, and quiet communion with a God higher indeed than she had been brought up to, high-church though she had always been? She had a pretty little apartment, where for very little – the bulk of her small wealth was habitually at the service of others – she could manage with one maid and no 'fuss'. She had some 'nice' French friends there, too. But more probably it was simply the war which kept her, waiting, like so many other people, till it seemed worth while to move and re-establish herself. The immensity and wickedness of this strange event held her suspended, body and spirit, high up on the hill which had seen the ancient peoples, the Romans, Gauls, Saracens, and still looked out towards the flat Camargue. Here in her three rooms, with a little kitchen, the maid Augustine, a parrot, and the Paris *Daily Mail*, she dwelt marooned by a world event which stunned her. Not that she worried, exactly. The defeat of her country and France never entered her head. She only grieved quietly over the dreadful things that were being done, and every now and then would glow with admiration at the beautiful way the King and Queen were behaving. It was no good to 'fuss', and one must make the best of things, as the 'dear little Queen' was doing – for each Queen in turn, and she had seen three reign in her time, was always that to her. Her ancestors had been uprooted from their lands, their house burned, her pedigree diverted, in the Stuart wars; and a reverence for royalty was fastened in her blood.

Quite early in the business she had begun to knit, moving her slim fingers not too fast, gazing at the grey wool through glasses, rimless and invisible, perched on the bridge of her firm, well-shaped nose, and now and then speaking to her parrot. The bird could say, 'Scratch a poll, Poll,' and 'Hullo!' – those keys to the English language. The maid Augustine, having completed some small duty, would come and stand, her head on one side, gazing down with inquiring compassion in her young, clear-brown eyes. It seemed to her, straight and sturdy as a young tree, both wonderful and sad that *Madame* should be seventy-seven, and so frail – *Madame* who had no lines in her face and such beautiful grey hair; who had so strong a will-power, too, and knitted such soft comforters '*pour nos braves chers poilus.*' And suddenly she would say: '*Madame n'est pas fatiguée?*' And *Madame* would answer: 'No. Speak English, Augustine – Polly will pick up your French!' And, reaching up a pale hand, she would set straight a stray fluff of the girl's dark-brown hair or improve the set of her fichu.

Those two got on extremely well, for though *Madame* was –

oh! but very particular, she was always '*très gentille et toujours grande dame*'. And that love of form deep in the French soul promoted the girl's admiration for one whom she could see would in no circumstances lose her dignity. Besides, *Madame* was full of dainty household devices, and could not bear waste; and these, though exacting, were qualities which appealed to Augustine. With her French passion for 'the family', she used to wonder how in days like these *Madame* could endure to be far away from her son and daughter and the grandchildren, whose photographs hung on the walls; and the long letters her mistress was always writing in a beautiful, fine hand, beginning, 'My darling Sybil,' 'My darling Reggie,' and ending always, 'Your devoted mother,' seemed to a warm and simple heart but meagre substitutes for flesh-and-blood realities. But, as *Madame* would inform her, they were so busy doing things for the dear soldiers, and working for the war; they could not come to her – that would never do. And to go to them would give so much trouble, when the railways were so wanted for the troops; and she had their lovely letters, which she kept – as Augustine observed – in a lavender-scented sachet, and frequently took out to read. Another point of sympathy between those two was their passion for military music and seeing soldiers pass. Augustine's brother and father were at the front, and *Madame's* dead brother had been a soldier in the Crimean War – 'long before you were born, Augustine, when the French and English fought the Russians: I was in France then, too, a little girl, and we lived at Nice; the flowers were so lovely, you can't think! And my poor brother was so cold in the siege of Sebastopol.' Somehow, that time and that war were more real to her than this.

In December, when the hospitals were already full, her French friends took her to the one which they attended. She went in, her face very calm with that curious inward composure which never deserted it, carrying in front of her a black silk bag, wherein she had concealed an astonishing collection of treasures for the poor men. A bottle of acidulated drops, packets of cigarettes, two of her own mufflers, a pocket set of draughts, some English riddles translated by herself into French (very curious), some ancient copies of an illustrated paper, boxes of chocolate, a ball of string to make 'cats' cradles' (such an amusing game), her own packs of patience cards, some photograph frames, postcards of Arles, and, most singular, a kettle-holder. At the head of each bed she would sit down and rummage in the bag, speaking in her slow but quite good French, to explain the use of the acidulated drops, or to give a lesson in cats' cradles. And the *poilus* would listen with their polite, ironic patience, and be left smiling, curiously fascinated, as if they had been visited by a creature from another world. She would move on to other beds, quite unconscious of the effect she had produced on them and of their remarks: '*L'ange aux chevaux gris*' became her name within those walls. And the habit of filling that black silk bag and going there to distribute its contents soon grew to be with her a ruling passion which neither weather nor her own aches and pains, not inconsiderable, must interfere with. The things she brought became more marvellous every week. But, however much she carried coals to Newcastle, or tobacco pouches to those who did not smoke, or homeopathic globules to such as crunched up the whole bottleful for the sake of the sugar as soon as her back was turned, no one ever smiled now with anything but real pleasure at the sight of her calm and truly sweet smile and the scent of soap on her pale hands. '*Cher fils, je croyais que ceci vous donnerait un peu de plaisir. Voyez-vous comme c'est commode, n'est ce pas?*' Each newcomer to the wards was warned by his comrades that the angel with the grey hair was to be taken without a smile, exactly as if she were his grandmother.

In the walk to the hospital Augustine would accompany her, carrying the bag and a large peasant's umbrella to cover them both, for the winter was hard and snowy, and carriages cost money, which must now be kept entirely for the almost daily replenishment of the bag and other calls of war. The girl, to her chagrin, was always left in a safe place, for it would never do to take her in and put fancies into her head, or excite the dear soldiers with anything so taking. The visit over, they would set forth home, walking very slowly in the high narrow streets, Augustine pouting a little and shooting swift glances at anything in uniform, and *Madame* making firm her lips against a fatigue which sometimes almost overcame her before she could get home and up the stairs. And the parrot would greet them indiscreetly with new phrases – 'Keep smiling!' and 'Kiss Augustine!' which he sometimes varied with 'Kiss a poll, Poll!' or 'Scratch Augustine!' to *Madame's* regret. Tea would revive her, and then she would knit, for as time went on and the war seemed to get farther from that end which, in common with so many, she had expected before now, it seemed dreadful not to be always doing something to help the poor dear soldiers; and for dinner, to Augustine's horror, she now had nothing but soup, or an egg beaten up with milk and brandy. It saved time and expense – she was sure people ate too much; and afterward she would read the *Daily Mail*, often putting it down to sigh, and press her lips together, and think, 'One must look on the bright side of things,' and wonder a little where it was. And Augustine, finishing her work in the tiny kitchen, would sigh too, and think of red trousers and peaked caps, not yet out of date in that southern region, and of her own heart saying 'Kiss Augustine!' and she would peer out between the shutters at the stars sparkling over the Camargue, or look down where the ground fell away beyond an old wall, and nobody walked in the winter night; and muse on her nineteenth birthday coming, and sigh with the thought that she would be old before anyone had loved her; and of how *Madame* was looking '*très fatiguée*'.

Indeed, *Madame* was '*très fatiguée*' in these days. The world's vitality and her own were at January ebb. But to think of oneself was impossible; it would be all right presently, and one must not fuss, or mention in one's letters to the dear children that one felt poorly. As for a doctor – that would be sinful waste, and besides, what use were they except to tell you what you knew? And she was terribly vexed when Augustine found her in a faint one morning, and she found Augustine in tears, with her hair all over her face. She rated the girl soundly for making such a fuss over 'a little thing like that', and with extremely trembling fingers pushed the brown hair back and told her to wash her face, while the parrot said reflectively, 'Scratch a poll – Hullo!' The girl, who had seen her own grandmother die not long before, and remembered how *'fatiguée'* she had been during her last days, was frightened. Coming back after washing her face, she found her mistress writing on a number of little envelopes the same words: *'En bonne Amitié'*.

'Take this hundred-franc note, Augustine, and get it changed into single francs – the ironmonger will do it if you say it's for me. I am going to take a rest. I shan't buy anything for the bag for a whole week. I shall take francs instead.'

'Oh *Madame*! you must not go out: *vous êtes trop fatiguée.*'

'Nonsense! How do you suppose our dear little Queen in England would get out with all she has to do, if she were to give in like that? We must none of us give up in these days. Help me to put on my things; I am going to church.'

'Oh, *Madame*! Must you go to church? It is not your kind of church. You do not pray there, do you?'

'Of course I pray there. I am very fond of the dear old church. God is in every church. Augustine; you ought to know that at your age.'

'But *Madame* has her own religion?'

'Don't be silly. What does that matter? Help me into my cloth coat – not the fur, it's too heavy – and then go and get that money changed.'

'But *Madame* should see a doctor. If *Madame* faints again I shall die with fright. *Madame* has no colour – but no colour at all; it must be that there is something wrong.'

Madame rose, and taking the girl's ear between thumb and finger pinched it gently.

'You are a very silly girl. What would our soldiers do if all the nurses were like you?'

Reaching the church she sat down gladly, turning her face up toward her favourite picture, a Virgin standing with her Baby in her arms. It was only faintly coloured now; but there were those who said that an Arlésienne must have sat for it. Why it pleased her so she never quite knew, unless by its cool, unrestored devotion, and the faint smiling in the eyes. Religion with her was strange yet very real. She was not clever, and never even began to try and understand what she believed. If she tried to be good she would go to God – wherever God might be; and rarely did she forget to try to be good. Sitting there she thought, or rather prayed: 'Let me forget that I have a body, and remember the poor soldiers.'

She shivered. It struck cold that morning in the church – the wind bitter from the north-east; some women in black were kneeling, and four candles burned in the gloom of a side aisle – thin, steady little spires of gold. There was no sound at all. A smile came on her lips. She was remembering all those young faces in the wards, the faces, too, of her own children far away, the faces of all she loved; and all the poor souls on land and sea, fighting and working and dying. Her lips moved in prayer: 'O God, who makes the birds sing and the stars shine and gives us little children, strengthen my heart so that I may forget my own aches and think of those of other people.'

On reaching home again she took gelsemium, her favourite remedy against that shivering, which would keep coming; then, covering herself with her fur coat, she lay down. Augustine, returning with the hundred single francs, placed them noiselessly beside the little pile of envelopes, and, after looking at the motionless face of her mistress, withdrew. Two tears came out of those closed eyes and clung on the pale cheeks below. The seeming sleeper was thinking of her children, away over there in England, her children and their children. Almost unbearably she was longing for a sight of them, recalling each face, voice, different way they had of saying 'Mother darling', or 'Granny, look what I've got!' and thinking that if only the war would end she would pack at once and go to them – that is, if they would not come to her for a nice long holiday in this beautiful place. She thought of spring and how lovely it would be to see the trees come out again, and almond blossom against a blue sky. The war seemed so long, and winter too. But she must not complain; others had much greater sorrows – the poor widowed women kneeling in the church; the poor boys freezing in the trenches. God in His great mercy could not allow it to last much longer! It would not be like Him! Her eyes rested gloatingly on the piles of francs and envelopes. How could she reduce still further her personal expenditure? It was so dreadful to spend on oneself – an old woman like her. Doctor, indeed! If Augustine fussed any more she would send her away and do for herself! And the parrot, leaving his cage, which he could always do, perched just behind her and said 'Hullo! Kiss me, too!'

That afternoon in the hospital everyone noticed what a beautiful colour she had. *'L'ange aux cheveux gris'* had never been more popular.

She had not meant to give all the francs that day, but she saw how pleased they were, and so the whole ninety-seven had their franc each. The three over would buy Augustine a little brooch to make up to the silly child for her fright in the morning. The buying of this brooch took a long time at the jeweller's, and she had only just fixed on an amethyst before feeling deadly ill with a dreadful pain through her lungs. She went out with her tiny package quickly, not wanting any fuss, and began to mount toward home. She had only three hundred yards to go, and with each step said to herself: 'Nonsense! What would the Queen think of you? Remember the poor soldiers with only one leg! You have got both your legs! And the poor men who walk from the battlefield with bullets through the lungs. What is your pain to theirs?' But the pain, like none she had ever felt – having sharp knife edges – kept passing through and through her; her legs had no strength at all, seeming to move simply because her will said: 'If you don't, I'll leave you behind. So there!' She felt as if perspiration were flowing down, yet her face was dry as a dead leaf when she put up her hand to it. Her brain stammered, came to sudden standstills. Her eyes searched painfully each grey-shuttered window for her own house, though she knew quite well that she had not reached it yet. From sheer pain she stood still, a wry smile on her lips, thinking how Polly would say: 'Keep smiling!' Then she moved on, holding out her hand, as if to pull on some imaginary rope. So, foot by foot, she crept to her door. A peculiar floating sensation had come over her. The pain ceased, and – as if she had passed through no doors, mounted no stairs – she was up in her room, lying on her sofa, conscious that she was not in control of her thoughts, and that Augustine must be thinking her ridiculous. Making a great effort, she said:

'I forbid you to send for a doctor, Augustine. I shall be all right in a day or two. And you must put on this little brooch – I bought it for you. The war will be over tomorrow, and then we will all go and have tea together in a wood. Granny will come to you, my darlings.'

And when the terrified girl had rushed out she thought: 'There now! I shall get up and do for myself.' The doctor found her half-dressed, trying to feed a perch in the empty cage with a spoon, while the parrot sat on the mantelpiece, with his head on one side.

When she had been properly undressed and made to lie down on the sofa, for she would not go to bed and they dared not oppose her, the doctor made his diagnosis. It was that of double pneumonia, which declares for life or death in forty-eight hours. At her age a desperate case. Her children must be wired to at once. She had sunk back, seemingly unconscious; and Augustine slipped out the lavender sachet where the letters were kept and gave it to the doctor. When he had left the room to extract addresses and send those telegrams, the girl sat down by the foot of the couch, staring at that motionless form, with tears running down her broad cheeks. For many minutes neither of them stirred, and the only sound was the restless stropping of the parrot's beak against a wire of his cage. Then the lips moved, and the girl bent forward. A whispering came forth:

'Mind, Augustine – no one is to tell my children – I can't have them disturbed – over a little thing – like this – and in my purse you'll find another – hundred-franc note. I shall want some more francs for the day after tomorrow. Be a good girl and don't fuss. Give me my gelsemium and my prayer-book. And go to bed just as usual – we must all – keep smiling – like the dear soldiers –' The whispering ceased; then began again in delirious incoherence. The girl sat trembling, covering her ears from those uncanny sounds. She could not follow – with her little English – the swerving, intricate flights of that old spirit mazed by fever – the memories released, the longings disclosed, the half-uttered prayers, the little half-conscious efforts to regain form and dignity. She could only pray to the Virgin. When relieved by the daughter of *Madame's* French friend, who spoke good English, she murmured: '*Oh! Mademoiselle, Madame est très, très fatigué – la pauvre tête – faut-il enlever les cheveux? Elle fait ça toujours pour elle-même.*' To the girl it seemed sacrilege to take off that crown of fine grey hair. Yet, when the old face was covered only by the thin white hair of nature, dignity still surmounted the wandering talk and the moaning from the parched lips, which smiled and pouted, as if remembering the maxims of the parrot. So the night passed. Once her spirit seemed to recover its coherence, and she was heard to whisper: 'God has given me this so that I may know what the poor soldiers suffer. Oh! they've forgotten to cover Polly's cage.' But high fever soon passes from the very old; and early morning brought a deathlike exhaustion, with utter silence, save for the licking of the flames at the olive-wood logs, and the sound as they slipped or settled down, calcined. The firelight crept fantastically about the walls covered with tapestry of French-grey silk, crept round the screen-head of the couch, and exhibited the pallor of that mask-like face, which covered such tenuous threads of life. Augustine, who had come on guard when the fever died away, sat in the armchair before those flames, trying to watch, but dropping off into the healthy sleep of youth. And out in the clear, hard, shivering Southern cold, the old clocks chimed the hours into the winter dark, where the old town brooded above plain and river under the morning stars. The girl dreamed – dreamed of a sweetheart under the acacias by her home, of his pinning their white flowers into her hair; and woke with a little laugh. Light was already coming through the shutter chinks, the fire was but red embers and white ash. She gathered it stealthily together, put on fresh logs, and stole over to the couch. How white! how still! Dead? She jerked her hands up to her full breast, and a cry mounted to her throat. The eyes opened. The lips parted, as if to smile; the voice whispered: 'Don't be silly!' The girl's cry changed into a little sob, and bending down she put her lips to the hand outside the quilt. It moved faintly, the lips whispered: 'The emerald ring is for you, Augustine. Is it morning? Uncover Polly's cage and open his door.'

A telegram had come. Her son and daughter would arrive next morning early. They waited for a moment of consciousness to tell her; but the day went by, and it did not come. She was sinking fast; her only movements were a tiny compression now and then of the lips, a half-opening of the eyes, and once a smile when the parrot spoke. The rally came at eight o'clock. *Mademoiselle* was sitting by the couch when the voice came fairly strong: 'Give my love to my dear soldiers, and take them their francs out of my purse, please. Augustine, take care of Polly. I want to see if the emerald ring fits you. Take it off, please. There, you see, it does. That's very nice. Your sweetheart will like that when you have one. What do you say, *Mademoiselle*? My son and daughter are coming? All that way?' The lips smiled, tears forced their way into her eyes. 'My darlings! How good of them! Oh! what a cold journey they'll have! Get my room ready, Augustine, with a good fire! What are you crying for? Remember what Polly says: "Keep smiling!"'

She did not seem anxious as to whether she would live to see her children. Her smile moved *Mademoiselle* to whisper: '*Elle a le sourire divine.*'

'*Ah! Mademoiselle, elle pense toujours aux autres.*' And the girl's tears dropped on the emerald ring.

The long night fell – would she wake again? Both watched, ready at the faintest movement to administer oxygen and brandy. She was still breathing when at six o'clock they heard the express come in and presently the carriage stop before the house. *Mademoiselle* stole down to let them in.

Still in their travelling coats, her son and daughter knelt down beside the couch, watching in the dim candle-light for a sign and cherishing her cold hands. Daylight came; they put the shutters back and blew out the candles. Augustine, huddled in the far corner, cried gently to herself. *Mademoiselle* had withdrawn. The two still knelt, tears running down their cheeks. The least twitching of just-opened lips showed that she breathed.

A tiny sigh escaped; her eyelids fluttered. The son, leaning forward, said:

'Sweetheart, we're here.'

The eyes opened then; something more than a simple human spirit seemed to look through – the lips parted. They bent to catch the sound.

'My darlings – don't cry; smile!' The eyes closed. A smile, so touching that it rent the heart, flickered and went out. Breath had ceased to pass the lips.

In the silence the French girl's sobbing rose; the parrot stirred in his still-covered cage. And the son and daughter knelt, pressing their faces against the couch.

1917

QUALITY

I KNEW him from the days of my extreme youth, because he made my father's boots; inhabiting with his elder brother two little shops let into one, in a small by-street — now no more, but then most fashionably placed in the West End.

That tenement had a certain quiet distinction; there was no sign upon its face that he made for any of the Royal Family — merely his own German name of Gessler Brothers; and in the window a few pairs of boots. I remember that it always troubled me to account for those unvarying boots in the window, for he made only what was ordered, reaching nothing down, and it seemed so inconceivable that what he made could ever have failed to fit. Had he bought them to put there? That, too, seemed inconceivable. He would never have tolerated in his house leather on which he had not worked himself. Besides, they were too beautiful — the pair of pumps, so inexpressibly slim, the patent leathers with cloth tops, making water come into one's mouth, the tall brown riding-boots with marvellous sooty glow, as if, though new, they had been worn a hundred years. Those pairs could only have been made by one who saw before him the Soul of Boot — so truly were they prototypes incarnating the very spirit of all footgear. These thoughts, of course, came to me later, though even when I was promoted to him, at the age of perhaps fourteen, some inkling haunted me of the dignity of himself and brother. For to make boots — such boots as he made — seemed to me then, and still seems to me, mysterious and wonderful.

I remember well my shy remark, one day, while stretching out to him my youthful foot:

'Isn't it awfully hard to do, Mr Gessler?'

And his answer, given with a sudden smile from out of the sardonic redness of his beard: 'Id is an Ardt!'

Himself, he was a little as if made from leather, with his yellow crinkly face, and crinkly reddish hair and beard, and neat folds slanting down his cheeks to the corners of his mouth, and his guttural and one-toned voice; for leather is a sardonic substance, and stiff and slow of purpose. And that was the character of his face, save that his eyes, which were grey-blue, had in them the simple gravity of one secretly possessed by the Ideal. His elder brother was so very like him – though watery, paler in every way, with a great industry – that sometimes in early days I was not quite sure of him until the interview was over. Then I knew that it was he, if the words, 'I will ask my brudder,' had not been spoken; and that, if they had, it was his elder brother.

When one grew old and wild and ran up bills, one somehow never ran them up with Gessler Brothers. It would not have seemed becoming to go in there and stretch out one's foot to that blue iron-spectacled glance, owing him for more than – say – two pairs, just the comfortable reassurance that one was still his client.

For it was not possible to go to him very often – his boots lasted terribly, having something beyond the temporary – some, as it were, essence of boot stitched into them.

One went in, not as into most shops, in the mood of: 'Please serve me, and let me go!' but restfully, as one enters a church; and, sitting on the single wooden chair, waited – for there was never anybody there. Soon, over the top edge of that sort of well – rather dark, and smelling soothingly of leather – which formed the shop, there would be seen his face, or that of his elder brother, peering down. A guttural sound, and the tip-tap of bast slippers beating the narrow wooden stairs, and he would stand before one without coat, a little bent, in leather apron, with sleeves turned back, blinking – as if awakened from some dream of boots, or like an owl surprised in daylight and annoyed at this interruption.

And I would say: 'How do you do, Mr Gessler? Could you make me a pair of Russia leather boots?'

Without a word he would leave me, retiring whence he came, or into the other portion of the shop, and I would continue to rest in the wooden chair, inhaling the incense of his trade. Soon he would come back, holding in his thin, veined hand a piece of gold-brown leather. With eyes fixed on it, he would remark: 'What a beaudiful biece!' When, I, too, had admired it, he would speak again. 'When do you wand dem?' And I would answer: 'Oh! As soon as you conveniently can.' And he would say: 'Tomorrow fordnighd?' Or if he were his elder brother: 'I will ask my brudder!'

Then I would murmur: 'Thank you! Good morning, Mr Gessler.' 'Goot morning!' he would reply, still looking at the leather in his hand. And as I moved to the door, I would hear the tip-tap of his bast slippers restoring him, up the stairs, to his dream of boots. But if it were some new kind of footgear that he had not yet made me, then indeed he would observe ceremony – divesting me of my boot and holding it long in his hand, looking at it with eyes at once critical and loving, as if recalling the glow with which he had created it, and rebuking the way in which one had disorganized this masterpiece. Then, placing my foot on a piece of paper, he would two or three times tickle the outer edges with a pencil and pass his nervous fingers over my toes, feeling himself into the heart of my requirements.

I cannot forget that day on which I had occasion to say to him: 'Mr Gessler, that last pair of town walking-boots creaked, you know.'

He looked at me for a time without replying, as if expecting me to withdraw or qualify the statement, then said:

'Id shouldn'd 'ave greaked.'

'It did, I'm afraid.'

'You goddem wed before dey found demselves?'

'I don't think so.'

At that he lowered his eyes, as if hunting for memory of those boots, and I felt sorry I had mentioned this grave thing.

'Zend dem back!' he said; 'I will look at dem.'

A feeling of compassion for my creaking boots surged up in me, so well could I imagine the sorrowful long curiosity of regard which he would bend on them.

'Zome boods,' he said slowly, 'are bad from birdt. If I can do noding wid dem, I dake dem off your bill.'

Once (once only) I went absent-mindedly into his shop in a pair of boots bought in an emergency at some large firm's. He took my order without showing me any leather, and I could feel his eyes penetrating the inferior integument of my foot. At last he said:

'Dose are nod my boods.'

The tone was not one of anger, nor of sorrow, not even of contempt, but there was in it something quiet that froze the blood. He put his hand down and pressed a finger on the place where the left boot, endeavouring to be fashionable, was not quite comfortable.

'Id 'urds you dere,' he said. 'Dose big virms 'ave no self-respect. Drash!' And then, as if something had given way within him, he spoke long and bitterly. It was the only time I ever heard him discuss the conditions and hardships of his trade.

'Dey get id all,' he said, 'dey get id by adverdisement, nod by work. Dey dake it away from us, who lofe our boods. Id gomes to this – bresently I haf no work. Every year id gets less – you will see.' And looking at his lined face I saw things I had never noticed before, bitter things and bitter struggle – and what a lot of grey hairs there seemed suddenly in his red beard!

As best I could, I explained the circumstances of the purchase of those ill-omened boots. But his face and voice made a so deep impression that during the next few minutes I ordered many pairs. Nemesis fell! They lasted more terribly than ever. And I was not able conscientiously to go to him for nearly two years.

When at last I went I was surprised to find that outside one of the two little windows of his shop another name was painted, also that of a bootmaker – making, of course, for the Royal Family. The old familiar boots, no longer in dignified isolation, were huddled in the single window. Inside, the now contracted well of the one little shop was more scented and darker than ever. And it was longer than usual, too, before a face peered down, and the tip-tap of the bast slippers began. At last he stood before me, and, gazing through those rusty iron spectacles, said:

'Mr —, isn'd it?'

'Ah! Mr Gessler,' I stammered, 'but your boots are really *too* good, you know! See, these are quite decent still!' And I stretched out to him my foot. He looked at it.

'Yes,' he said, 'beople do nod wand good boods, id seems.'

To get away from his reproachful eyes and voice I hastily remarked: 'What have you done to your shop?'

He answered quietly: 'Id was too exbensif. Do you wand some boods?'

I ordered three pairs, though I had only wanted two, and quickly left. I had, I know not quite what feeling of being part, in his mind, of a conspiracy against him; or not perhaps so much against him as against his idea of boot. One does not, I suppose, care to feel like that; for it was again many months before my next visit to his shop, paid, I remember, with the feeling: 'Oh! well, I can't leave the old boy — so here goes! Perhaps it'll be his elder brother!'

For his elder brother, I knew, had not character enough to reproach me, even dumbly.

And, to my relief, in the shop there did appear to be his elder brother, handling a piece of leather.

'Well, Mr Gessler,' I said, 'how are you?'

He came close, and peered at me.

'I am breddy well,' he said slowly; 'but my elder brudder is dead.'

And I saw that it was indeed himself — but how aged and wan! And never before had I heard him mention his brother. Much shocked, I murmured: 'Oh! I am sorry!'

'Yes,' he answered, 'he was a good man, he made a good bood; but he is dead.' And he touched the top of his head, where the hair had suddenly gone as thin as it had been on that of his poor brother, to indicate, I suppose, the cause of death. 'He could nod ged over losing de oder shop. Do you wand any boods?' And he held up the leather in his hand: 'Id's a beaudiful biece.'

I ordered several pairs. It was very long before they came — but they were better than ever. One simply could not wear them out. And soon after that I went abroad.

It was over a year before I was again in London. And the first shop I went to was my old friend's. I had left a man of sixty, I came back to one of seventy-five, pinched and worn and tremulous, who genuinely, this time, did not at first know me.

'Oh! Mr Gessler,' I said, sick at heart; 'how splendid your boots are! See, I've been wearing this pair nearly all the time I've been abroad; and they're not halfworn out, are they?'

He looked long at my boots – a pair of Russian leather, and his face seemed to regain steadiness. Putting his hand on my instep, he said:

'Do dey vid you here? I'ad drouble wid dat bair, I remember.'

I assured him that they had fitted beautifully.

'Do you wand any boods?' he said. 'I can make dem quickly; id is a slack dime.'

I answered: 'Please, please! I want boots all round – every kind!'

'I will make a vresh model. Your food must be bigger.' And with utter slowness, he traced round my foot, and felt my toes, only once looking up to say:

'Did I tell you my brudder was dead?'

To watch him was painful, so feeble had he grown; I was glad to get away.

I had given those boots up, when one evening they came. Opening the parcel, I set the four pairs out in a row. Then one by one I tried them on. There was no doubt about it. In shape and fit, in finish and quality of leather, they were the best he had ever made me. And in the mouth of one of the town walking-boots I found his bill. The amount was the same as usual, but it gave me quite a shock. He had never before sent it in till quarter day. I flew downstairs and wrote a cheque, and posted it at once with my own hand.

A week later, passing the little street, I thought I would go in and tell him how splendidly the new boots fitted. But when I came to where his shop had been, his name was gone. Still there, in the window, were the slim pumps, the patent leathers with cloth tops, the sooty riding-boots.

I went in, very much disturbed. In the two little shops – again made into one – was a young man with an English face. 'Mr Gessler in?' I said.

He gave me a strange, ingratiating look.

'No, sir,' he said, 'no. But we can attend to anything with pleasure. We've taken the shop over. You've seen our name, no doubt, next door. We make for some very good people.'

'Yes, yes,' I said; 'but Mr Gessler?'

'Oh!' he answered; 'dead.'

'Dead! But I only received these boots from him last Wednesday week.'

'Ah!' he said; 'a shockin' go. Poor old man starved 'imself.'

'Good God!'

'Slow starvation, the doctor called it! You see he went to work in such a way! Would keep the shop on; wouldn't have a soul touch his boots except himself. When he got an order, it took him such a time. People won't wait. He lost everybody. And there he'd sit, goin' on and on – I will say that for him – not a man in London made a better boot! But look at the competition! He never advertised! Would 'ave the best leather, too, and do it all 'imself. Well, there it is. What could you expect with his ideas?'

'But starvation –!'

'That may be a bit flowery, as the sayin' is – but I know myself he was sittin' over his boots day and night, to the very last. You see I used to watch him. Never gave 'imself time to eat; never had a penny in the house. All went in rent and leather. How he lived so long I don't know. He regular let his fire go out. He was a character. But he made good boots.'

'Yes,' I said, 'he made good boots.'

1911

THE MAN WHO KEPT HIS FORM

◄◄◄‹·›►►►

IN these days every landmark is like Alice's flamingo-croquet-mallet – when you refer to it, the creature curls up into an interrogation mark and looks into your face; and every cornerstone resembles her hedgehog-croquet-ball, which, just before you can use it, gets up and walks away. The old flavours of life are out of fashion, the old scents considered stale; 'gentleman' is a word to sneer at, and 'form' a sign of idiocy.

And yet there are families in the British Isles in which gentility has persisted for hundreds of years, and though you may think me old-fashioned and romantic, I am convinced that such gentlefolk often have a certain quality, a kind of inner pluck bred into them, which is not to be despised at all.

This is why I tell you my recollections of Miles Ruding.

My first sight of him – if a new boy may look at a monitor – was on my rather wretched second day at a Public School. The three other pups who occupied an attic with me had gone out, and I was ruefully considering whether I had a right to any wall-space on which to hang two small oleographs depicting very scarlet horsemen on very bay horses, jumping very brown hedges, which my mother had bought me, thinking they might be suitable to the manly taste for which Public Schools are celebrated. I had taken them out of my playbox, together with the photographs of my parents and eldest sister, and spread them all on the window-seat. I was gazing at the little show lugubriously when the door was opened by a boy in 'tails'.

'Hallo!' he said. 'You new?'

'Yes,' I answered in a mouse-like voice.

'I'm Ruding. Head of the House. You get an allowance of two bob weekly when it's not stopped. You'll see the fagging lists on the board. You don't get any fagging the first fortnight. What's your name?'

'Bartlet.'

'Oh! Ah!' he examined a piece of paper in his hand. 'You're one of mine. How are you getting on?'

'Pretty well.'

'That's all right.' He seemed about to withdraw, so I asked him hastily: 'Please, am I allowed to hang these pictures?'

'Rather – any pictures you like. Let's look at them!' He came forward. When his eyes fell on the array, he said abruptly: 'Oh! Sorry!' and, taking up the oleos, he turned his back on the photographs. A new boy is something of a psychologist out of sheer fright, and when he said 'Sorry!' because his eyes had fallen on the effigies of my people, I felt somehow that he couldn't be a beast. 'You got these at Tompkins',' he said. 'I had the same my first term. Not bad. I should put 'em up here.'

While he was holding them to the wall I took a 'squint' at him. He seemed to me of a fabulous height – about five feet ten, I suppose; thin, and bolt upright. He had a stick-up collar – 'barmaids' had not yet come in – but not a very high one, and his neck was rather long. His hair was peculiar, dark and crisp, with a reddish tinge; and his dark-grey eyes were small and deep in, his cheekbones rather high, his cheeks thin and touched with freckles. His nose, chin, and cheekbones all seemed a little large for his face as yet. If I may put it so, there was a sort of unfinished finish about him. But he looked straight, and had a nice smile.

'Well, young Bartlet,' he said, handing me back the pictures, 'buck up, and you'll be all right.'

I put away my photographs, and hung the oleos. Ruding! The name was familiar. Among the marriages in my family pedigree, such as '– daughter of Fitzherbert', 'daughter of Tastborough', occurred the entry: 'daughter of Ruding' – some time before the Civil War. Daughter of Ruding! This demigod might be a far-off kinsman. But I felt I should never dare to tell him of the coincidence.

Miles Ruding was not brilliant, but pretty good at everything. He was not well dressed – you did not think of dress in connection with him either one way or the other. He was not exactly popular – being reserved, far from showy, and not rich

– but he had no 'side', and never either patronized or abused his juniors. He was not indulgent to himself or others, but he was very just; and, unlike many monitors, seemed to take no pleasure in 'whopping'. He never fell off in 'trials' at the end of a term, and was always playing as hard at the finish of a match as at the start. One would have said he had an exacting conscience, but he was certainly the last person to mention such a thing. He never showed his feelings, yet he never seemed trying to hide them, as I used always to be. He was greatly respected without seeming to care; an independent, self-dependent bird, who would have cut a greater dash if he hadn't been so, as it were, uncreative. In all those two years I only had one at all intimate talk with him, which, after all, was perhaps above the average number, considering the difference in our ages. In my fifth term and Ruding's last but one, there had been some disciplinary rumpus in the house, which had hurt the dignity of the captain of the football 'torpid' eleven – a big Irish boy who played back and was the mainstay of the side. It happened on the eve of our first house match, and the sensation may be imagined when this important person refused to play; physically and spiritually sore, he declared for the part of Achilles and withdrew to his tent. The house rocked with pro and con. My sympathies, in common with nearly all below the second fifth, lay with Donelly against the sixth form. His defection had left me captain of the side, so that the question whether we could play at all depended on me. If I declared a sympathetic strike, the rest would follow. That evening, after long hours of '*fronde*' with other rebellious spirits, I was alone and still in two minds, when Ruding came into my room. He leaned against the door, and said: 'Well, Bartlet, *you're* not going to rat?'

'I – I don't think Donelly ought to have been – been whopped,' I stammered.

'That's as may be,' he said, 'but the house comes first. You know that.'

Torn between the loyalties, I was silent.

'Look here, young Bartlet,' he said suddenly, 'it'll be a disgrace to us all, and it hangs on you.'

'All right,' I said sulkily, 'I'll play.'

'Good chap!'

'But I don't think Donelly ought to have been whopped,' I repeated inanely; 'he's – he's too big.'

Ruding approached till he looked right down on me in my old 'froust,' as we called armchairs. 'One of these days,' he said slowly, 'you'll be head of the house yourself. You'll have to keep up the prestige of the sixth form. If you let great louts like Donelly cheek little weak six-formers with impunity' (I remember how impressed I was by the word), 'you'll let the whole show down. My old governor runs a district in Bengal, about as big as Wales, entirely on prestige. He's often talked to me about it. I hate whopping anybody, but I'd much rather whop a lout like Donelly than I would a little new chap. He's a swine, anyway, for turning the house down because his back is sore.'

'It isn't that,' I said, 'it – it wasn't just.'

'If it was unjust,' said Ruding, with what seems to me now extraordinary patience, 'then the whole system's wrong, and that's a pretty big question, young Bartlet. Anyway, it's not for me to decide. I've got to administer what is. Shake hands, and do your damnedest tomorrow, won't you?'

I put out my hand with a show of reluctance, though secretly won over.

We got an awful hiding, but I can still hear Ruding's voice yelling: 'Well played, Bartlet! Well pla-a-ayed!'

I have only one other school recollection of Miles Ruding which lets any real light in on him. On the day he left for good I happened to travel up to Town in the same carriage. He sat looking through the window back at the old Hill, and I distinctly saw a tear run down his cheek. He must have been conscious that I had remarked the phenomenon, for he said suddenly:

'Damn! I've got a grit in my eye,' and began to pull the eyelid down in a manner which did not deceive me in the least.

I then lost sight of him completely for several years. His people were not well off, and he did not go up to the 'Varsity. He once said to me: 'My family's beastly old, and beastly poor.'

It was during one of my Odysseys in connection with sport that

I saw him again. He was growing fruit on a ranch in Vancouver Island. Nothing used to strike a young Englishman travelling in the Colonies more than the difference between what he saw and what all printed matter led him to expect. When I ran across Ruding in the Club at Victoria and he invited me to stay with him, I expected rows of fine trees with large pears and apples hanging on them, a colonial house with a broad verandah, and Ruding in ducks, among rifles and fishing rods, and spirited horses. What I found was a bare new wooden house, not yet painted, in a clearing of the heavy forest. His fruit trees had only just been planted, and he would be lucky if he got a crop within three years. He wore, not white ducks, but blue jeans, and worked about twelve hours a day, felling timber and clearing fresh ground. He had one horse to ride and drive, and got off for a day's shooting or fishing about once a month. He had three Chinese boys working under him, and lived nearly as sparingly as they. He had been out of England eight years, and this was his second venture – the first in Southern California had failed after three years of drought. He would be all right for water here, he said; which seemed likely enough in a country whose rainfall is superior to that of England.

'How the devil do you stand the loneliness?' I said.

'Oh! one gets used to it. Besides, this isn't lonely – good Lord, no! You should see some places!'

Living this sort of life, he yet seemed exactly what he used to be – in fact, he had kept his form. He didn't precisely dress for dinner, but he washed. He had English papers sent out to him, and read Victorian poetry, and history natural and unnatural, in the evenings over his pipe. He shaved every day, had his cold tub every morning, and treated his Chinese boys just as he used to treat us new boys at school; so far as I could tell, they seemed to have for him much the feelings we used to have – a respect not amounting to fear, and a liking not quite rising to affection.

'I couldn't live here without a woman,' I said one evening.

He sighed. 'I don't want to mess myself up with anything short of a wife; and I couldn't ask a girl to marry me till the place is fit for her. This fruit-growing's always a gamble at first.'

'You're an idealist,' I said.

He seemed to shrink, and it occurred to me suddenly that if there were anything he hated, it would be a generalization like that. But I was in a teasing mood.

'You're keeping up the prestige of the English gentleman.'

His teeth gritted on his pipe-stem. 'I'm dashed if I'm keeping up anything except my end; that's quite enough.'

'And exactly the same thing,' I murmured.

He turned away. I felt he was much annoyed with me for trying to introduce him to self-consciousness. And he was right! It's destructive; and his life held too many destructive elements – silence, solitude, distance from home, and this daily mixing with members of an Eastern race. I used to watch the faces of his Chinese boys – remote as cats, wonderfully carved, and old, and self-sufficient. I appreciate now how much of what was carved and old and self-sufficient Ruding needed in himself to live year in, year out, alone among them, without losing his form. All that week of my visit I looked with diabolical curiosity for some sign of deterioration – of the coarsening or softening which one felt ought naturally to come of such a life. Honestly, I could not find a trace, save that he wouldn't touch whisky, as if he were afraid of it, and shied away at any mention of women.

'Aren't you ever coming home?' I asked when I was taking leave.

'When I've made good here,' he said, 'I shall come back and marry.'

'And then out again?'

'I expect so. I've got no money, you know.'

Four years later I happened to see the following in *The Times*: 'Ruding – Fuljambe: At St Thomas's, Market Harborough, Miles Ruding of Bear Ranch, Vancouver Island, to Blanche, daughter of Charles Fuljambe, J.P., Market Harborough.' So it seemed he *had* made good! But I wondered what 'daughter of Fuljambe' would make of it out there. Well, I came across Ruding and his wife that very summer at Eastbourne, where they were spending the butt end of their long honeymoon. She was pleasant, pretty, vivacious – too vivacious I felt when I thought of Bear Ranch; and Ruding himself, under the stimulus of his new venture, was as nearly creative as I ever saw him. We dined and bathed, played tennis and went riding on the Downs together. Daughter of Fuljambe was quite 'a sport' – though, indeed, in 1899 that word had hardly come into use. I confess to wondering why, exactly, she had married my friend, till she gave me the history of it one evening. It seems their families were old neighbours, and when Ruding came back after having been away in the New World for twelve years, he was something of a curiosity, if not of a hero. He had been used to take her out hunting when she was a small child, so that she had an old-time reverence for him. He seemed, in his absence of small-talk and 'side', superior to the rattle-pated young men about her – here daughter of Fuljambe gave me a sidelong glance – and one day he had done a thing which toppled her into his arms. She was to go to a fancy dress ball one evening as a Chinese lady. But in the morning a cat upset a bottle of ink over her dress and reduced it to ruin. What was to be done? All the elaborate mask of make-up and head-dressing, which she had rehearsed to such perfection, sacrificed for want of a dress to wear it with! Ruding left that scene of desolation possessed by his one great creative impulse. It seemed that he had in London a Chinese lady's dress which he had brought home with him from San Francisco. No trains from Market Harborough could possibly get him up to Town and back in time, so he had promptly commandered the only neighbouring motor car, driven it up at a rate which must have approached forty miles an hour – a really fabulous speed for those days – got the dress, sent daughter of Fuljambe a wire, motored back at the same furious pace, and appeared before her door with the dress at eight forty-five. Daughter of Fuljambe received him in her dressing-gown, with her hair combed up, and her face beautifully painted. Ruding said quietly: 'Here you are; it's the genuine thing,' and disappeared before she had time to thank him. The dress was superior to the one the cat had spoiled. That night she accepted him. 'Miles didn't properly propose to me,' she said; 'I saw he couldn't bear to, because of what he'd done, so I just had to tell him not to keep his form so awfully. And here we are! He *is* a dear, isn't he?'

In his dealings with her he certainly was, for she was a self-centred little person.

They went off to Vancouver Island in September. The following January I heard that he had joined a Yeomanry contingent and gone out to fight the Boers. He left his wife in England with her people on his way. I met her once or twice before he was invalided home with enteric. She told me that she had opposed his going, till she found out it was making him quite miserable. 'And yet, you know,' she said, 'he's really frightfully devoted.'

When he recovered they went back to Vancouver Island, where he found his ranch so let down that he had to begin nearly all over again. I can imagine what he went through with his dainty and exacting helpmate. She came home in 1904, to get over it, and again I met her out hunting.

'Miles is too good for me,' she said the second day as we were jogging home; 'he's got such fearful pluck. If only he'd kick his conscience out of the window sometimes. Oh! Mr Bartlet, I don't want to go back there – I really don't; it's simply deadly. But he says if he gives this up he'll be thirty-eight without a thing to show for it, and just have to cadge round for a job, and he won't do that; but I don't believe I can stand it much longer.'

I wrote to Ruding. His answer was dry and inexpressive, but I could read between the lines: Heaven forbid that he should drag his wife out to him again, but he would have to stick it there another two years; then, perhaps, he could sell and buy a farm in England. To clear out now would be ruination. He missed his wife awfully, but – one must hoe one's row, and he would rather she stayed with her people than force herself to rough it out there with him.

Then, of course, came that which a man like Ruding, with his loyalty and his sense of form, is the last to imagine possible. Daughter of Fuljambe met a young man in the Buffs or Greens or Blues, and after, I am sure, a struggle – she was not a bad little sort — went off with him. That happened early in 1906, just as he was beginning to see the end of his struggle with Bear Ranch. I felt very sorry for him, yet inclined to say: 'My dear man, where was your imagination; couldn't you see this was bound to happen with "daughter of Fuljambe" once she got away from you?' And yet, poor devil, what could he have done?

He came home six thousand miles to give her a divorce. A ghoulish curiosity took me into Court. I never had more whole-hearted admiration for Ruding than I had that day, watching him in that pretentiously crooked Court among us tight-lipped, curly-minded lawyers, giving his unemotional evidence. Straight, thin, lined and brown, with grey already in his peculiar-coloured hair, his voice low, his eyes unwavering, in all his lonely figure a sad, quiet protest — it was not I only who was moved by the little speech he made to the Judge: 'My Lord, I should like to say that I have no bitter feelings; I think it was my fault for asking a woman to share a rough, lonely life, so far away.' It gave me a queer pleasure to see the little bow the Judge made him, as if saying: 'Sir, as one gentleman to another.' I had meant to get hold of him after the case, but when it came to the point I felt it was the last thing he would want of anyone. He went straight back the six thousand miles and sold his ranch. Cunningham, who used to be in our house, and had a Government post in Esquimault, told me that Ruding made himself quite unpopular over that sale. Some enterprising gentleman, interested in real estate, had reported the discovery of coal seams, which greatly enhanced the value of Bear Ranch and several neighbouring properties. Ruding was offered a big sum. He took it, and had already left the neighbourhood when the report about coal was duly disproved. Ruding at once offered to cancel the price, and take the agricultural value of the property. His offer was naturally accepted, and the disgust of other owners who had sold on the original report may be imagined. More wedded to the rights of property, they upheld the principle 'Caveat emptor', and justified themselves by calling Ruding names. With his diminished proceeds he bought another ranch on the mainland.

How he spent the next eight years I only vaguely know. I

don't think he came home at all. Cunningham spoke of him as 'Still the same steady-going old chap, awfully respected; but no one knows him very well. He looks much as he did, except that he's gone grey.'

Then, like a bolt from hell, came the Great War. I can imagine Ruding almost glad. His imagination would not give him the big horror of the thing; he would see it as the inevitable struggle, the long-expected chance to show what he and his country were made of. And I must confess that on the evidence he seems to have been made of even better stuff than his country. He began by dyeing his hair. By dint of this and by slurring the eight of his age so that it sounded like forty-odd, he was accepted, and, owing to his Transvaal experience, given a commission in Kitchener's army. But he did not get out to France till early in 1916. He was considered by his Colonel the best officer in the regiment for training recruits, and his hair, of course, had soon gone grey again. They said he chafed terribly at being kept at home. In the spring of 1916 he was mentioned in despatches, and that summer was badly gassed on the Somme. I went to see him in hospital. He had grown a little grey moustache, but otherwise seemed quite unchanged. I grasped at once that he was one of those whose nerve – no matter what happened to him – would see it through. One had the feeling that this would be so as a matter of course, that he himself had not envisaged any other possibility. He was so completely lost in the winning of the war that his own sensations seemed to pass him by. He had become as much of a soldier as the best of those professionally unimaginative stoical creatures, and quite naturally, as if it were in his blood. He dwelt quietly, without visible emotion, in that universal atmosphere of death. All was in the day's work, so long as the country emerged victorious; nor did there seem the least doubt in his mind but that it would so emerge. A part of me went with him all the way, but a part of me stared at him in curiosity, surprise, admiration, and a sort of contempt, as at a creature too single-hearted and uncomplicated. One side of me was bred like him – armorial bearings, daughter of Ruding, and all the rest of it – the other had new blood with all its doubts and ferments.

I saw him several times in that hospital at Teignmouth, where he recovered slowly.

One day I asked him point blank whether one's nerve was not bound to go in time. He looked a little surprised and said rather coldly: 'Not if your heart's in the right place.'

That was it to a T. His heart was so deeply rooted in exactly the right place that nothing external could get at it. Whatever downed Ruding would have to blow him up bodily – there was no detaching his heart from the rest of him. And that's what I mean by an inbred quality, the inner pluck that you can bet on. I don't say it's not to be found in private soldiers and 'new' people, but not in quite the same – shall we say? – matter-of-course way. When those others have it, they're proud of it or conscious of it, or simply primitively virile and thick-skinned; they don't – like such as Ruding – regard not having it as 'impossible,' a sort of disgrace. If scientists could examine the nerves of men like him, would they discern a faint difference in their colour or texture – the result of generations of nourishment above the average and of a traditional philosophy which for hundreds of years has held fear to be *the* cardinal offence? I wonder.

He went out again in 1917, and was out for the rest of the war. He did nothing very startling or brilliant; but, as at school, he was always on the ball, finishing as hard as when he started. At the Armistice he was a Lieutenant-Colonel, and a Major when he was gazetted out, at the age of fifty-three, with the various weaknesses which gas and a prolonged strain leave in a man of that age, but no pensionable disability. He went back to Vancouver. Anyone at all familiar with fruit-growing knows it for a pursuit demanding the most even and constant attention. When Ruding joined up he had perforce left his ranch in the first hands which came along; and at that time, with almost every rancher in like case, those hands were very poor substitutes for the hands of an owner. He went back to a property practically valueless. He was not in sufficient health to sit down for another long struggle to pull it round, as after the Boer War, so he sold it for a song and came home again, full of confidence that, with his record, he would get a job. He found that his case was that of thousands. They didn't want him back in the Army. They were awfully sorry, but they didn't know what they could do for him. The Governmental education and employment schemes, too, seemed all for younger men. He sat down on the song and the savings from his pay to wait for some ship or other out of his fleet of applications to come home. It did not come; his savings went. How did I know all this? I will tell you.

One night last January I had occasion to take a cab from a restaurant in Soho to my Club in Pall Mall. It was wet, and I got in hastily. I was sitting there comatose from my good dinner when I had a queer feeling that I knew the back of the driver. It had – what shall I call it? – a refined look. The man's hair was grey; and I began trying to recollect the profile I had glimpsed when bolting in. Suddenly with a sort of horror the thought flashed through me: Miles Ruding!

It was!

When I got out and we looked each other in the face, he smiled and my lips quivered. 'Old chap,' I said, 'draw your cab up on that stand and get in with me.'

When we were sitting together in his cab we lighted cigarettes, and didn't speak for quite a minute, till I burst out:

'Look here! What does this mean?'

'Bread and butter.'

'Good God! And this is what the country –'

'Bartlet,' he said, through curiously set lips, with a little fixed smile about the corners, 'cut out all that about the country. I prefer this to any more cadging for a job; that's all.'

Silent from shame, I broke out at last: 'It's the limit! What about the Government schemes?'

'No go! they're all for younger men.'

'My dear chap!' was all I could find to say.

'This isn't a bad life in good weather,' he went on with that queer smile; 'I haven't much of a chest now.'

'Do you mean to say you contemplate going on with this?'

'Till something turns up; but I'm no good at asking for things, Bartlet; I simply can't do it.'

'What about your people?'

'Dead or broke.'

'Come and stay with me till your ship comes home.'

He squeezed my arm and shook his head. That's what's so queer about gentility! If only I could have established a blood tie! Ruding would have taken help or support from his kinfolk – would have inherited without a qualm from a second cousin that he'd never seen; but from the rest of the world it would be charity. Sitting in that cab of his, he told me, without bitterness, the tale which is that of hundreds since the war. Ruding one could not pity to his face, it would have been impossible. And, when he had finished, I could only mutter:

'Well, I think it's damnable, considering what the country owes you.'

He did not answer. You can say what you like about his limitations, but Miles Ruding was bred to keep his form.

I nearly shook his hand off when I left him, and I could see that he disliked that excessive display of feeling. From my Club doorway I looked round. He had resumed his driver's seat, and, through the rain, I saw him with the cigarette between his lips, and the lamplight shining on his profile. Very still he sat – symbol of that lost cause, gentility.

1920

THE JAPANESE QUINCE

As Mr Nilson, well known in the City, opened the window of his dressing-room on Campden Hill, he experienced a peculiar sweetish sensation in the back of his throat, and a feeling of emptiness just under his fifth rib. Hooking the window back, he noticed that a little tree in the Square Gardens had come out in blossom, and that the thermometer stood at sixty. 'Perfect morning,' he thought; 'spring at last!'

Resuming some meditations on the price of Tintos, he took up an ivory-backed hand-glass and scrutinized his face. His firm, well-coloured cheeks, with their neat brown moustaches, and his round, well-opened, clear grey eyes, wore a reassuring appearance of good health. Putting on his black frock-coat, he went downstairs.

In the dining-room his morning paper was laid out on the sideboard. Mr Nilson had scarcely taken it in his hand when he again became aware of that queer feeling. Somewhat concerned, he went to the French window and descended the scrolled iron steps into the fresh air. A cuckoo clock struck eight.

'Half an hour to breakfast,' he thought; 'I'll take a turn in the Gardens.'

He had them to himself, and proceeded to pace the circular path with his morning paper clasped behind him. He had scarcely made two revolutions, however, when it was borne in on him that, instead of going away in the fresh air, the feeling had increased. He drew several deep breaths, having heard deep breathing recommended by his wife's doctor; but they augmented rather than diminished the sensation – as of some sweetish liquor in course within him, together with a faint aching just above his heart. Running over what he had eaten the night

before, he could recollect no unusual dish, and it occurred to
him that it might possibly be some smell affecting him. But he
could detect nothing except a faint sweet lemony scent, rather
agreeable than otherwise, which evidently emanated from the
bushes budding in the sunshine. He was on the point of resuming his promenade, when a blackbird close by burst into song,
and, looking up, Mr Nilson saw at a distance of perhaps five
yards a little tree, in the heart of whose branches the bird was
perched. He stood staring curiously at this tree, recognizing it
for that which he had noticed from his window. It was covered
with young blossoms, pink and white, and little bright green
leaves both round and spiky; and on all this blossom and these
leaves the sunlight glistened. Mr Nilson smiled; the little tree
was so alive and pretty! And instead of passing on, he stayed
there smiling at the tree.

'Morning like this!' he thought; 'and here I am the only
person in the Square who has the – to come out and –!' But he
had no sooner conceived this thought than he saw quite near
him a man with his hands behind him, who was also staring
up and smiling at the little tree. Rather taken aback, Mr Nilson
ceased to smile, and looked furtively at the stranger. It was his
next-door neighbour, Mr Tandram, well known in the City,
who had occupied the adjoining house for some five years. Mr
Nilson perceived at once the awkwardness of his position, for,
being married, they had not yet had occasion to speak to
one another. Doubtful as to his proper conduct, he decided at
last to murmur: 'Fine morning!' and was passing on, when Mr
Tandram answered: 'Beautiful, for the time of year!' Detect-
ing a slight nervousness in his neighbour's voice, Mr Nilson
was emboldened to regard him openly. He was of about Mr
Nilson's own height, with firm, well-coloured cheeks, neat
brown moustaches, and round, well-opened, clear grey eyes; and
he was wearing a black frock-coat. Mr Nilson noticed that he
had his morning paper clasped behind him as he looked up at
the little tree. And visited somehow by the feeling that he had
been caught out, he said abruptly:

'Er – can you give me the name of that tree?'

Mr Tandram answered:

'I was about to ask you that,' and stepped towards it. Mr Nilson also approached the tree.

'Sure to have its name on, I should think,' he said.

Mr Tandram was the first to see the little label, close to where the blackbird had been sitting. He read it out.

'Japanese quince!'

'Ah!' said Mr Nilson, 'thought so. Early flowerers.'

'Very,' assented Mr Tandram, and added: 'Quite a feelin' in the air today.'

Mr Nilson nodded.

'It was a blackbird singin',' he said.

'Blackbirds,' answered Mr Tandram, 'I prefer them to thrushes myself; more body in the note.' And he looked at Mr Nilson in an almost friendly way.

'Quite,' murmured Mr Nilson. 'These exotics, they don't bear fruit. Pretty blossom!' and he again glanced up at the blossom, thinking: 'Nice fellow, this, I rather like him.'

Mr Tandram also gazed up at the blossom. And the little tree, as if appreciating their attention, quivered and glowed. From a distance the blackbird gave a loud, clear call. Mr Nilson dropped his eyes. It struck him suddenly that Mr Tandram looked a little foolish; and, as if he had seen himself, he said: 'I must be going in. Good morning!'

A shade passed over Mr Tandram's face, as if he, too, had suddenly noticed something about Mr Nilson.

'Good morning,' he replied, and clasping their journals to their backs they separated.

Mr Nilson retraced his steps towards his garden window, walking slowly so as to avoid arriving at the same time as his neighbour. Having seen Mr Tandram mount his scrolled iron steps, he ascended his own in turn. On the top step he paused.

With the slanting spring sunlight darting and quivering into it, the Japanese quince seemed more living than a tree. The blackbird had returned to it, and was chanting out his heart.

Mr Nilson sighed; again he felt that queer sensation, that choky feeling in his throat.

The sound of a cough or sigh attracted his attention. There, in the shadow of his French window, stood Mr Tandram, also looking forth across the Gardens at the little quince tree.

Unaccountably upset, Mr Nilson turned abruptly into the house, and opened his morning paper.

1910

THE BROKEN BOOT

><++>

THE actor, Gilbert Caister, who had been 'out' for six months, emerged from his East-coast seaside lodging about noon in the day, after the opening of 'Shooting the Rapids', on tour, in which he was playing Dr Dominick in the last act. A salary of four pounds a week would not, he was conscious, remake his fortunes, but a certain jauntiness had returned to the gait and manner of one employed again at last.

Fixing his monocle, he stopped before a fishmonger's and, with a faint smile on his face, regarded a lobster. Ages since he had eaten a lobster! One could long for a lobster without paying, but the pleasure was not solid enough to detain him. He moved upstreet and stopped again, before a tailor's window. Together with the actual tweeds, in which he could so easily fancy himself refitted, he could see a reflection of himself, in the faded brown suit wangled out of the production of 'Marmaduke Mandeville' the year before the war. The sunlight in this damned town was very strong, very hard on seams and buttonholes, on knees and elbows! Yet he received the ghost of aesthetic pleasure from the reflected elegance of a man long fed only twice a day, of an eyeglass well rimmed out from a soft brown eye, of a velour hat salved from the production of 'Educating Simon' in 1912; and in front of the window he removed that hat, for under it was his new phenomenon, not yet quite evaluated, his *mêche blanche*. Was it an asset, or the beginning of the end? It reclined backwards on the right side, conspicuous in his dark hair, above the shadowy face always interesting to Gilbert Caister. They said it came from atrophy of the – something nerve, an effect of the war, or of undernourished tissue. Rather distinguished, perhaps, but – !

He walked on, and became conscious that he had passed a face he knew. Turning, he saw it also turned on a short and dapper figure – a face rosy, bright, round, with an air of cherubic knowledge, as of a getter-up of amateur theatricals.

Bryce-Green, by George!

'Caister? It is! Haven't seen you since you left the old camp. Remember what sport we had over "Gotta-Grampus"? By Jove! I am glad to see you. Doing anything with yourself? Come and have lunch with me.'

Bryce-Green, the wealthy patron, the moving spirit of entertainment in that south-coast convalescent camp. And, drawling slightly, Caister answered:

'I shall be delighted.' But within him something did not drawl: 'By God, you're going to have a feed, my boy!'

And – elegantly threadbare, roundabout and dapper – the two walked side by side.

'Know this place? Let's go in here! Phyllis, cocktails for my friend Mr Caister and myself, and caviare on biscuits. Mr Caister is playing here; you must go and see him.'

The girl who served the cocktails and the caviare looked up at Caister with interested blue eyes. Precious! – he had been 'out' for six months!

'Nothing of a part,' he drawled; 'took it to fill a gap.' And below his waistcoat the gap echoed: 'Yes, and it'll take some filling.'

'Bring your cocktail along, Caister; we'll go into the little further room, there'll be nobody there. What shall we have – a lobstah?'

And Caister murmured: 'I love lobstahs.'

'Very fine and large here. And how are you, Caister? So awfully glad to see you – only real actor we had.'

'Thanks,' said Caister, 'I'm all right.' And he thought: 'He's a damned amateur, but a nice little man.'

'Sit here. Waiter, bring us a good big lobstah and a salad; and then – er – a small fillet of beef with potatoes fried crisp, and a bottle of my special hock. Ah! and a rum omelette – plenty of rum and sugah. Twig?'

And Caister thought: 'Thank God, I do.'

They had sat down opposite each other at one of two small tables in the little recessed room.

'Luck!' said Bryce-Green.

'Luck!' replied Caister; and the cocktail trickling down him echoed: 'Luck!'

'And what do you think of the state of the drama?'

Oh! ho! A question after his own heart. Balancing his monocle by a sweetish smile on the opposite side of his mouth, Caister drawled his answer: 'Quite too bally awful!'

'H'm! Yes,' said Bryce-Green; 'nobody with any genius, is there?'

And Caister thought: 'Nobody with any money.'

'Have you been playing anything great? You were so awfully good in "Gotta-Grampus"!'

'Nothing particular. I've been – er – rather slack.' And with their feel around his waist his trousers seemed to echo: 'Slack!'

'Ah!' said Bryce-Green. 'Here we are! Do you like claws?'

'Tha-a-nks. Anything!' To eat – until warned by the pressure of his waist against his trousers! What a feast! And what a flow of his own tongue suddenly released – on drama, music, art; mellow and critical, stimulated by the round eyes and interjections of his little provincial host.

'By Jove, Caister! You've got a *mêche blanche*. Never noticed. I'm awfully interested in *mêches blanches*. Don't think me too frightfully rude – but did it come suddenly?'

'No, gradually.'

'And how do you account for it?'

'Try starvation,' trembled on Caister's lips.

'I don't,' he said.

'I think it's ripping. Have some more omelette? I often wish I'd gone on the regular stage myself. Must be a topping life, if one has talent, like you.'

Topping?

'Have a cigar. Waiter! Coffee, and cigars. I shall come and see you tonight. Suppose you'll be here a week?'

Topping! The laughter and applause – 'Mr Caister's rendering left nothing to be desired; its – and its – are in the true spirit of –!'

Silence recalled him from his rings of smoke. Bryce-Green was sitting, with cigar held out and mouth a little open, and bright eyes round as pebbles, fixed – fixed on some object near the floor, past the corner of the tablecloth. Had he burnt his mouth? The eyelids fluttered; he looked at Caister, licked his lips like a dog, nervously, and said:

'I say, old chap, don't think me a beast, but are you at all – er – er – rocky? I mean – if I can be of any service, don't hesitate! Old acquaintance, don't you know, and all that –'

His eyes rolled out again towards the object, and Caister followed them. Out there above the carpet he saw it – his own boot. It dangled slightly, six inches off the ground – split – right across, twice, between lace and toecap. Quite! He knew it. A boot left him from the role of Bertie Carstairs, in 'The Dupe', just before the war. Good boots. His only pair, except the boots of Dr. Dominick, which he was nursing. And from the boot he looked back at Bryce-Green, sleek and concerned. A drop, black when it left his heart, suffused his eye behind the monocle; his smile curled bitterly; he said:

'Not at all, thanks! Why?'

'Oh! n-n-nothing. It just occurred to me.' His eyes – but Caister had withdrawn the boot. Bryce-Green paid the bill and rose.

'Old chap, if you'll excuse me; engagement at half-past two. So awf'ly glad to have seen you. Good-bye!'

'Good-bye!' said Caister. 'Thanks.'

He was alone. And, chin on hand, he stared through his monocle into an empty coffee cup. Alone with his heart, his boot, his life to come... 'And what have you been in lately, Mr Caister?' 'Nothing very much lately. Of course, I've played almost everything.' 'Quite so. Perhaps you'll leave your address; can't say anything definite, I'm afraid.' 'I – I should – er – be willing to rehearse on approval; or – if I could read the part?' 'Thank you, afraid we haven't got as far as that.' 'No? Quite! Well, I shall hear from you, perhaps.' And Caister could see his own eyes looking at the manager. God! What a look! ... A topping life! A dog's life! Cadging – cadging – cadging for work! A life of draughty waiting, of concealed beggary, of terrible depressions, of want of food!

The waiter came skating round as if he desired to clear. Must go! Two young women had come in and were sitting at the other table between him and the door. He saw them look at him, and his sharpened sense caught the whisper:

'Sure – in the last act. Don't you see his *mèche blanche*?'

'Oh! yes – of course! Isn't it – wasn't he –!'

Caister straightened his back; his smile crept out, he fixed his monocle. They had spotted his Dr Dominick!

'If you've quite finished, sir, may I clear?'

'Certainly. I'm going.' He gathered himself and rose. The young women were gazing up. Elegant, with faint smile, he passed them close, so that they could not see, managing – his broken boot.

1922

THE CHOICE

SOME years ago in Chelsea there used to stand at the crossing of a street leading to the Embankment an old man whose living was derived from the cleanliness of boots. In the intervals of plying his broom he could generally be seen seated on an up-turned wooden box, talking to an Irish terrier, who belonged to a house near by, and had taken a fancy to him. He was a Cornishman by birth, had been a plumber by trade, and was a cheerful, independent old fellow with ruddy cheeks, grey hair and beard, and little, bright, rather watery, grey eyes. But he was a great sufferer from a variety of ailments. He had gout, and some trouble in his side, and feet that were like barometers in their susceptibility to weather. Of all these matters he would speak to us in a very impersonal and uncomplaining way, diagnosing himself, as it were, for the benefit of his listeners. He was, it seems, alone in the world, not having of course at that time anything to look forward to in the way of a pension, nor, one fancies, very much to look back on except the death of his near relatives and the decline of the plumbing trade. It had declined him for years, but, even before a long illness ousted him in favour of younger men, he had felt very severely the palpable difference in things. In old days plumbing had been a quiet, steady business, in which you were apparently 'on your own, and knew where you were'; but latterly 'you had just had to do what the builders told you, and of course they weren't going to make allowances; if you couldn't do the job as fast as a young man – out you went, and there you were.' This long illness and the death of his wife coming close together (and sweeping away the last of his savings), had determined him therefore to buy a broom and seek for other occupation. To sweep a crossing was not a profession that he himself would have chosen before all others, still it was 'better than the 'house – and you were your own master'. The climate in those days not being the most suitable for a business which necessitated constant exposure to all elements but that of fire, his ailments were proportionally active; but the one remarkable feature of his perpetual illness was that he was always 'better' than he had been. We could not at times help thinking that this continual crescendo of good health should have gradually raised him to a pinnacle of paramount robustness; and it was with a certain disappointment, in the face of his assurances, that we watched him getting, on the contrary, slowly stiffer and feebler, and noted the sure increase of the egg-like deposits, which he would proudly have us remark, about his wrists and fingers.

He was so entirely fixed and certain that he was 'going in the river' before he went 'in the 'house', that one hesitated to suggest that the time was at hand when he should cease to expose himself all day and every day. He had evidently pondered long and with a certain deep philosophy on this particular subject, and fortified himself by hearsay.

'The 'house ain't for a man that respects himself,' he would remark. And, since that was his conviction, such as respected themselves could not very well beg him to act against it. At the same time, it became increasingly difficult to pass him without wondering how much longer it would be before he finally sought shelter in the element of water, which was so apt to pour down on him day by day.

It is uncertain whether he discussed this matter of the river *versus* the 'house with the dog, to whom he was always talking; but that they shared a certain fellow-feeling on the subject of exposure and advancing age is more than probable; for, as he would point out: The poor old feller's teeth were going; and the stiffness across his loins was always worse when it was wet. In fact, he was afraid that the old dog was gettin' old! And the dog would sit patiently for an hour at a time looking up at him, trying to find out, perhaps, from his friend's face what a dog should do, when the enemy weighed on him till he could no longer tolerate himself, not knowing, of course, that kindly humans would see to it that he did not suffer more than a dog could bear. On his face with its grizzled muzzle and rheumy eyes, thus turned up, there was never a sign of debate: it was full of confidence that, whatever decision his friend came to, in this momentous question between the river and the 'house, would be all right, perfectly satisfactory in every way to dogs and men.

One very rainy summer our old friend in a burst of confidence disclosed the wish of his heart. It was that he might be suffered to go down once more to Fowey in Cornwall, where he had been born, but had not been for fifty years. By some means or other the money was procured for this enterprise, and he was enabled to set off by excursion train for a fortnight's holiday. He was observed the day before his start talking at great length to the dog, and feeding it out of a paper bag with carraway-seed biscuits. A letter was received from him during his absence, observing certain strange laws of calligraphy, and beginning 'Honoured Sir and Lady'. It was full of an almost passionate description of a regatta, of a certain 'Joe Petherick' who had remembered him, of the 'luvly weather' and other sources of his great happiness; and ended 'Yours truley obedient'. On the fifteenth day he was back at his corner seated on his box in the pouring rain, saying that he was 'a different man, ten years younger, and ready to "go" now, any day'; nor could anything dissuade him from the theory that Heaven had made a special lodgement in our persons on his behalf. But only four days later, the sun being for once in the heavens, he was so long in answering a salutation that we feared he had been visited by some kind of stroke; his old face had lost colour, it seemed stiff, and his eyes had almost disappeared.

Inquiry elicited from him the information that he was better than he had been, but that the dog was dead. They had put it away while he had been gone, and he was afraid that he should miss the 'faithful old feller'.

'He was very good to me,' he said; 'always came for a bit of bread or biscuit. And he was company to me; I never knew such a sensible creature.' He seemed to think that the dog must have pined during his absence, and that this had accelerated his end by making his owners think he was more decrepit than he really was.

The death of the dog, and the cold damp autumn that year, told heavily on the old man, but it was not till mid-November that he was noted one morning absent from his post. As he did not reappear his lodging was sought out. It was in a humble street, but the house was neat and clean, and the landlady seemed a good, rough woman. She informed us that our old friend was laid up 'with pleurisy and the gouty rheumatics'; that by rights, of course, he ought to be in the infirmary, but she didn't like to turn him out, though where she would get her rent from she didn't know, to say nothing of his food, because she couldn't let him starve while there he was cryin' out with the pain, and no one but herself to turn a hand to him, with his door open at the top of the house, where he could holler for her if he wanted. An awful independent old feller, too, or else she wouldn't hesitate, for that was where he ought to be, and no mistake, not having a soul in the world to close his eyes, and that's what it would come to, though she would never be surprised if he got up and went out tomorrow, he was that stubborn!

Leaving her to the avocations which we had interrupted by coming in, we went upstairs.

The door of the back room at the top was, as indeed she had led us to suppose, open; and through it the sound of our friend's voice could be heard travelling forth:

'O Lord God, that took the dog from me, and gave me this here rheumatics, help me to keep a stiff and contrite heart. I am an old man, O Lord God, and I am not one to go into that *place*. So God give me a stiff heart, and I will remember you in my prayers, for that's about all I can do now, O God. I have been a good one in my time, O Lord, and cannot remember doing harm to any man for a long while now, and I have tried to keep upsides with it; so, good Lord, remember and do not forget me, now that I am down, a-lying here all day, and the rent goin' on. For ever and ever, O Lord, Amen.'

We allowed a little time to pass before we went in, unwilling that he should think we had overheard that prayer. He was lying in a small dingy bed, with a medicine bottle and glass beside him on an old tin trunk. There was no fire.

He was – it seemed – better than he had been; the doctor's stuff was doing him good.

Certain arrangements were made for his benefit, and in less than three weeks he was back again at his corner.

In the spring of the following year we went abroad and were absent several months. He was no longer at his post when at last we came back, and a policeman informed us that he had not been there for some weeks. We made a second pilgrimage to his lodgings. The house had changed hands. The new landlady was a thin, anxious-looking young woman, who spoke in a thin anxious voice. Yes, the old man had been taken very ill – double pneumonia and heart disease, she thought. Anyway, she couldn't have the worry and responsibility of him, let alone her rent. She had had the doctor, and had him taken off. Yes, it had upset him a bit; he would never have gone if he'd had his choice; but of course she had her living to get. She had his bits of things locked up all right; he owed her a little rent. In her opinion he'd never come out again. She was very sorry for him, too; he'd given no trouble till he was took ill.

Following up her information we repaired with heavy hearts to the 'house, which he had so often declared he would never enter. Having ascertained the number of his ward we mounted the beautifully clean stairs. In the fifth of a row of beds, our old friend was lying, apparently asleep. But watching him carefully, we saw that his lips, deep sunk between his frosty moustache and beard, were continually moving.

'He's not asleep,' said the nurse; 'he'll lie like that all the time. He frets.'

At the sound of his name he had opened his eyes, which, though paler and smaller and more rheumy, were still almost bright. He fixed them on us with a peculiar stare, as much as to say: 'You've taken an advantage of me, finding me here.' We could hardly bear that look, and hurriedly asked him how he was. He tried to raise himself and answered huskily that he was better than he had been. We begged him not to exert himself, and told him how it was that we had been away, and so forth. He seemed to pay no attention, but suddenly said: 'I'm in here; I don't mean to stay, I'll be goin' out in a day or two.'

We tried to confirm that theory, but the expression of his eyes seemed to take away our power of comfort, and make us ashamed of looking at him. He beckoned us closer.

'If I'd a had the use of my legs,' he whispered, 'they'd never have had me. I'd a-gone in the river first. But I don't mean to stay – I'm goin' back home.'

The nurse told us, however, that this was out of the question; he was still very ill.

Four days later we went again to see him. He was no longer there. He had gone home. They had buried him that morning.

1910

ULTIMA THULE

ULTIMA THULE! The words come into my head this winter night. That is why I write down the story, as I know it, of a little old friend.

I used to see him first in Kensington Gardens, where he came in the afternoons, accompanied by a very small girl. One would see them silent before a shrub or flower, or with their heads inclined to heaven before a tree, or leaning above water and the ducks, or stretched on their stomachs watching a beetle, or on their backs watching the sky. Often they would stand holding crumbs out to the birds, who would perch about them, and even drop on their arms little white marks of affection and esteem. They were admittedly a noticeable couple. The child, who was fair-haired and elfinlike, with dark eyes and a pointed chin, wore clothes that seemed somewhat hard put to it. And, if the two were not standing still, she went along pulling at his hand, eager to get there; and, since he was a very little, light old man, he seemed always in advance of his own feet. He was garbed, if I remember, in a daverdy brown overcoat and broad-brimmed soft grey hat, and his trousers, what was visible of them, were tucked into half-length black gaiters which tried to join with very old brown shoes. Indeed, his costume did not indicate any great share of prosperity. But it was his face that riveted attention. Thin, cherry-red, and wind-dried as old wood, it had a special sort of brightness, with its spikes and waves of silvery hair, and blue eyes which seemed to shine. Rather mad, I used to think. Standing by the rails of an enclosure, with his withered lips pursed and his cheeks drawn in till you would think the wind might blow through them, he would emit the most enticing trills and pipings, exactly imitating various birds.

Those who rouse our interest are generally the last people we speak to, for interest seems to set up a kind of special shyness; so it was long before I made his acquaintance. But one day by the Serpentine, I saw him coming along alone, looking sad, but still with that queer brightness about him. He sat down on my bench with his little dried hands on his thin little knees, and began talking to himself in a sort of whisper. Presently I caught the words: 'God cannot be like us.' And for fear that he might go on uttering such precious remarks that were obviously not intended to be heard, I had either to go away or else address him. So, on an impulse, I said:

'Why?'

He turned without surprise.

'I've lost my landlady's little girl,' he said. 'Dead! And only seven years old.'

'That little thing I used to watch you with?'

'Did you? Did you? I'm glad you saw her.'

'I used to see you looking at flowers, and trees, and those ducks.'

His face brightened wistfully. 'Yes; she was a great companion to an old man like me.' And he relapsed into his contemplation of the water. He had a curious, precise way of speaking, that matched his pipchinesque little old face. At last he again turned to me those blue youthful eyes which seemed to shine out of a perfect little nest of crow's-feet.

'We were great friends! But I couldn't expect it. Things don't last, do they?' I was glad to notice that his voice was getting cheerful. 'When I was in the orchestra at the Harmony Theatre, it never used to occur to me that some day I shouldn't play there any more. One felt like a bird. That's the beauty of music, sir. You lose yourself; like that blackbird there.' He imitated the note of a blackbird so perfectly that I could have sworn the bird started.

'Birds and flowers! Wonderful things; wonderful! Why, even a buttercup –!' He pointed at one of those little golden flowers with his toe. 'Did you ever see such a marvellous thing?' And he turned his face up at me. 'And yet, somebody told me once that they don't agree with cows. Now can that be? I'm not a countryman – though I was born at Kingston.'

'The cows do well enough on them', I said, 'in my part of

the world. In fact, the farmers say they like to see buttercups.'

'I'm glad to hear you say that. I was always sorry to think they disagreed.'

When I got up to go, he rose, too.

'I take it as very kind of you', he said, 'to have spoken to me.'

'The pleasure was mine. I am generally to be found hereabouts in the afternoons any time you like a talk.'

'Delighted,' he said; 'delighted. I make friends of the creatures and flowers as much as possible, but they can't always make us understand.' And after we had taken off our respective hats, he reseated himself, with his hands on his knees.

Next time I came across him standing by the rails of an enclosure, and, in his arms, an old and really wretched-looking cat.

'I don't like boys,' he said, without preliminary of any sort. 'What do you think they were doing to this poor old cat? Dragging it along by a string to drown it; see where it's cut into the fur! I think boys despise the old and weak!' He held it out to me. At the ends of those little sticks of arms the beast looked more dead than alive; I had never seen a more miserable creature.

'I think a cat', he said, 'is one of the most marvellous things in the world. Such a depth of life in it.'

And, as he spoke, the cat opened its mouth as if protesting at that assertion. It *was* the sorriest-looking beast.

'What are you going to do with it?'

'Take it home; it looks to me as if it might die.'

'You don't think that might be more merciful?'

'It depends; it depends. I shall see. I fancy a little kindness might do a great deal for it. It's got plenty of spirit. I can see from its eye.'

'May I come along with you a bit?'

'Oh!' he said; 'delighted.'

We walked on side by side, exciting the derision of nearly everyone we passed – his face looked so like a mother's when she is feeding her baby!

'You'll find this'll be quite a different cat tomorrow,' he said. 'I shall have to get in, though, without my landlady seeing; a funny woman! I have two or three strays already.'

'Can I help in any way?'

'Thank you,' he said. 'I shall ring the area bell, and as she comes out below I shall go in above. She'll think it's boys. They *are* like that.'

'But doesn't she do your rooms, or anything?'

A smile puckered his face. 'I've only one; I do it myself. Oh, it'd never do to have her about, even if I could afford it. But,' he added, 'if you're so kind as to come with me to the door, you might engage her by asking where Mr Thompson lives. That's me. In the musical world my name was Moronelli; not that I have Italian blood in me, of course.'

'And shall I come up?'

'Honoured; but I live very quietly.'

We passed out of the gardens at Lancaster Gate, where all the house-fronts seem so successful, and out of it into a little street that was extremely like a grubby child trying to hide under its mother's skirts. Here he took a newspaper from his pocket and wrapped it round the cat.

'She's a funny woman!' he repeated; 'Scotch descent, you know.' Suddenly he pulled an area bell and scuttled up the steps.

When he had opened the door, however, I saw before him in the hall a short, thin woman dressed in black, with a sharp and bumpy face. Her voice sounded brisk and resolute.

'What have you got there, Mr Thompson?'

'Newspaper, Mrs March.'

'Oh, indeed! Now, you're not going to take that cat upstairs!'

The little old fellow's voice acquired a sudden shrill determination. 'Stand aside, please. If you stop me, I'll give you notice. The cat is going up. It's ill, and it is going up.'

It was then I said:

'Does Mr Thompson live here?'

In that second he shot past her, and ascended.

'That's him,' she said, 'and I wish it wasn't, with his dirty cats. Do you want him?'

'I do.'

'He lives at the top.' Then, with a grudging apology: 'I can't help it; he tries me – he's very trying.'

'I am sure he is.'

She looked at me. The longing to talk that comes over those who answer bells all day, and the peculiar Scottish desire to justify oneself, rose together in that face which seemed all promontories dried by an east wind.

'Ah!' she said; 'he is. I don't deny his heart; but he's got no sense of anything. Goodness knows what he hasn't got up there. I wonder I keep him. An old man like that ought to know better; half-starving himself to feed them.' She paused, and her eyes, which had a cold and honest glitter, searched me closely.

'If you're going up,' she said, 'I hope you'll give him good advice. He never lets me in. I wonder I keep him.'

There were three flights of stairs, narrow, clean, and smelling of oilcloth. Selecting one of two doors at random, I knocked. His silvery head and bright, pinched face were cautiously poked out.

'Ah!' he said; 'I thought it might be her!'

The room, which was fairly large, had a bare floor with little on it save a camp-bed and chest of drawers with jug and basin. A large bird-cage on the wall hung wide open. The place smelt of soap and a little of beasts and birds. Into the walls, whitewashed over a green wall-paper which stared through in places, were driven nails with their heads knocked off, on to which bits of wood had been spiked, so that they stood out as bird-perches high above the ground. Over the open window a piece of wire-netting had been fixed. A little spirit-stove and an old dressing-gown hanging on a peg completed the accoutrements of a room which one entered with a certain diffidence. He had not exaggerated. Besides the new cat, there were three other cats and four birds, all – save one, a bullfinch – invalids. The cats kept close to the walls, avoiding me, but wherever my little old friend went they followed him with their eyes. The birds were in the cage, except the bullfinch, which had perched on his shoulder.

'How on earth,' I said, 'do you manage to keep cats and birds in one room?'

'There is danger,' he answered, 'but I have not had a disaster yet. Till their legs or wings are mended, they hardly come out of the cage; and after that they keep up on my perches. But they don't stay long, you know, when they're once well. That wire is only put over the window while they're mending; it'll be off tomorrow for this lot.'

'And then they'll go?'

'Yes. The sparrow first, and then the two thrushes.'

'And this fellow?'

'Ask him,' he said. 'Would *you* go, bully?' But the bullfinch did not deign to answer.

'And were all those cats, too, in trouble?'

'Yes,' he said. 'They wouldn't want me if they weren't.'

Thereupon he began to warm some blue-looking milk, contemplating the new cat, which he had placed in a round basket close to the little stove, while the bullfinch sat on his head. It seemed time to go.

'Delighted to see you, sir,' he said, 'any day.' And, pointing up at the bullfinch on his head, he added: 'Did you ever see anything so wonderful as that bird? The size of its heart! Really marvellous.'

To the rapt sound of that word marvellous, and full of the memory of his mysterious brightness while he stood pointing upward to the bird perched on his thick, silvery hair, I went.

The landlady was still at the bottom of the stairs, and began at once: 'So you found him! I don't know why I keep him. Of course, he was kind to my little girl.' I saw tears gather in her eyes.

'With his cats and his birds, I wonder I keep him! But where would he go? He's no relations, and no friends – not a friend in the world, I think! He's a character. Lives on air – feeding them cats! I've no patience with them, eating him up. He never lets me in. Cats and birds! I wonder I keep him. Losing himself for those rubbishy things! It's my belief he was always like that; and that's why he never got on. He's no sense of anything.'

And she gave me a shrewd look, wondering, no doubt, what the deuce I had come about.

I did not come across him again in the gardens for some time, and went at last to pay him a call. At the entrance to a mews just round the corner of his grubby little street, I found a knot of people collected round one of those bears that are sometimes led through the less conspicuous streets of our huge towns. The yellowish beast was sitting up in deference to its master's rod, uttering little grunts, and moving its uplifted snout from side to side, in the way bears have. But it seemed to be extracting more amusement than money from its audience.

'Let your bear down off its hind legs and I'll give you a penny.' And suddenly I saw my little old friend under his flopping grey hat, amongst the spectators, all taller than himself. But the bear's master only grinned and prodded the animal in the chest. He evidently knew a good thing when he saw it.

'I'll give you twopence to let him down.'

Again the bear-man grinned. 'More!' he said, and again prodded the bear's chest. The spectators were laughing now.

'Threepence! And if you don't let him down for that, I'll hit you in the eye.'

The bear-man held out his hand. 'All a-right,' he said, 'threepence: I let him down.'

I saw the coins pass and the beast dropping on his forefeet; but just then a policeman coming in sight, the man led his bear off, and I was left alone with my little old friend.

'I wish I had that poor bear,' he said; 'I could teach him to be happy. But, even if I could buy him, what could I do with him up there? She's such a funny woman.'

He looked quite dim, but brightened as we went along.

'A bear', he said, 'is really an extraordinary animal. What wise little eyes he has! I do think he's a marvellous creation! My cats will have to go without their dinner, though. I was going to buy it with that threepence.'

I begged to be allowed the privilege.

'Willingly!' he said. 'Shall we go in here? They like cod's head best.'

While we stood waiting to be served I saw the usual derisive smile pass over the fishmonger's face. But my little old friend by no means noticed it; he was too busy looking at the fish. 'A fish is a marvellous thing, when you come to think of it,' he murmured. 'Look at its scales. Did you ever see such mechanism?'

We bought five cod's heads, and I left him carrying them in a bag, evidently lost in the anticipation of five cats eating them.

After that I saw him often, going with him sometimes to buy food for his cats, which seemed ever to increase in numbers. His talk was always of his strays, and the marvels of creation, and that time of his life when he played the flute at the Harmony Theatre. He had been out of a job, it seemed, for more than ten years; and, when questioned, only sighed and answered: 'Don't talk about it, please!'

His bumpy landlady never failed to favour me with a little conversation. She was one of those women who have terrific consciences, and terrible grudges against them.

'I never get out,' she would say.

'Why not?'

'Couldn't leave the house.'

'It won't run away!'

But she would look at me as if she thought it might, and repeat:

'Oh! I never get out.'

An extremely Scottish temperament.

Considering her descent, however, she was curiously devoid of success, struggling on apparently from week to week, cleaning, and answering the bell, and never getting out, and wondering why she kept my little old friend; just as he struggled on from week to week, getting out and collecting strays, and discovering the marvels of creation, and finding her a funny woman. Their hands were joined, one must suppose, by that dead child.

One July afternoon, however, I found her very much upset. He had been taken dangerously ill three days before.

'There he is,' she said; 'can't touch a thing. It's my belief he's done for himself, giving his food away all these years to those cats of his. I shooed 'em out today, the nasty creatures; they won't get in again.'

'Oh!' I said, 'you shouldn't have done that. It'll only make him miserable.'

She flounced her head up. 'Hoh!' she said; 'I wonder I've kept him all this time, with his birds and his cats dirtying my house. And there he lies, talking gibberish about them. He made me write to a Mr Jackson, of some theatre or other – I've no patience with him. And that little bullfinch all the time perching on his pillow, the dirty little thing! I'd have turned it out, too, only it wouldn't let me catch it.'

'What does the doctor say?'

'Double pneumonia – caught it getting his feet wet, after some stray, I'll be bound. I'm nursing him. There has to be someone with him all the time.'

He was lying very still when I went up, with the sunlight falling across the foot of his bed, and, sure enough, the bullfinch perching on his pillow. In that high fever he looked brighter than ever. He was not exactly delirious, yet not exactly master of his thoughts.

'Mr Jackson! He'll be here soon. Mr Jackson! He'll do it for me. I can ask him, if I die. A funny woman. I don't want to eat; I'm not a great eater – I want my breath, that's all.'

At sound of his voice the bullfinch fluttered off the pillow and flew round and round the room, as if alarmed at something new in the tones that were coming from its master.

Then he seemed to recognize me. 'I think I'm going to die,' he said; 'I'm very weak. It's lucky there's nobody to mind. If only he'd come soon. I wish' – and he raised himself with feeble excitement – 'I wish you'd take that wire off the window; I want my cats. She turned them out. I want him to promise me to take them, and bully-boy, and feed them with my money, when I'm dead.'

Seeing that excitement was certainly worse for him than cats, I took the wire off. He fell back, quiet at once; and presently, first one and then another cat came stealing in, till there were four or five seated against the walls. The moment he ceased to speak the bullfinch, too, came back to his pillow. His eyes looked most supernaturally bright, staring out of his little, withered-up old face at the sunlight playing on his bed; he said just audibly: 'Did you ever see anything more wonderful than that sunlight? It's really marvellous!' After that he fell into a sort of doze or stupor. And I continued to sit there in the window, relieved, but rather humiliated, that he had not asked me to take care of his cats and bullfinch.

Presently there came the sound of a motor-car in the little

street below. And almost at once the landlady appeared. For such an abrupt woman, she entered very softly.

'Here he is,' she whispered.

I went out and found a gentleman, perhaps sixty years of age, in a black coat, buff waistcoat, gold watch-chain, light trousers, patent-leather boots, and a wonderfully shining hat. His face was plump and red, with a glossy grey moustache; indeed, he seemed to shine everywhere, save in the eyes, which were of a dull and somewhat liverish hue.

'Mr Jackson?'

'The same. How is the little old chap?'

Opening the door of the next room, which I knew was always empty, I beckoned Mr Jackson in.

'He's really very ill; I'd better tell you what he wants to see you about.'

He looked at me with that air of 'You can't get at me — whoever you may be,' which belongs to the very successful.

'Right-o!' he said. 'Well?'

I described the situation. 'He seems to think,' I ended, 'that you'll be kind enough to charge yourself with his strays, in case he should die.'

Mr Jackson prodded the unpainted washstand with his gold-headed cane.

'Is he really going to kick it?'

'I'm afraid so; he's nothing but skin, bone, and spirit, as it is.'

'H'm! Stray cats, you say, and a bird! Well, there's no accounting. He was always a cracky little chap. So that's it! When I got the letter I wondered what the deuce! We pay him his five quid a quarter regular to this day. To tell truth, he deserved it. Thirty years he was at our shop; never missed a night. First-rate flute he was. He ought never to have given it up, though I always thought it showed a bit of heart in him. If a man don't look after number one, he's as good as gone; that's what I've always found. Why, I was no more than he was when I started. Shouldn't have been worth a plum if I'd gone on his plan, that's certain.' And he gave that profound chuckle which comes from the very stomach of success. 'We were having a rocky time at the Harmony; had to cut down everything we could – music, well, that came about first. Little old Moronelli, as we used to call him – old Italian days before English names came in, you know – he was far the best of the flutes; so I went to him and said: "Look here, Moronelli, which of these other boys had better go?" "Oh!" he said – I remember his funny little old mug now – "has one of them to go, Mr Jackson? Timminsa" – that was the elder – "he's a wife and family; and Smetoni" – Smith, you know – "he's only a boy. Times are bad for flutes." "I know it's a bit hard," I said, "but this theatre's goin' to be run much cheaper; one of 'em's got to get." "Oh!" he said, "dear me!" he said. What a funny little old chap it was! Well – what do you think? Next day I had his resignation. Give you my word I did my best to turn him. Why, he was sixty then if he was a day – at sixty a man don't get jobs in a hurry. But, not a bit of it! All he'd say was: "I shall get a place all right!" But that's it, you know – he never did. Too long in one shop. I heard by accident he was on the rocks; that's how I make him that allowance. But that's the sort of hopeless little old chap he is – no idea of himself. Cats! Why not? I'll take his old cats on; don't you let him worry about that. I'll see to his bird, too. If I can't give 'em a better time than ever they have here, it'll be funny!' And, looking round the little empty room, he again uttered that profound chuckle: 'Why, he was with us at the Harmony thirty years – that's time, you know; I made my fortune in it.'

'I'm sure,' I said, 'it'll be a great relief to him.'

'Oh! Ah! That's all right. You come down to my place' – he handed me a card: "Mr Cyril Porteous Jackson, Ultima Thule, Wimbledon" ' – 'and see how I fix 'em up. But if he's really going to kick it, I'd like to have a look at the little old chap, just for old times' sake.'

We went, as quietly as Mr Jackson's bright boots would permit, into his room, where the landlady was sitting gazing angrily at the cats. She went out without noise, flouncing her head as much as to say: 'Well, now you can see what I have to go through, sitting up here. I never get out.'

Our little old friend was still in that curious stupor. He

seemed unconscious, but his blue eyes were not closed, staring brightly out before them at things we did not see. With his silvery hair and his flushed frailty, he had an unearthly look. After standing perhaps three minutes at the foot of the bed, Mr Jackson whispered:

'Well, he does look queer. Poor little old chap! You tell him from me I'll look after his cats and bird; he needn't worry. And now, I think I won't keep the car. Makes me feel a bit throaty, you know. Don't move; he might come to.'

And, leaning all the weight of his substantial form on those bright and creaking toes, he made his way to the door, flashed at me a diamond ring, whispered hoarsely: 'So long! That'll be all right!' and vanished. And soon I heard the whirring of his car and just saw the top of his shiny hat travelling down the little street.

Some time I sat on there, wanting to deliver that message. An uncanny vigil in the failing light, with those five cats – yes, five at least – lying or sitting against the walls, staring like sphinxes at their motionless protector. I could not make out whether it was he in his stupor with his bright eyes that fascinated them, or the bullfinch perched on his pillow, who they knew perhaps might soon be in their power. I was glad when the landlady came up and I could leave the message with her.

When she opened the door to me next day at six o'clock I knew that he was gone. There was about her that sorrowful, unmistakable importance, that peculiar mournful excitement, which hovers over houses where death has entered.

'Yes,' she said, 'he went this morning. Never came round after you left. Would you like to see him?'

We went up.

He lay, covered with a sheet, in the darkened room. The landlady pulled the window-curtains apart. His face, as white now almost as his silvery head, had in the sunlight a radiance like that of a small, bright angel gone to sleep. No growth of hair, such as comes on most dead faces, showed on those frail cheeks that were now smooth and lineless as porcelain. And on the sheet above his chest the bullfinch sat, looking into his face.

The landlady let the curtains fall, and we went out.

'I've got the cats in here' – she pointed to the room where Mr Jackson and I had talked – 'all ready for that gentleman when he sends. But that little bird, I don't know what to do; he won't let me catch him, and there he sits. It makes me feel all funny.'

It had made me feel all funny, too.

'He hasn't left the money for his funeral. Dreadful, the way he never thought about himself. I'm glad I kept him, though.' And, not to my astonishment, she suddenly began to cry.

A wire was sent to Mr Jackson, and on the day of the funeral I went down to 'Ultima Thule,' Wimbledon, to see if he had carried out his promise.

He had. In the grounds, past the vinery, an outhouse had been cleaned and sanded, with cushions placed at intervals against the wall, and a little trough of milk. Nothing could have been more suitable or luxurious.

'How's that?' he said. 'I've done it thoroughly.' But I noticed that he looked a little glum.

'The only thing,' he said, 'is the cats. First night they seemed all right; and the second, there were three of 'em left. But today the gardener tells me there's not the ghost of one anywhere. It's not for want of feeding. They've had tripe, and liver, and milk – as much as ever they liked. And cods' heads, you know – they're very fond of them. I must say it's a bit of a disappointment to me.'

As he spoke, a sandy cat which I perfectly remembered, for it had only half its left ear, appeared in the doorway, and stood, crouching, with its green eyes turned on us; then, hearing Mr Jackson murmur, 'Puss, puss!' it ran for its life, slinking almost into the ground, and vanished among some shrubs.

Mr Jackson sighed. 'Peversity of the brutes!' he said. He led me back to the house through a conservatory full of choice orchids. A gilt bird-cage was hanging there, one of the largest I had ever seen, replete with every luxury the heart of bird could want.

'Is that for the bullfinch?' I asked him.

'Oh!' he said; 'didn't you know? The little beggar wouldn't let himself be caught, and the second morning, when they went up, there he lay on the old chap's body, dead. I thought it was very touchin'. But I kept the cage hung up for you to see that I should have given him a good time here. Oh, yes, "Ultima Thule" would have done him well!'

And from a bright leather case Mr Jackson offered me a cigar.

The question I had long been wishing to ask him slipped out of me then:

'Do you mind telling me why you called your house "Ultima Thule"?'

'Why?' he said. 'Found it on the gate. Think it's rather distingué, don't you?' and he uttered his profound chuckle.

'First-rate. The whole place is the last word in comfort.'

'Very good of you to say so,' he said. 'I've laid out a goodish bit on it. A man must have a warm corner to end his days in. "Ultima Thule," as you say – it isn't bad. There's success about it, somehow.'

And with that word in my ears, and in my eyes a vision of the little old fellow in *his* 'Ultima Thule,' with the bullfinch lying dead on a heart that had never known success, I travelled back to town.

1914

COURAGE

⏤❬❭⏤

AT that time (said Ferrand) I was in poverty. Not the kind of poverty that goes without dinner, but the sort that goes without breakfast, lunch, and dinner, and exists as it can on bread and tobacco. I lived in one of those fourpenny lodging-houses, Westminster way. Three, five, seven beds in a room; if you pay regularly, you keep your own bed; if not, they put someone else there who will certainly leave you a memento of himself. It's not the foreigners' quarter; they are nearly all English, and drunkards. Three-quarters of them don't eat — can't; they have no capacity for solid food. They drink and drink. They're not worth wasting your money on — cab-runners, newspaper-boys, sellers of laces and what you call sandwich-men; three-fourths of them brutalized beyond the power of recovery. What can you expect? They just live to scrape enough together to keep their souls in their bodies; they have no time or strength to think of anything but that. They come back at night and fall asleep — and how dead that sleep is! No, they never eat — just a bit of bread; the rest is drink!

There used to come to that house a little Frenchman, with a yellow, crow's-footed face; not old either, about thirty. But his life had been hard — no one comes to these houses if life is soft, especially no Frenchman; a Frenchman hates to leave his country. He came to shave us — charged a penny; most of us forgot to pay him, so that in all he shaved about three for a penny. He went to others of these houses — this gave him his income — he kept the little shop next door, too, but he never sold anything. How he worked! He also went to one of your Public Institutions; this was not so profitable, for there he was paid a penny for ten shaves. He used to say to me, moving his tired fingers like little yellow sticks: 'Pff! I slave! To gain a penny, friend, I'm spending fourpence. What would you have? One must nourish oneself to have the strength to shave ten people for a penny.' He was like an ant, running round and round in his little hole, without any chance but just to live; and always in hopes of saving enough to take him back to France, and set him up there. We had a liking for each other. He was the only one, in fact – except a sandwichman who had been an actor, and was very intelligent, when he wasn't drunk – the only one in all that warren who had ideas. He was fond of pleasure and loved his music-hall – must have gone at least twice a year, and was always talking of it. He had little knowledge of its joys, it's true – hadn't the money for that, but his intentions were good. He used to keep me till the last, and shave me slowly.

'This rests me,' he would say. It was amusement for me, too, for I had got into the habit of going for days without opening my lips. It's only a man here and there one can talk with; the rest only laugh; you seem to them a fool, a freak – something that should be put into a cage or tied by the leg.

'Yes,' the little man would say, 'when I came here first I thought I should soon go back, but now I'm not so sure. I'm losing my illusions. Money has wings, but it's not to *me* it flies. Believe me, friend, I am shaving my soul into these specimens. And how unhappy they are, poor creatures; how they must suffer! Drink! you say. Yes, that saves them – they get a little happiness from that. Unfortunately, I haven't the constitution for it – here.' And he would show me where he had no constitution. 'You, too, comrade, you don't seem to be in luck; but then, you're young. Ah, well, *faut être philosophe* – but imagine what sort of a game it is in this climate, especially if you come from the South!'

When I went away, which was as soon as I had nothing left to pawn, he gave me money – there's no question of lending in those houses: if a man parts with money he *gives* it; and lucky if he's not robbed into the bargain. There are fellows there who watch for a new pair of shoes, or a good overcoat, profit by their wakefulness as soon as the other is asleep, and promptly disappear. There's no morality in the face of destitution – it needs a man of iron, and these are men of straw. But one thing I will say of the low English – they are not bloodthirsty, like the low French and Italians.

Well, I got a job as fireman on a steamer, made a tour tramping, and six months later I was back again. The first morning I saw the Frenchman. It was shaving-day; he was more like an ant than ever, working away with all his legs and arms; a little yellower, and perhaps more wrinkled.

'Ah!' he called out to me in French, 'there you are – back again. I knew you'd come. Wait till I've finished with this specimen – I've a lot to talk about.'

We went into the kitchen, a big stone-floored room, with tables for eating – and sat down by the fire. It was January, but, summer or winter, there's always a fire burning in that kitchen.

'So,' he said, 'you have come back? No luck? Eh! Patience! A few more days won't kill you at your age. What fogs, though! You see, I'm still here, but my comrade, Pigon, is dead. You remember him – the big man with black hair who had the shop down the street. Amiable fellow, good friend to me; and married. Fine woman his wife – a little ripe, seeing she has had children, but of good family. He died suddenly of heart disease. Wait a bit; I'll tell you about that. . .

'It was not long after you went away, one fine day in October, when I had just finished with these specimens here, and was taking my coffee in the shop, and thinking of that poor Pigon – dead then just three days – when *pom!* comes a knock, and there is Madame Pigon! Very calm – a woman of good family, well brought up, well made – fine woman. But the cheeks pale, and the eyes so red, poor soul.

'"Well, Madame," I asked her, "what can I do for you?"

'It seems this poor Pigon died bankrupt; there was not a cent in the shop. He was two days in his grave, and the bailiffs in already.

'"Ah, Monsieur!" she says to me, "what am I to do?"

' "Wait a bit, Madame!" I get my hat and go back to the shop with her.

'What a scene! Two bailiffs, who would have been the better for a shave, sitting in a shop before the basins; and everywhere, *ma foi*, everywhere, children! Tk! Tk! A little girl of ten, very like her mother; two little boys with little trousers, and one with nothing but a chemise; and others – two, quite small, all rolling on the floor; and what a horrible noise! – all crying, all but the little girl, fit to break themselves in two. The bailiffs seemed perplexed. It was enough to make one weep! Seven! some quite small! That poor Pigon, I had no idea he was so good a rabbit!

'The bailiffs behaved very well.

'"Well," said the biggest, "you can have four-and-twenty hours to find this money; my mate can camp out here in the shop – we don't want to be hard on you!"

'I helped Madame to soothe the children.

'"If I had the money," I said, "it should be at your service, Madame – in each well-born heart there should exist humanity; but I have no money. Try and think whether you have no friends to help you."

'"Monsieur," she answered, "I have none. Have I had time to make friends – I, with seven children?"

'"But in France, Madame?"

'"None, Monsieur. I have quarrelled with my family; and reflect – it is now seven years since we came to England, and then only because no one would help us." That seemed to me bad, but what could I do? I could only say:

'"Hope always, Madame – trust in me!"

'I went away. All day long I thought how calm she was – magnificent! And I kept saying to myself: "Come, tap your head! tap your head! Something must be done!" But nothing came.

'The next morning it was my day to go to that sacred Institution, and I started off still thinking what on earth could be done for the poor woman; it was as if the little ones had got hold of my legs and were dragging at me. I arrived late, and, to make up time, I shaved them as I have never shaved them; a hot morning – I perspired! Ten for a penny! Ten for a penny! I thought of that, and of the poor woman. At last I finished and sat down. I thought to myself: "It's too strong! Why do you do it? It's stupid! You are wasting yourself!" And then, my idea came to me! I asked for the manager.

'"Monsieur," I said, "it is impossible for me to come here again."

'"What do you mean?" says he.

'"I have had enough of your – 'ten for a penny' – I am going to get married; I can't afford to come here any longer. I lose too much flesh for the money."

'"What?" he says, "you're a lucky man if you can afford to throw away your money like this!"

'"Throw away my money! Pardon, Monsieur, but look at me" – I was still very hot – "for every penny I make I lose threepence, not counting the boot leather to and fro. While I was still a bachelor, Monsieur, it was my own affair – I could afford these extravagances; but now – it must finish – I have the honour, Monsieur!"

'I left him, and walked away. I went to the Pigons' shop. The bailiff was still there – Pfui! He must have been smoking all the time.

'"I can't give them much longer," he said to me.

'"It is of no importance," I replied; and I knocked, and went into the back room.

'The children were playing in the corner, that little girl, a heart of gold, watching them like a mother; and Madame at the table with a pair of old black gloves on her hands. My friend, I have never seen such a face – calm, but so pale, so frightfully discouraged, so overwhelmed. One would say she was waiting for her death. It was bad, it was bad – with winter coming on!

'"Good morning, Madame," I said. "What news? Have you been able to arrange anything?"

'"No, Monsieur. And you?"

'"No!" And I looked at her again – a fine woman; ah! a fine woman.

'"But," I said, "an idea has come to me this morning. Now, what would you say if I asked you to marry me? It might possibly be better than nothing."

'She regarded me with her black eyes, and answered:

'"But willingly, Monsieur!" and then, comrade, but not till then, she cried.'

The little Frenchman stopped, and stared at me hard.

'H'm!' I said at last, 'you have courage!'

He looked at me again; his eyes were troubled, as if I had paid him a bad compliment.

'You think so?' he said at last, and I saw that the thought was gnawing at him, as if I had turned the light on some desperate, dark feeling in his heart.

'Yes!' he said, taking his time, while his good yellow face wrinkled and wrinkled, and each wrinkle seemed to darken: 'I was afraid of it even when I did it. Seven children!' Once more he looked at me: 'And since! – sometimes – sometimes – I could –' he broke off, then burst out again:

'Life is hard! What would you have? I knew her husband. Could I leave her to the streets?'

1904

THE BRIGHT SIDE

A LITTLE Englishwoman, married to a German, had dwelt with him eighteen years in humble happiness and the district of Putney, where her husband worked in the finer kinds of leather. He was a harmless, busy little man with the gift for turning his hand to anything, which is bred into the peasants of the Black Forest, who on their upland farms make all the necessaries of daily life – their coarse linen from home-grown flax, their leather gear from the hides of their beasts, their clothes from the wool thereof, their furniture from the pine logs of the forest, their bread from home-grown flour milled in simple fashion and baked in the home-made ovens, their cheese from the milk of their own goats. Why he had come to England he probably did not remember – it was so long ago; but he would still know why he had married Dora, the daughter of the Putney carpenter, she being, as it were, salt of the earth: one of those Cockney women, deeply sensitive beneath a well-nigh impermeable mask of humour and philosophy, who quite unselfconsciously are always doing things for others. In their little grey Putney house they had dwelt those eighteen years, without perhaps ever having had time to move, though they had often had the intention of doing so for the sake of the children, of whom they had three, a boy and two girls. Mrs Gerhardt – as I will call her, for her husband had a very German name, and there is more in a name than Shakespeare dreamed of – Mrs Gerhardt was a little woman with large hazel eyes and dark crinkly hair, in which there were already a few threads of grey when the war broke out. Her boy David, the eldest, was fourteen at that date, and her girls, Minnie and Violet, were eight and five, rather pretty children, especially the little one. Gerhardt, perhaps because he was so handy, had never risen. His firm regarded him as indispensable and paid him fair wages, but he had no 'push', having the craftsman's temperament, and employing his spare time in little neat jobs for his house and his neighbours, which brought him no return. They made their way, therefore, without that provision for the future which necessitates the employment of one's time for one's own ends. But they were happy, and had no enemies; and each year saw some mild improvements in their studiously clean house and tiny back garden. Mrs Gerhardt, who was cook, seamstress, washerwoman, besides being wife and mother, was almost notorious in that street of semi-detached houses for being at the disposal of anyone in sickness or trouble. She was not strong in body, for things had gone wrong when she bore her first, but her spirit had that peculiar power of seeing things as they were, and yet refusing to be dismayed, which so embarrasses Fate. She saw her husband's defects clearly, and his good qualities no less distinctly – they never quarrelled. She gauged her children's characters, too, with an admirable precision, which left, however, loopholes of wonder as to what they would become.

The outbreak of the war found them on the point of going to Margate for Bank Holiday, an almost unparalleled event; so that the importance of the world catastrophe was brought home to them with a vividness which would otherwise have been absent from folk so simple, domestic, and far-removed from that atmosphere in which the egg of war is hatched. Over the origin and merits of the struggle, beyond saying to each other several times that it was a dreadful thing, Mr and Mrs Gerhardt held but one little conversation, lying in their iron bed with an immortal brown eiderdown, patterned with red wriggles, over them. They agreed that it was a cruel, wicked thing to invade 'that little Belgium', and there left a matter which seemed to them a mysterious and insane perversion of all they had hitherto been accustomed to think of as life. Reading their papers – a daily and a weekly, in which they had as much implicit faith as a million other readers – they were soon duly horrified by the reports therein of 'Hun' atrocities; so horrified that they would express their condemnation of the Kaiser and his militarism as freely as if they had been British subjects. It was, therefore, with an uneasy surprise that they began to find these papers talking of 'the Huns at large in our midst', of 'spies', and the national danger of 'nourishing such vipers'. They were deeply conscious of not being 'vipers,' and such sayings began to awaken in both their breasts a humble sense of injustice, as it were. This was more acute in the breast of little Mrs Gerhardt, because, of course, the shafts were directed not at her, but at her husband. She knew her husband so well, knew him incapable of anything but homely kindly sayings, and that he should be lumped into the category of 'Huns' and 'spies' and tarred with the brush of mass hatred amazed and stirred her indignation, or would have, if her Cockney temperament had allowed her to take it very seriously. As for Gerhardt, he became extremely silent, so that it was ever more and more difficult to tell what he was feeling. The patriotism of the newspapers took a considerable time to affect the charity of the citizens of Putney, and so long as no neighbour showed signs of thinking that little Gerhardt was a monster and a spy, it was fairly easy for Mrs Gerhardt to sleep at night, with the feeling that the remarks in the papers were not really intended for Gerhardt and herself. But she noticed that her man had given up reading them and would push them away, if, in the tiny sitting-room with the heavily-flowered walls, they happened to rest beside him. He had perhaps a closer sense of impending Fate than she. The boy, David, went to his first work, and the girls to their school, and so things dragged on through that first long war winter and spring. Mrs Gerhardt, in the intervals of doing everything, knitted socks for 'our poor cold boys in the trenches', but Gerhardt no longer sought out little jobs to do in the houses of his neighbours. Mrs Gerhardt thought that he 'fancied' they would not like it. It was early in that spring that she took a deaf aunt to live with them, the wife of her mother's brother, no blood-relation, but the poor woman had nowhere else to go; so David was put to sleep on the horsehair sofa in the sitting-room because she 'couldn't refuse the poor thing'. And then, of a May afternoon, while she was washing the household sheets, her neighbour, Mrs Clirehugh, a little spare woman, all eyes, cheek-bones, hair and decision, came in breathless and burst out:

'Oh! Mrs Gerhardt, 'ave you 'eard? They've sunk the *Loositania!* Has I said to Will: Isn't it horful?'

Mrs Gerhardt, her round arms, dripping soapsuds, answered: 'What a dreadful thing! The poor drowning people! Dear! Oh, dear!'

'Oh! those Huns! I'd shoot the lot, I would!'

'They *are* wicked!' Mrs Gerhardt echoed: 'that was a dreadful thing to do.'

But it was not till Gerhardt came in at five o'clock, white as a sheet, that she perceived how this catastrophe affected them.

'I have been called a German,' were the first words he uttered; 'Dollee, I have been called a German.'

'Well, so you are, my dear,' said Mrs Gerhardt.

'You do not see,' he answered, with a heat and agitation which surprised her. 'I tell you this *Lusitania* will finish our business. They will have me. They will take me away from you all. Already the papers have: "Intern all the Huns."' He sat down at the kitchen table and buried his face in hands still grimy from his leather work. Mrs Gerhardt stood beside him, her eyes unnaturally big.

'But, Max,' she said, 'what has it to do with you? You couldn't help it, Max!'

Gerhardt looked up; his white face, broad in the brow and tapering to a thin chin, seemed distraught.

'What do they care for that? Is my name Max Gerhardt? What do they care if I hate war? I am a German. That's enough. You will see.'

'Oh!' murmured Mrs Gerhardt, 'they won't be so unjust.'

Gerhardt reached up and caught her chin in his hand, and for a moment those two pairs of eyes gazed, straining, into each other. Then he said:

'I don't want to be taken, Dollee. What shall I do away from you and the children? I don't want to be taken, Dollee.'

Mrs Gerhardt, with a feeling of terror and a cheerful smile, answered:

'You mustn't go fancyin' things, Max. I'll make you a nice cup of tea. Cheer up, old man! Look on the bright side!'

But Gerhardt lapsed into the silence which of late she had begun to dread.

That night some shop windows were broken, some German names effaced. The Gerhardts had no shop, no name painted up, and they escaped. In Press and Parliament the cry against 'the Huns in our midst' rose with a fresh fury; but, for the Gerhardts, the face of Fate was withdrawn. Gerhardt went to his work as usual, and their laborious and quiet existence remain undisturbed; nor could Mrs Gerhardt tell whether her 'man's' ever-deepening silence was due to his 'fancying things' or to the demeanour of his neighbours and fellow-workmen. One would have said that he, like the derelict aunt, was deaf, so difficult to converse with had he become. His length of sojourn in England and his value to his employers, for he had real skill, had saved him for the time being; but, behind the screen, Fate twitched her grinning chaps.

Not till the howl which followed some air raids in 1916 did they take off Gerhardt, with a variety of other elderly men, whose crime it was to have been born in Germany. They did it suddenly, and perhaps it was as well, for a prolonged sight of his silent misery must have upset his family till they would have been unable to look on that bright side of things which Mrs Gerhardt had, as it were, always up her sleeve. When, in charge of a big and sympathetic constable, he was gone, taking all she could hurriedly get together for him, she hastened to the police station. They were friendly to her there – she must cheer up, 'e'd be all right, she needn't worry. Ah! she could go down to the 'Ome Office, if she liked, and see what could be done. But they 'eld out no 'ope! Mrs Gerhardt waited till the morrow, having the little Violet in bed with her, and crying quietly into her pillow; then, putting on her Sunday best, she went down to a building in Whitehall, larger than any she had ever entered. Two hours she waited, sitting unobtrusive, with big, anxious eyes, and a line between her brows. At intervals of half an hour she would get up and ask the messenger cheerfully: 'I 'ope they haven't forgotten me, sir. Perhaps you'd see to it.' And because she was cheerful the messenger took her under his protection, and answered: 'All right, Missis. They're very busy, but *I'll* wangle you in some'ow.'

When at length she was 'wangled' into the presence of a

grave gentleman in eye-glasses, realization of the utter importance of this moment overcame her so that she could not speak.
'Oh! dear,' she thought, while her heart fluttered like a bird –
'he'll never understand; I'll never be able to make him.' She
saw her husband buried under the dead leaves of despair; she
saw her children getting too little food; the deaf aunt, now bedridden, neglected in the new pressure of work which must fall
on the only breadwinner left. And choking a little, she said:

'I'm sure I'm very sorry to take up your time, sir; but my
'usband's been taken to the Palace; and we've been married
over twenty years, and he's been in England twenty-five; and
he's a very good man and a good workman; and I thought perhaps they didn't understand that; and we've got three children
and a relation that's bedridden. And of course, we understand
that the Germans have been very wicked; Gerhardt always said
that himself. And it isn't as if he was a spy; so I thought if you
could do something for us, sir, I being English myself.'

The gentleman, looking past her at the wall, answered
wearily:

'Gerhardt – I'll look into it. We have to do very hard things,
Mrs Gerhardt.'

Little Mrs Gerhardt, with big eyes almost starting out of her
head, for she was no fool, and perceived that this was the end,
said eagerly:

'Of course I know that there's a big outcry, and the papers
are askin' for it; but the people in our street don't mind 'im, sir.
He's always done little things for them; so I thought perhaps
you might make an exception in his case.'

She noticed that the gentleman's lips tightened at the word
outcry, and that he was looking at her now.

'His case was before the Committee, no doubt; but I'll in-
quire. Good morning.'

Mrs Gerhardt, accustomed to not being troublesome, rose; a
tear rolled down her cheek and was arrested by her smile.

'Thank you, sir, I'm sure. Good morning, sir.'

And she went out. Meeting the messenger in the corridor,
and hearing his: 'Well, Missis?' she answered: 'I don't know.
I must look on the bright side. Good-bye, and thank you for

your trouble.' And she turned away feeling as if she had been beaten all over.

The bright side on which she looked did not include the return to her of little Gerhardt, who was duly detained for the safety of the country. Obedient to economy, and with a dim sense that her favourite papers were in some way responsible for this, she ceased to take them in, and took in sewing instead. It had become necessary to do so, for the allowance she received from the Government was about a quarter of Gerhardt's weekly earnings. In spite of its inadequacy it was something, and she felt she must be grateful. But, curiously enough, she could not forget that she was English, and it seemed strange to her that, in addition to the grief caused by separation from her husband, from whom she had never been parted, not even for a night, she should now be compelled to work twice as hard and eat half as much because that husband had paid her country the compliment of preferring it to his own. But, after all, many other people had much worse trouble to grieve over, so she looked on the bright side of all this, especially on those days once a week when alone, or accompanied by the little Violet, she visited that Palace where she had read in her favourite journals to her great comfort that her husband was treated like a prince. Since he had no money, he was in what they called 'the battalion', and their meetings were held in the bazaar, where things that 'the princes' made were exposed for sale. Here Mr and Mrs Gerhardt would stand in front of some doll, some blotting-book, calendar, or walking-stick, which had been fashioned by one of 'the princes'. There they would hold each other's hands and try to imagine themselves unsurrounded by other men and wives, while the little Violet would stray and return to embrace her father's leg spasmodically. Standing there, Mrs Gerhardt would look on the bright side, and explain to Gerhardt how well everything was going, and he mustn't fret about them, and how kind the police were, and how auntie asked after him, and Minnie would get a prize; and how he oughtn't to mope but eat his food, and look on the bright side. And Gerhardt would smile the smile which went into her heart just like a sword, and say:

'All right, Dollee. I'm getting on fine.' Then, when the whistle blew and he had kissed little Violet, they would be quite silent, looking at each other. And she would say in a voice so matter-of-fact that it could have deceived no one:

'Well, I must go now. Good-bye, old man.'

And he would say:

'Good-bye, Dollee. Kiss me.'

They would kiss, and holding little Violet's hand very hard, she would hurry away in the crowd, taking care not to look back for fear she might suddenly lose sight of the bright side. But as the months went on, became a year, eighteen months, two years, and still she went weekly to see her 'prince' in his Palace, that visit became for her the hardest experience of all her hard week's doings. For she was a realist, as well as a heroine, and she could see the lines of despair not only in her man's heart, but in his face. For a long time he had not said: 'I'm getting on fine, Dollee.' His face had a beaten look, his figure had wasted, he complained of his head.

'It's so noisy,' he would say constantly; 'oh! it's so noisy, never a quiet moment – never alone – never – never – never. And not enough to eat; it's all reduced now, Dollee.'

She learned to smuggle food into his hands, but it was very little, for they had not enough at home either, with the price of living ever going up and her depleted income ever stationary. They had – her 'man' told her – made a fuss in the papers about their being fed like turkey-cocks, while the 'Huns' were sinking the ships. Gerhardt, always a spare little man, had lost eighteen pounds. She, naturally well-covered, was getting thin herself, but that she did not notice, too busy all day long, and too occupied in thinking of her 'man'. To watch him week by week, more hopeless as the months dragged on, was an acute torture, to disguise which was torture even more acute. She had long seen that there *was* no bright side, but if she admitted that, she knew she would go down; so she did not. And she carefully kept from Gerhardt such matters as David's overgrowing his strength because she could not feed him properly; the completely bedridden nature of auntie; and, worse than these, the growing coldness and unkindness of her neighbours. Perhaps they did not mean to be unkind, perhaps they did, for it was not in their nature to withstand the pressure of mass sentiment, the continual personal discomfort of having to stand in queues, the fear of air raids, the cumulative indignation caused by stories of atrocities, true and untrue. In spite of her record of kindliness towards them, she became tarred with the brush at last, for her nerves had given way once or twice, and she had said it was a shame to keep her 'man' like that gettin' iller and iller, who had never done a thing. Even her reasonableness – and she was very reasonable – succumbed to the strain of that weekly sight of him, till she could no longer allow for the difficulties which Mrs Clirehugh assured her the Government had to deal with. Then one day she used the words 'fair play', and at once it became current that she had 'German sympathies'. From that time on she was somewhat doomed. Those who had received kindnesses from her were foremost in showing her coldness, being wounded in their self-esteem. To have received little benefits, such as being nursed when they were sick, from one who had 'German sympathies' was too much for the pride which is in every human being, however humble an inhabitant of Putney. Mrs Gerhardt's Cockney spirit could support this for herself, but she could not bear it for her children. David came home with a black eye and would not say why he had got it. Minnie missed her prize at school, though she had clearly won it. That was just after the last German offensive began; but Mrs Gerhardt refused to see that this was any reason. Little Violet twice put the heart-rending question to her: 'Aren't I English, mummy?'

She was answered: 'Yes, my dear, of course.'

But the child obviously remained unconvinced in her troubled mind.

And then they took David for the British Army. It was that which so upset the apple-cart in Mrs Gerhardt that she broke out to her last friend, Mrs Clirehugh:

'I do think it's hard, Eliza. They take his father and keep him there for a dangerous Hun, year after year like that; and then they take his boy for the army to fight against him. And how I'm to get on without him I don't know.'

Little Mrs Clirehugh, who was Scotch, with a Gloucester-
shire accent, replied:

'Well, we've got to beat them. They're such a wicked lot. I
daresay it's 'ard on you, but we've got to beat them.'

'But *we* never did nothing,' cried Mrs Gerhardt; 'it isn't us
that's wicked. We never wanted the war; it's nothing but ruin
to him. They did ought to let me have my man or my boy, one
or the other.'

'You should 'ave some feeling for the Government, Dora;
they 'ave to do 'ard things.'

Mrs Gerhardt, with a quivering face, had looked at her
friend.

'I have,' she said at last in a tone which implanted in Mrs
Clirehugh's heart the feeling that Dora was 'bitter'.

She could not forget it; and she would flaunt her head at
any mention of her former friend. It was a blow to Mrs Gerhardt, who had now no friends, except the deaf and bedridden
aunt, to whom all things where the same, war or no war, Germans or no Germans, so long as she was fed.

About then it was that the tide turned, and the Germans began to know defeat. Even Mrs Gerhardt, who read the papers
no longer, learned it daily, and her heart relaxed; that bright
side began to reappear a little. She felt they could not feel so
hardly toward her 'man' now as when they were all in fear;
and perhaps the war would be over before her boy went out.
But Gerhardt puzzled her. He did not brighten up. The iron
seemed to have entered his soul too deeply. And one day, in the
bazaar, passing an open doorway, Mrs Gerhardt had a glimpse
of why. There, stretching before her astonished eyes, was a
great, as it were, encampment of brown blankets, slung and
looped up anyhow, dividing from each other countless sordid
beds, which were almost touching, and a whiff of huddled humanity came out to her keen nostrils, and a hum of sound to
her ears. So that was where her 'man' had dwelt these thirty
months, in that dirty, crowded, noisy place with dirty looking
men, such as those she could see lying on the beds, or crouching
by the side of them over their work. He had kept neat somehow, at least on the days when she came to him – but *that*

was where he lived! Alone again (for she no longer brought the little Violet to see her German father), she grieved all the way home. Whatever happened to him now, even if she got him back, she knew he would never quite get over it.

And then came the morning when she came out of her door like the other inhabitants of Putney, at sound of the maroons, thinking it was an air raid; and, catching the smile on the toothless mouth of one of her old neighbours, hearing the cheers of the boys in the school round the corner, knew that it was Peace. Her heart overflowed then, and, withdrawing hastily, she sat down on a shiny chair in her empty parlour. Her face crumpled suddenly, the tears came welling forth, and she cried, alone in the little cold room. She cried from relief and utter thankfulness. It was over – over at last! The long waiting – the long misery – the yearning for her 'man' – the grieving for all those poor boys in the mud and the dreadful shell-holes and the fighting, the growing terror of anxiety for her own boy – over, all over! Now they would let Max out, now David would come back from the army; and people would not be unkind and spiteful to her and the children any more!

For all she was a Cockney, hers was a simple soul, associating peace with goodwill. Drying her tears, she stood up, and in the little cheap mirror above the empty grate looked at her face. It was lined, and she was grey; for more than two years her 'man' had not seen her without her hat. Whatever would he say? And she rubbed and rubbed her cheeks, trying to smooth them out. Then her conscience smote her, and she ran upstairs to the back bedroom, where the deaf aunt lay. Taking up the amateur ear-trumpet which Gerhardt himself had made for 'auntie', before he was taken away, she bawled into it:

'Peace, Auntie; it's Peace! Think of that. It's Peace!'

'What's that?' answered the deaf woman.

'It's Peace, Auntie, Peace!'

The deaf lady roused herself a little, and some meaning came into the lack-lustre black eyes of her long, leathery face. 'You don't say,' she said in her wooden voice. 'I'm so hungry, Dolly; isn't it time for my dinner?'

'I was just goin' to get it, dearie,' replied Mrs Gerhardt, and hurried back downstairs with her brain teeming, to make the deaf woman's bowl of bread, pepper, salt and onions.

All that day and the next and the next she saw the bright side of things with almost dazzling clearness, waiting to visit her 'prince' in his Palace. She found him in a strange and pitiful state of nerves. The news had produced too intense and varied emotions among those crowded thousands of men buried away from normal life so long. She spent all her hour and a half trying desperately to make him see the bright side, but he was too full of fears and doubts, and she went away smiling, but utterly exhausted. Slowly in the weeks which followed she learned that nothing was changed. In the fond hope that Gerhardt might be home now any day, she was taking care that his slippers and some clothes of David's were ready for him, and the hip bath handy for him to have a lovely hot wash. She had even bought a bottle of beer and some of his favourite pickle, saving the price out of her own food, and was taking in the paper again, letting bygones be bygones. But he did not come. And soon the paper informed her that the English prisoners were returning – many in wretched state, poor things, so that her heart bled for them, and made her fiercely angry with the cruel men who had treated them so; but it informed her too that, if the paper had its way, no 'Huns' would be tolerated in this country for the future. 'Send them all back!' were the words it used. She did not realize at first that this applied to Gerhardt; but when she did she dropped the journal as if it had been a living coal of fire. Not let him come back to his home, and family, not let him stay, after all they'd done to him, and he never did anything to them! Not let him stay, but send him out to that dreadful country, which he had almost forgotten in these thirty years; and he with an English wife and children! In this new terror of utter dislocation the bright side so slipped from her that she was obliged to go out into the back garden in the dark, where a sou'westerly wind was driving the rain. There, lifting her eyes to the evening sky, she uttered her little moan. It couldn't be true; and yet, what they said in her paper had always turned out true, like the taking of Gerhardt away, and the reduction of his food. And the face of the gentleman in the building at Whitehall came before her out of the long past, with his lips tightening, and his words: 'We have to do very hard things, Mrs Gerhardt.' Why had they to do them? Her 'man' had never done no harm to no one! A flood, bitter as sea water, surged in her, and seemed to choke her very being. Those gentlemen in the papers – why should they go on like that? Had they no hearts, no eyes to see the misery they brought to humble folk? 'I wish them nothing worse than what they've brought to him and me,' she thought wildly, 'nothing worse!'

The rain beat on her face, wetted her grey hair, cooled her eyeballs. 'I mustn't be spiteful,' she thought; and, bending down in the dark, she touched the glass of the tiny conservatory up against the warm kitchen wall, heated by the cunning hot-water pipe that her 'man' had put there in his old handy days. Under it were one monthly rose, which still had blossoms, and some strangely small chrysanthemums. She had been keeping them for the feast when he came home; but if he wasn't to come, what should she do? She raised herself. Above the wet roofs, sky-rack was passing wild and dark, but in a cleared space one or two stars shone the brighter for the blackness below. 'I must look on the bright side,' she thought, 'or I can't bear myself.' And she went in to cook the porridge for the evening meal.

The winter passed for her in the most dreadful anxiety. 'Repatriate the Huns!' That cry continued to spurt up in her paper like a terrible face seen in some recurrent nightmare; and each week that she went to visit Gerhardt brought solid confirmation to her terror. He was taking it hard, so that sometimes she was afraid that 'something' was happening in him. This was the umost she went towards defining what doctors might have diagnosed as incipient softening of the brain. He seemed to dread the prospect of being sent to his native country.

'I couldn't stick it, Dollee,' he would say. 'What should I do – whatever should I do? I haven't a friend. I haven't a spot to go to. I should be lost. I'm afraid, Dollee. How could you come out there, you and the children? I couldn't make a living for you. I couldn't make one for myself now.'

And she would say: 'Cheer up, old man. Look on the bright

side. Think of the others.' For, though those others were not precisely the bright side, the mental picture of their sufferings, all those poor 'princes' and their families, somehow helped her to bear her own. But he shook his head:

'No, I should never see you again.'

'I'd follow you,' she answered. 'Never fear, Max, we'd work in the fields – me and the children. We'd get on somehow. Bear up, my dearie. It'll soon be over now. I'll stick to you, Max, never you fear. But they won't send you, they never will.'

And then, like a lump of ice pressed on her breast, came the thought: 'But if they do! Auntie! My boy! My girls! However shall I manage if they do?'

Then long lists began to appear, and in great batches men were shovelled wholesale back to the country whose speech some of them had well-nigh forgotten. Gerhardt's name had not appeared yet. The lists were hung up the day after Mrs Gerhardt's weekly visit, but she urged him if his name did appear to appeal against repatriation. It was with the greatest difficulty that she roused in him the energy to promise. 'Look on the bright side, Max,' she implored him. 'You've got a son in the British Army; they'll never send you. They wouldn't be so cruel. Never say die, old man.'

His name appeared, but was taken out, and the matter hung again in awful suspense, while the evil face of the recurrent nightmare confronted Mrs Gerhardt out of her favourite journal. She read that journal again, because so far as in her gentle spirit lay, she hated it. It was slowly killing her 'man', and all her chance of future happiness; she hated it, and read it every morning. To the monthly rose and straggly brown-red chrysanthemums in the tiny hot house there had succeeded spring flowers – a few hardy January snowdrops, and one by one blue scillas, and pale daffodils called 'angels' tears'.

Peace tarried, but the flowers came up long before their time in their tiny hothouse against the kitchen flue. Then one wonderful day there came to Mrs Gerhardt a strange letter, announcing that Gerhardt was coming home. He would not be sent to Germany – he was coming home! Today, that very day – any moment he might be with her. When she received it, who had long received no letters save the weekly letters of her boy still in the army, she was spreading margarine on auntie's bread for breakfast, and, moved beyond all control, she spread it thick, wickedly, wastefully thick, then dropped the knife, sobbed, laughed, clasped her hands on her breast, and without rhyme or reason began singing, 'Hark! the herald angels sing'. The girls had gone to school already, auntie in the room above could not hear her, no one heard her, nor saw her drop suddenly into the wooden chair, and, with her bare arms stretched out one on either side of the plate of bread and margarine, cry her heart out against the clean white table. Coming home, coming home, coming home! The bright side! The white stars!

It was a quarter of an hour before she could trust herself to answer the knocking on the floor, which meant that auntie was missing her breakfast. Hastily she made the tea and went up. The woman's dim long face gleamed greedily when she saw how thick the margarine was spread; but little Mrs Gerhardt said no word of the reason for that feast. She just watched her only friend eating it, while moisture still trickled out from her eyes on to her flushed cheeks, and the words still hummed in her brain:

> Peace on earth and mercy mild,
> Jesus Christ a little child.

Then, still speaking no word, she ran out and put clean sheets on her and her 'man's' bed. She was on wires, she could not keep still, and all the morning she polished. About noon she went out into her garden, and from under the glass plucked every flower that grew there – snowdrops, scillas, 'angels' tears', quite two dozen blossoms. She brought them into the parlour and opened its window wide. The sun was shining, and fell on the flowers strewn on the table, ready to be made into the nosegay of triumphant happiness. While she stood fingering them, delicately breaking half an inch off their stalks so that they should last the longer in water, she became conscious of someone on the pavement outside the window, and looking up saw Mrs Clirehugh. The past, the sense of having been deserted by her friends, left her, and she called out:

'Come in, Eliza; look at my flowers!'

Mrs Clirehugh came in; she was in black, her cheekbones higher, her hair looser, her eyes bigger. Mrs Gerhardt saw tears starting from those eyes, wetting those high cheekbones, and cried out:

'Why, what's the matter, dear?'

Mrs Clirehugh choked. 'My baby!'

Mrs Gerhardt dropped an 'angels' tear' and went up to her. 'Whatever's happened?' she cried.

'Dead!' replied Mrs Clirehugh. 'Dead o' the influenza. 'E's to be buried today. I can't – I can't –' Wild choking stopped her utterance. Mrs Gerhardt put an arm round her and drew her head on to her shoulder.

'I can't' – sobbed Mrs Clirehugh – 'find any flowers. It's seein' yours made me cry.'

'There, there!' cried Mrs Gerhardt. 'Have them. I'm sure you're welcome, dearie. Have them – I'm so sorry!'

'I don't know,' choked Mrs Clirehugh; 'I 'aven't deserved them.' Mrs Gerhardt gathered up the flowers.

'Take them,' she said. 'I couldn't think of it. Your poor little baby. Take them! There, there, he's spared a lot of trouble. You must look on the bright side, dearie.'

Mrs Clirehugh tossed up her head.

'You're an angel, that's what *you* are!' And grasping the flowers, she hurried out, a black figure passing the window in the sunlight.

Mrs Gerhardt stood above the emptied table, thinking: 'Poor dear – I'm glad she had the flowers. It was a mercy I didn't call out that Max was coming!' And from the floor she picked up the 'angel's tear' she had dropped, and set it in a glass of water, where the sunlight fell. She was still gazing at it, pale, slender, lonely in that coarse tumbler, when she heard a knock on the parlour door and went to open it. There stood her 'man', with a large brown-paper parcel in his hand. He stood quite still, his head down, the face very grey. She cried out: 'Max!' but the thought flashed through her: 'He knocked on the door! It's *his* door – he knocked on the door!'

'Dollee?' he said, with a sort of question in his voice.

She threw her arms round him, drew him into the room, and, shutting the door, looked hard into his face. Yes, it was his face, but in the eyes something wandered – lit up, went out, lit up.

'Dollee,' he said again, and clutched her hand.

She strained him to her with a sob.

'I'm not well, Dollee,' he murmured.

'No, of course not, my dearie man; but you'll soon be all right now – home again with me. Cheer up, cheer up!'

'I'm not well,' he said again.

She caught the parcel out of his hand, and, taking the 'angel's tear' from the tumbler, fixed it in his coat.

'Here's a spring flower for you, Max; out of your own little hothouse. You're home again; home again, my dearie. Auntie's upstairs, and the girls'll be coming soon. And we'll have dinner.'

'I'm not well, Dollee,' he said.

Terrified by that reiteration, she drew him down on the little horsehair sofa, and sat on his knee. 'You're home, Max; kiss me. There's my man!' and she rocked him to and fro against her, yearning yet fearing to look into his face and see that 'something' wander there – light up, go out, light up. 'Look, dearie,' she said, 'I've got some beer for you. You'd like a glass of beer?'

He made a motion of his lips, a sound that was like the ghost of a smack. It terrified her, so little life was there in it.

He clutched her close, and repeated feebly:

'Yes, all right in a day or two. They let me come – I'm not well, Dollee.' He touched his head.

Straining him to her, rocking him, she murmured over and over again, like a cat purring to its kitten:

'It's all right, my dearie – soon be well – soon be well. We must look on the bright side – My man!'

1919

THE BLACK GODMOTHER

SITTING out on the lawn at tea with our friend and his retriever, we had been discussing those massacres of the helpless which had of late occurred, and wondering that they should have been committed by the soldiery of so civilized a State, when, in a momentary pause of our astonishment, our friend, who had been listening in silence, crumpling the drooping soft ear of his dog, looked up and said: 'The cause of atrocities is generally the violence of Fear. Panic's at the back of most crimes and follies.'

Knowing that his philosophical statements were always the result of concrete instance, and that he would not tell us what that instance was if we asked him – such being his nature – we were careful not to agree.

He gave us a look out of those eyes of his, so like the eyes of a mild eagle, and said abruptly: 'What do you say to this, then? ... I was out in the dog-days last year with this fellow of mine, looking for Osmunda, and stayed some days in a village – never mind the name. Coming back one evening from my tramp, I saw some boys stoning a mealy-coloured dog. I went up and told the young devils to stop it. They only looked at me in the injured way boys do, and one of them called out, "It's mad, guv'nor!" I told them to clear off, and they took to their heels. The dog followed me. It was a young, leggy, mild-looking mongrel, cross – I should say – between a brown retriever and an Irish terrier. There was froth about its lips, and its eyes were watery; it looked indeed as if it might be in distemper. I was afraid of infection for this fellow of mine, and whenever it came too close shooed it away, till at last it slunk off altogether. Well, about nine o'clock, when I was settling down to write by the open window of my sitting-room – still daylight, and very quiet and warm – there began that most maddening sound, the barking of an unhappy dog. I could do nothing with that continual "Yap – yap!" going on, and it was too hot to shut the window; so I went out to see if I could stop it. The men were all at the pub, and the women just finished with their gossip; there was no sound at all but the continual barking of this dog somewhere away out in the fields. I travelled by ear across three meadows, till I came on a haystack by a pool of water. There was the dog sure enough – the same mealy-coloured mongrel, tied to a stake, yapping, and making frantic little runs on a bit of rusty chain; whirling round and round the stake, then standing quite still, and shivering. I went up and spoke to it, but it backed into the hay-stack, and there it stayed shrinking away from me, with its tongue hanging out. It had been heavily struck by something on the head; the cheek was cut, one eye half-closed, and an ear badly swollen. I tried to get hold of it, but the poor thing was beside itself with fear. It snapped and flew round so that I had to give it up and sit down with this fellow here beside me to try and quiet it – a strange dog, you know, will generally form his estimate of you from the way it sees you treat another dog. I had to sit there quite half an hour before it would let me go up to it, pull the stake out, and lead it away. The poor beast, though it was so feeble from the blows it had received, was still half-frantic, and I didn't dare to touch it; and all the time I took good care that this fellow here didn't come too near. Then came the question what was to be done. There was no vet, of course, and I'd no place to put it except my sitting-room, which didn't belong to me. But, looking at its battered head, and its half-mad eyes, I thought: "No trusting you with these bumpkins; you'll have to come in here for the night!" Well, I got it in, and heaped two or three of those hairy little red rugs landladies are so fond of, up in a corner, and got it on to them, and put down my bread and milk. But it wouldn't eat – its sense of proportion was all gone, fairly destroyed by terror. It lay there moaning, and every now and then it raised its head with a "yap" of sheer fright, dreadful to hear, and bit the air, as if its enemies were on it again; and this fellow of mine lay in the opposite corner, with his head on his paw, watching it. I sat up for a long time with that poor beast, sick enough, and wondering how it had come to be stoned and kicked and battered into this state; and next day I made it my business to find out.' Our friend paused, scanned us a little angrily, and then went on: 'It had made its first appearance, it seems, following a bicyclist. There are men, you know – save the mark – who, when their beasts get ill or too expensive, jump on their bicycles and take them for a quick run, taking care never to look behind them. When they get back home they say: "Hullo! Where's Fido?" Fido is nowhere, and there's an end! Well, this poor puppy gave up just as it got to our village; and, roaming about in search of water, attached itself to a farm labourer. The man – with excellent intentions, as he told me himself – tried to take hold of it, but too abruptly, so that it was startled, and snapped at him. Whereon he kicked it for a dangerous cur, and it went drifting back towards the village, and fell in with the boys coming home from school. It thought, no doubt, that they were going to kick it too, and nipped one of them who took it by the collar. Thereupon they hullabalooed and stoned it down the road to where I found them. Then I put in my little bit of torture, and drove it away, through fear of infection to my own dog. After that it seems to have fallen in with a man who told me: "Well, you see, he came sneakin' round my house, with the children playin', and snapped at them when they went to stroke him, so that they came running in to their mother, an' she called to me in a fine takin' about a mad dog. I ran out with a shovel and gave 'im one, and drove him out. I'm sorry if he wasn't mad; he looked it right enough. You can't be too careful with strange dogs." Its next acquaintance was an old stone-breaker, a very decent sort. "Well! you see," the old man explained to me, "the dog came smellin' round my stones, an' it wouldn't come near, an' it wouldn' go away; it was all froth and blood about the jaw, and its eyes glared green at me. I thought to meself, bein' the dog-days – I don't like the look o' you, you look funny! So I took a stone, an' got it here, just on the ear; an' it fell over. And *I* thought to meself: Well, you've got to finish it, or it'll go bitin' somebody, for sure! But when I come to it with my hammer, the dog it got up – an' you know how it is when there's somethin' you've 'alf killed, and you feel sorry, and yet you feel you must finish it, an' you hit at it blind, you hit at it agen an' agen. The poor thing, it wriggled and snapped, an' I was terrified it'd bite me, an' some'ow it got away."' Again our friend paused, and this time we dared not look at him.

'The next hospitality it was shown,' he went on presently, 'was by a farmer who, seeing it all bloody, drove it off, thinking it had been digging up a lamb that he'd just buried. The poor homeless beast came sneaking back, so he told his men to get rid of it. Well, they got hold of it somehow – there was a hole in its neck that looked as if they'd used a pitchfork – and, mortally afraid of its biting them, but not liking, as they told me, to drown it, for fear the owner might come on them, they got a stake and a chain, and fastened it up, and left it in the water by the hay-stack where I found it. *I* had some conversation with that farmer. "That's right," he said, "but who was to know? I couldn't have my sheep worried. The brute had blood on his muzzle. These curs do a lot of harm when they've once been blooded. You can't run risks."' Our friend cut viciously at a dandelion with his stick. 'Run risks!' he broke out suddenly. 'That was it – from beginning to end of that poor beast's sufferings, fear! From that fellow on the bicycle, afraid of the worry and expense, as soon as it showed signs of distemper, to myself and the man with the pitchfork – not one of us, I daresay, would have gone out of our way to do it a harm. But we felt fear, and so – by the law of self-preservation, or whatever you like – it all began, till there the poor thing was, with a battered head and a hole in its neck, ravenous with hunger, and too distraught even to lap my bread and milk. Yes, and there's something uncanny about a suffering animal – we sat watching it, and again we were afraid, looking at its eyes and the way it bit the air. Fear! It's the black godmother of all damnable things!'

Our friend bent down, crumpling and crumpling at his dog's ears. We, too, gazed at the ground, thinking of that poor lost puppy, and the horrible inevitability of all that happens, seeing men are what they are; thinking of all the foul doings in the world, whose black godmother is Fear.

'And what became of the poor dog?' one of us asked at last.

'When', said our friend slowly, 'I'd had my fill of watching, I covered it with a rug, took this fellow away with me, and went to bed. There was nothing else to do. At dawn I was awakened by three dreadful cries – not like a dog's at all. I hurried down. There was the poor beast – wriggled out from under the rug – stretched on its side, dead. This fellow of mine had followed me in, and he went and sat down by the body. When I spoke to him he just looked round, and wagged his tail along the ground, but would not come away; and there he sat till it was buried, very interested but not sorry at all.'

Our friend was silent, looking angrily at something in the distance.

And we, too, were silent, seeing in spirit that vigil of early morning: The thin, lifeless, sandy-coloured body, stretched on those red mats; and this black creature – now lying at our feet – propped on its haunches like the dog in 'The Death of Procris', patient, curious, ungrieved, staring down at it with his bright, interested eyes.

1912

PHILANTHROPY

<<->>

Mist enwrapped Restington-on-Sea; not very thick, but exceedingly clammy. It decked the autumn trees in weirdness, cobwebbed the tamarisks, and compelled Henry Ivor to shut his window, excluding the faint hiss and rustle from the beach. He seldom wrote after tea without the accompaniment of fresh air, and was drowsing over his pen when his housekeeper entered.

'A couple to see you, sir; they came once before, when you was away.'

Ivor blinked. 'Well, show them in.'

When the door was again opened a scent of whisky came in first, then a man, a woman, and a dog.

Ivor laid down his pen and rose; he had never seen any of them before, and immediately doubted whether he wanted to see any of them again. Never able, however, to be disagreeable at a moment's notice, he waited defensively. The man, who might have been thirty-five, pale, warped, and thin, seemed to extract his face from the grip of nerves.

'Hearing you were down here, sir, and being in the printing trade, if you understand my meaning –'

Ivor nodded; he did not want to nod, but it seemed unavoidable; and he looked at the woman. Her face was buttoned, the most expressionless he had ever seen.

'Well?' he said.

The man's lips, thin and down at one corner, writhed again.

'You being a well-known writer,' he said, and the scent of whisky deepened.

Ivor thought: 'It wants courage to beg; it's damp too. Perhaps he's only primed himself.'

'Well?' he said again.

'If you understand me,' said the man, 'I'm in a very delicate position. I expect you know Mr Gloy – Charles Gloy – editor of *Cribbage* –'

'No,' said Ivor. 'But will you sit down?' And he placed two chairs.

The man and the woman sat down on their edges, the dog, too, sat on its edge! Ivor regarded it – a Schipperke – thinking. 'Did they bring their dog to undermine me?' As to that, it was the only kind of dog he did not like, but it looked damp and woeful.

'My brother works for Mr Gloy,' said the man; 'so, being at Beachhampton – out of a job, if you understand my meaning – I brought my wife – you being a well-known philanthropist –'

Ivor nervously took out a cigarette, and nervously put it back.

'I don't know what I can do for you,' he murmured.

'I'm one to speak the truth,' resumed the man, 'if you follow me –' And Ivor did – he followed on and on behind a wandering tale of printing, the war, ill-health. At last he said in despair:

'I really can't recommend people I know nothing about. What exactly do you want me to do?'

The woman's face seemed suddenly to lose a button, as if she were going to cry, but just then the dog whimpered; she took it up on her lap. Ivor thought:

'How much have I got on me?'

'The fact is, Mr Ivor,' said the man, 'I'm broke to the world, if you understand my meaning. If once I could get back to London –'

'What do you say, madam?'

The woman's mouth quivered and mumbled; Ivor stopped her with his hand.

'Well,' he said, 'I can give you enough to get up to London with, and a little over. But that's all, I'm afraid. And, forgive me, I'm very busy.' He stood up. The man rose also.

'I don't want to say anything about my wife; you'll forgive my mentioning it, but there's not a lady in England that's her equal at makin' babies' slippers.'

'Indeed!' said Ivor. 'Well, here you are!' And he held out some pound notes. The man took the notes; one of his trouser-legs was pitiably patched.

'I'm sure I'm more than grateful –' he said; and looking at Ivor as if he expected to be contradicted, added: 'I can't say better than that, can I?'

' No,' said Ivor, and opened the door.

'I'll be ready to repay you as soon as ever I can – if you understand my meaning.'

'Yes,' said Ivor. 'Good day! Good day, Mrs –! Good-bye, little dog!'

One by one the three passed him and went out into the mist. Ivor saw them trailing down the road, shut the outer door, returned to his chair, sighed profoundly, and took up his pen.

When he had written three pages, and it was getting too dusk to see, his housekeeper came in.

'There's a boy from the Black Cow, sir, come to say they want you down there.'

'Want *me*?'

'Yes, sir. That couple – the boy says they don't know what to do with them. They gave your name as being a friend.'

'Good Lord!'

'Yes, sir; and the landlord says they don't seem to know where they come from like.'

'Heavens!' said Ivor. He got up, however, put on his overcoat, and went out.

In the lighted doorway of the Black Cow stood the landlord.

'Sorry to have troubled you, sir, but really I can't tell how to deal with these friends of yours.'

Ivor frowned. 'I only saw them for the first time this afternoon. I just gave them money to go up to London with. Are they drunk?'

'Drunk!' said the landlord. 'Well, if I'd known the man was half gone when he came in – of course I'd never – As to the woman, she sits and smiles. I can't get them to budge, and it's early closin' –'

'Well,' muttered Ivor, 'let's look at them!' And he followed the landlord in.

On the window-seat in the bar parlour those two were sitting, with mugs beside them, and the dog asleep on the feet of the woman, whose lips were unbuttoned in a foolish smile. Ivor looked at the man; his face was blank and beatific. Specimens of a damp and doleful world, they now seemed almost blissful.

'Mist' Ivor,' he said. 'Thought so – I'm not tight –'

'Yes,' said Ivor, 'but I thought you wanted to go up to London. The station's not half a mile.'

'Cert'nly – go up to London.'

'Come along, then; I'll show you the way.'

'Ve'y good, we can walk, if you understand my meaning.' And the man stood up, the dog and the woman also. All three passed unsteadily out.

The man walked first, then the woman, then the dog, wavering into the dusky mist. Ivor followed, praying that they might meet no traffic. The man's voice broke the silence in front.

'Hen'y Ivor!' Ivor closed up nervously.

'Hen'y Ivor! I see 'm sayin' to 'mself: "What'll they move on for!" I see him, if y' understand my meaning. Wha'sh he good for – Hen'y Ivor – only writer o' books. Is he any better than me – no! Not 's good, if you f-follow me. I see 'm thinkin': "How can I get rid of 'm?"' He stood still suddenly, almost on Ivor's toes. 'Where's dog – carry th' dog – get 'is feet wet.'

The woman stooped unsteadily, picked up the dog, and they both wavered on again. Ivor walked alongside now, grim and apprehensive. The man seemed to have become aware of him.

''Mist' Ivor,' he said. 'Thought so – I'm not tight – can't say better than that, can I? – I'm not writer of books like you – not plutocrat, if you understand my meaning. Want to ask you question: What would you do if you was me?'

There was silence, but for the slip-slippering of the woman's feet behind.

'I don' blame you,' said the man, whose speech was getting thicker; 'you can't help being a plutothrist. But whash the good of anything for me, except ob-oblivion, if you follow me?'

A faint radiance shone through the mist. The station building loomed suddenly quite close. Ivor steered towards it.

'Goin' up t' London,' said the man. 'Qui' right!'

He lurched past into the lighted entry, and the woman followed with the dog. Ivor saw them waver through the doorway. And, spinning round, he ran into the mist. 'Perfectly true!' he thought while he was running. Perfectly true! Why had he helped them? What did he care so long as he got rid of man, woman, and dog?

1922